THE HOSTESSES

3-26-17

THE HOSTESSES
THE CASE OF WHO'S TRYING TO KILL THEM

JOHN GARDNER

TATE PUBLISHING
AND ENTERPRISES, LLC

Published by Tate Publishing & Enterprises, LLC
127 E. Trade Center Terrace | Mustang, Oklahoma 73064 USA
1.888.361.9473 | www.tatepublishing.com

Tate Publishing is committed to excellence in the publishing industry. The company reflects the philosophy established by the founders, based on Psalm 68:11,
"The Lord gave the word and great was the company of those who published it."

Book design copyright © 2016 by Tate Publishing, LLC. All rights reserved.
Cover design by Joshua Rafols
Interior design by Mary Jean Archival

Published in the United States of America

ISBN: 978-1-68301-254-2
Fiction / Mystery & Detective / General
16.05.02

Acknowledgments

I would like to thank my family and friends for encouraging me to write this story. The good people at Tate Publishing for their help along the way.

To the men and women of TV home-shopping networks from the number one to the number twenty-one, they all have one thing in common. They are so very good at what they do. They take an extraordinarily difficult job day after day and make it look so easy. These men and women are highly intelligent, well educated, and very professional. They come into our homes and into our hearts. When they hurt, we hurt. When they are happy, we are happy. They are our children, and we love them as such.

You buy from him or her and not the company. You believe what they tell you as if he or she were your own child. They would rather quit the show than to mislead you on something. These people hold themselves to the highest standards of any celebrity I can think have today. The men and women of home shopping have proven what I have been saying for years. "People buy from people." The brick-and-mortar stores have yet to learn this technique. They think their so-called salespeople should spend all day straightening merchandise and ignoring customers. I built a successful retail business and ran it for over a decade, personally meeting every customer, and it paid off for me. I competed against some of the largest retailers that are, by the way, no longer in business.

Every day you hear a retailer complaining about low sales. You go to their store, and they act as if you are too much trouble for them to serve you. They won't even say hi or thank you.

The men and women of TV shopping sell more in fifteen minutes than the big boys sell in a day, yet they still don't understand "buy from people."

It is with the utmost of love and respect that I write this story. I have never had the honor or pleasure of meeting any of them. I, like most of us, do have a favorite. But I've got to tell you—and I'm sure you know this—picking one is not an easy thing to do; so I picked all of them as my favorite. However, there are a few that I lean toward sometimes.

Thank you (all the people at the home-shopping networks) for being there for all of us. You are appreciated.

John Gardner

Special note

Sit back with your favorite brand of coffee, iced tea, or perhaps a cold glass of milk. I sincerely hope you enjoy reading this story as much as I did writing it for you.

Warning!

It has been said that once you start reading this story, you can't put it down.

I would love to hear your opinions of this story. Any remarks, suggestions, or criticisms are welcome. Please feel free to e-mail gardner196@gmail.com at any time.

Note

Watch for one of the hostesses to take over a corrupt corporation in book two, *From Hostess to CEO*, which is coming soon.

And be sure to get a copy of *Thoughts*. It will tell you why HOA is so bad for you and some of the funny things happening to me.

Thank you for buying and reading this book.

John Gardner

Contents

1

Introducing John Garfield

John Garfield—a former US marshal, former businessman, and former husband—had a major setback in his life. There were a lot of reasons that made that happened—mostly the high tax increase of the nineties, large competitors moving in, and the rent and utilities going up every year. His wife and his girlfriend had left. Surely all of this and so much more had to do with the closing of his business. John would not make any excuses for his failure. He was his own man. He made the decisions. He called the shots. It was his decisions, and his alone, that caused the business to close. He felt so badly about letting his employees go; he felt bad about letting his friends down.

This was a pain he could never imagine. The hurt was so much more painful than anything he had ever experienced.

No one, but no one, in his family had ever failed, certainly not bankruptcy of all things, not bankruptcy. This was unheard of in his family.

How in the world could he ever look anyone in the eye again? He had done the worst possible thing. He had let down all the people who had believed in him, counted on him for a living, and the creditors who loaned him money. They were all now at a loss just because they believed in him. This was so new to John; for the first time in his life, he did not know how to deal with a problem.

How can he handle a problem of such magnitude? This time, the mistake was not just about him. There were other people, good people, who depended on him; and he had let them all down. John had been a winner in life, although he had some setbacks, as we all had; but John Garfield never thought of a setback as failure. Instead, he looked on it as one of life's learning experiences. John prided himself on not making the same mistake twice. He also admitted he had made a lot of new mistakes, but never the same one twice.

The has made the final decision in his life, sober and clear-minded, he opened the door to his upscale one-bedroom apartment while knowing he would never open that door again. He paused for a moment to look around to see everything he would be leaving behind, things which came with a high price tags, things that he could never finest paying for now. The eviction notice would be arriving at any time today. The thirty-five-hundred-square-foot house he once lived in was already gone. The forty-eight-thousand-dollar sports car, his ex-wife's new car, and the new twelve-thousand-dollar car he had brought to drive on days when the weather wasn't just right for his sports car now occupied spaces at the bank's parking lot. All the gold credit cards were gone, and John's business of seventeen years was bankrupted.

Earlier that year, his wife left him. Karen Carter, John's girlfriend of five-plus years, was also gone. John paid for her last year in college and got her a job on TV as a reporter. She left before the bankruptcy and did not know of it.

John was deeply hurt by the way Karen was acting toward him. Her new boyfriend was everything that John hated in life and everything he had always believed Karen hated as well. Karen left with a new company car that John had paid off. They agreed not to ask for help from each other and not to ever call or write. They both kept their word.

He walked one more time through the apartment, stopping to pick up this and that, remembering things of the past while tears trotted out of his eyes. He thought about Karen, Patty his ex-wife, and everything that lead up to this point.

John stopped at the new American-made dresser he bought just a year ago. All his furniture was American made. John believed in buying American made when possible, even if it cost more.

Knowing what's in that drawer, he pulled it open. He could see a gun there. He had brought that gun a few weeks earlier. His reason for buying that gun was to kill Karen's new lowlife boyfriend. After getting the opportunity to kill him and not doing so, John Garfield learned that night he was not a cold-blooded murderer.

He grabbed the gun in his sweaty hands and pulled it out, opening the chamber, but the chamber was empty. There was a new box of bullets in the drawer, lying next to where the gun had just been retrieved. Reaching for only one, he turned. Walking slowly toward the window, he could see Jan, a pretty young lady about his age. Jan had talked to John several times while walking around the pool. John thought, *I apologize, Jan. You will never get the chance to enjoy the greatest sexes of your life*, laughing at himself.

Slowly, he headed back to the living room holding that one bullet, then depositing that single bullet into the chamber, turning it fast. Hands shaking like a jug of beer on a table during a heavy earthquake, John knew what he must do next. John also knew that his life would be over in a matter of minutes.

Dropping to his knees on the living room floor, he placed the gun next to his temper and pulled the trigger once, twice, three times—he had squeezed that trigger. Next would be the fourth time. Then came the fifth, and John was still alive. He knew the next squeezing of that trigger would be the charm, and John Garfield's life would be over. One and only one more squeeze and it will be the final move he would ever make. John Garfield's life would end there, alone on the floor, and no one would know he was dead.

Grasping the trigger for the sixth and final time, he applied light pressure on to it when the apartment doors open, just in time before he could complete the squeezing of the sixth trigger. Lisa King, a very good friend and a sometime lover of his, entered the apartment with her key. She saw what he was about to do and ran fast to him, pulling the gun away from his head. It fired but missed him. She held him in her arms so tightly and yet so gentle.

Lisa spent the rest of the week with him and paid his rent in full. John Garfield's life was saved that night. It has been said that God has a reason for everything, and that day was not his time.

Six years later, the century was changing numbers. It was now the twentieth century, and things had change. Karen never married, dumped her lowlife boyfriend, and moved to Atlanta, then New York City. She could be seen on a daily national morning news show. Her life is getting better every day. John was big part of her early success. He paid for her last year in college and helped her in getting on TV in Dallas, on a morning news show. That show made it easier for her to go to Atlanta and then to New York.

John was just beginning to get things back in his life. Patty has returned. His credit rating was improving, and he had a new large apartment. John and Patty still have two old used cars to drive. He was beginning to quite feeling so sorry for himself, but John Garfield was desperately in need of attention, for some new excitement in his life. He wanted to be his own man again even if it kills him.

A small man in stature but big in ideas was John Garfield. He liked to think of himself as being somewhat of a look-alike of Michael J. Fox. They are about the same size; John certainly could relate to some of the characters that Fox had played. His life, like some of Fox's characters' life, had been filled with excitement, danger, and romance during his high school days at Thomas Jefferson High in Richmond. The young ladies and his college days at the University of Virginia were even better.

John Garfield could tell some good tales, like most of us. The tales he told had more excitement, more adventure, and, of course, a lot more romance as the years went by. One tale he liked to tell was about the shoot-out with drug lords when he was an undercover US marshal in Miami. That never did happen. John was only there for twenty-two days. He never even had a gun; however, the marshals did bust a large group of drug pushers in a small town that he was part of, but it grew in size to drug lords as John told the story. He did, however, have a small part in capturing a small drug lord there, just a little bit smaller part than the way he told it. It sounded real good the way he told it. In fact, it got better every time he told it. One thing he never talked about, but actually did receive credit for, was saving another officer's life.

A few years later, Patty had returned after everything fell apart. She didn't know about Karen Carter or Lisa King, and

John was not about to tell her the story. She was unhappy with the closing of the business, the bankruptcy, the losing of her home, the house she picked out herself, the house she decorated herself, and the three new cars. The high-limit credit cards and now the pride were all gone, gone along with all the rest. An eleven-hundred-square-foot two-bedroom apartment replaced the thirty-five-hundred-square-foot house.

This apartment was not in the low-rent district. Instead, it was one of the nicer, larger, newer apartments available. It was one thing that did make it hard for John. He could not have gotten this nice apartment without Patty's cousin cosigning the lease. The same cousin John had helped when he got into a tax jam and was about to lose everything to the IRS a few years back. John did not look on this as payback. He never would have asked for help from anyone; however, Patty had other thoughts. She was not willing to go all the way to the bottom while John was so busy feeling sorry for himself. There were times he did not seem to care anymore. She still believed in him, although not as strongly as before.

Patty had no intention of giving up on him at this point. She had no idea of how or when they could get back to the top again. Patty only knew in her heart that someday someway they would be back on top and they would be stronger and better people because of it. She believed that bad things happen to good people for a reason.

The people John had helped, the same people with the money that could have helped him in his time of need, were nowhere in sight. Some of them John had made rich.

He did not expect a handout from any of them, but he darn sure did expected some support from them, emotionally at the very least. There was no one willing to help in any shape, form, or fashion. It was John and Patty alone.

A few years later, John's life was really well. He was thankful for what he had; however, there is something missing from his life. John wanted to get back in charge again. He wanted his own business. He did not want to work for someone else anymore. But he realized he could not just walk off the job. He had a wife depending on him, and he had no intention of letting her down again.

John continued to look for a business of some kind, not wanting a storefront, employees, or anyone depending on him for a paycheck. Earlier this year, he had found a company that would let him sell their products under his name. All John had to do was to sell the merchandise. They had the entire overhead. This was just what John had been looking for. No big investment, no employees, no inventory. All he had to do was get out and hustle. What he didn't know was that because of this new adventure, John's life would change or maybe end it for real.

2

The Hostesses

Katie Richard stood five feet, five inches tall in her stocking feet, with beautiful auburn hair, a body that would make a grown man act like a half-witted teenager, and a face so beautiful that it was hard to find the words to describe it. Katie's face was definitely one of a kind. No movie star or any other celebrity anywhere could come close to matching Katie's beauty. One vendor had remarked, "When Katie walks into a room, the whole room lights up."

A graduate of the University of Tennessee with a degree in journalism, she was also the winner of the Miss National Journalist Pageant, a beauty pageant for female journalists. The best part, her Aunt Annie thought, was she had a brain to match her looks.

Katie had worked for several small television stations in the south and won some awards for her investigative reporting as well. Katie was not happy with the small-time station where she was working. She got very little airtime, and the pay was pathetic. She was looking for something more in life than what she was getting. She moved to another small station in Oklahoma, where she met Katie Morgan.

Katie Morgan was also a very beautiful lady, about the same age as Katie Richard—a little shorter, with light-brown hair and a smile that could lift anyone's spirits regardless of the kind of day they were having. Katie Morgan had a face and body that most women would die for. She was completely happy with being Katie Morgan, very sure of herself; and like Katie Richard, she was very happy with life in general.

A graduate of the University of Texas with a degree in journalism, she had won many awards for her investigative reporting as well. Katie Morgan was also not happy with her job. And for the same reasons, Katie Richard was unhappy with hers.

Katie Richard met Katie Morgan at a small NBC station outside of Oklahoma City, where they became very good friends.

Katie Morgan was just called Morgan. Shortly after arriving at that station, Morgan got a job offer from a large cable network in Atlanta, Georgia. Discussing it with Katie, Morgan decided to take the job in Atlanta. She told Katie that she would drop her resume on her new boss's desk and mention her name every time she got a chance in the hope that they would give her a call one day soon.

Because they worked in a male-dominated industry, they had promised early on in their relationship to look out for one another. They had formed such a close bond that each knew the other would do their utmost to follow through on whatever was promised. Morgan was watching one of those home-shopping shows, AHS (American home-shopping shows), in Landover, only twenty miles from Atlanta. They were looking for a new hostess.

She drove the twenty miles to Landover and spoke with the program manager. He was so impressed that he made her an offer on the spot. He had seen her work on cable news and one of the special reports she had done for that NBC station.

Morgan was so happy. She went back to the cable network. It only took Morgan a few short months to not like her new job any more than the others. They promised her good hours, good pay, and a lot of airtime. She had only a little more airtime now than before. The airtime she did get was only at night, from 11:00 p.m. to 2:00 a.m., doing special reports, one minute per hour. Seeing the high turnover at that station and the way she was being treated, she started looking for something better.

Wednesday, the next day, was Morgan's day off. She turned in her two weeks' notice immediately. She did not need to do that, however, because they told her to leave on the same day. That made Katie Morgan a very happy girl. She had done the right thing, and now she was free of that job. Morgan had a good feeling about this new job. She would not be a journalist; however, she would be on national TV.

Morgan called the program manager at AHS to tell him she could report to work anytime now. He told her to come to work tomorrow. She was so excited about her new job that she arrived well over an hour before the manager got there.

Beth, a very attractive hostess who had been there since the opening and considered to be the mother of the show, was more than gladded to train Morgan. They became very close friends.

After working there for only a few weeks, she gave the program manager a tape of Katie Richard. He liked what he saw and told Morgan to have Katie come in for an interview. Katie was there the next Monday. She too was hired on the spot.

Five years later, both of them were still on AHS. Morgan got married. Katie had a bad relationship with Wayne Becker, whom Morgan later married. Katie seemed to be okay with that. She love to sing and did some singing when she wasn't working. Both Katies were very popular with everyone—the old, the young, the men, and the women. They all loved the two Katies. Things were good for them. Lots of fans, good friends, and good pay. The network was doing good as well.

AHS was hiring another hostess. One of the hostesses had quit to have her baby and decided to stay home with her new one. They had narrowed the list down to two girls.

Nicky, a very beautiful tall lady of thirtysomething. The other—Lynn, who had worked for another home-shopping network for the last ten years—was looking forward to coming back to Atlanta. Her mother, who lived close by, had been sick for a while; and she wanted to be near her.

The program manager was out when Lynn called. It seemed she had changed her mind. Nicky now had the job. Lyn called to see about the job. She told them she did not call and tell them she didn't want the job. Susan, the program manager assistant told Chad, the program manager. "I know her voice. It was her on the phone."

Nicky quickly became friends with Morgan and Katie. She was a hit on the air, but she did require a lot more training than most of the others. She talked to Katie and asked for her help. She told Katie that she was afraid she might be fired if she doesn't get better fast. Katie was more than glad to help. Together with Katie, Nicky became a big success.

The hostesses are a big family. They are very close to each other. This love and respect they have for each other can be a very good thing. Sometime this closeness could become deadly.

3

Garfield Sees an Ad

Katie Richard and Katie Morgan, now known as Katie and Morgan, were starting their fifth season on AHS; and John Garfield was moving to his new apartment. The moved was a short one to Plano, just south of Allen, Texas, and just north of Dallas. The cable company there was different from the one in Allen. This one had AHS on it, and it had no other shopping network. It was there where John first saw Morgan and Katie.

John's first thought was, *Yeah, they're cute.* He never really gave much thought to either one of them. Patty would order and order and order more from them—not just from the either of the two Katies, but from any of them. The TV was on to AHS a lot, and John would watch it too, especially if Morgan was the hostess.

As the years went by, John, like most viewers, picked a favorite. It was so hard for him to pick just one. There was no one he didn't like, but there were four that he really did like: Beth, Kim, Katie, and Morgan. John favored Morgan more than the others. Why? Maybe it was her smile; her charms; her personality; and, of course, her beautiful face did not go unnoticed. Over the next few years, he saw more of Morgan and Katie than the others. Although he liked everything about both of them, he never thought of them except when they were on the air. John was not the kind to e-mail anyone on TV; that just wasn't his style.

In Texas, the mid-August sun was glaring down on John as he ran the garden department at a big box store when a customer that he was talking with, a heavyset man looking to do some yard work today, told John about his partnership he had with his brother, Sam, and their gift shop in Dallas. John had about twenty gift products he believed Sam might to add to his inventory. He told John to call his brother. "Tell him I told you to call," he told John.

That afternoon when John got off of work, he did call. A man calling himself Sam answered. They set up a 1:00 p.m. appointment for Wednesday. That was John's next day off. On Wednesday, John, keeping that appointment in mind, drove over to Dallas. This gift store was located close to a bad neighborhood: prostitutes, bars, topless bars, adult bookstores, nude modeling studios, peep shows, and cheap motels.

John arrived on time at the gift shop, parked his car, went in, and asked for Sam. He was told that he had to leave but would be back in about an hour and a half. John felt disappointed but determined to talk with Sam. And the drive back to Plano was too long to make, so he decided to just get a bite to eat and wait for Sam to return.

The neighborhood close by was getting the best of John's curiosity. He drove a few miles to the neighborhood he had heard so much about. Driving south on Harry Hines Boulevard, and looking to his left and then to his right, he was hoping to see some real prostitutes walking the streets.

There would be no streetwalkers today. The Dallas police were seeing to that. He made a U-turn after about a mile or two down the road—driving back, looking just as hard as he had before, but still not seeing anyone on the street.

He pulled into the parking lot of a small cafe and found himself a seat. The waitress, a very attractive young girl in a short uniform, came up. "May I help you?" she asked.

John, looking up at her, said, "Hi, how are you today?"

"Okay, thanks for asking," she replied.

He was thinking how good she looked, wondering if she was one of those prostitutes. It wouldn't have made any difference anyway. He wouldn't have known what to do if she had offered for free. And John's limit would be ten dollars. You can't even get a haircut for ten dollars then. So putting that thought out of mind, John ordered a hamburger and fries. There was a paper-type magazine lying on the table next to him. "Here, I will take that for you," the waitress told him.

"No, it's all right. Gives me something to look at while I'm waiting."

"It sure will give you something to look at, all right," the waitress said as she walked off.

She was right. This publication was all about the nightlife in Dallas. The friendly ladies of the evening—ladies who will make house calls—and information on where to find them, the price they charged, all the sexual toys one might ever want, this magazine had it all. Instead of a ladies-rental-by-the-hour section, a half-page ad for condoms got John's attention. He found a beautiful girl in a near-nothing bikini. This is what got his attention. John kept looking at her. He knew that he knew this girl. Thinking and thinking, it came to him. It was Katie Richard of AHS. John could not believe what he was looking at. Surely, it was not Katie Richard. Not Katie Richard of all people. Katie would not pose for that kind of ad. Dressed like that. Not Katie. *What the heck is going on?* John was thinking. *This is just a look-alike. That's it. This girl is only a look-alike. A very close look-alike*, he thought.

"I see you picked out one for today," the waitress remarked.

"No, ha…No, I know this girl. She used to work for me," John explained. He didn't want to mention Katie's name to her.

"I will bet you, you will be calling her now," the waitress added.

"No, it's probably not her anyway. I can't see her posing in this ad."

"Let me see it," she said while pulling it out of John's hands.

"She's very beautiful. You know what? She looks familiar to me."

She handed the magazine back to him. John finished eating and headed back to meet with Sam.

Not being able to get that ad out of his mind, he took that magazine with him. At the traffic light, he opened the magazine to that ad. Glancing at it from time to time, even picking it up while waiting for the light to change, he decided to put it away. It was none of his business anyway, he was now thinking.

Later that night, AHS was on, and of all people, it was Katie Richard herself. He could do nothing except stare at her. The more he watched, the more he thought about the ad. John turned on the VCR and recorded her show. The next day, he played the tape, pausing on her face. He placed the ad next to her on the TV screen. It was Katie Richard. Katie Richard of AHS. Why? This did not fit her image. AHS was a family show. What would happen if the management found out? Would they fire her? There were too many questions and not enough answers. One thing was for sure. The girl was Katie Richard.

While watching *Fox & Friends* the next morning, they were talking about a tennis player who appeared in one of these girlie magazines. The story was that the picture was not all her.

Someone had taken her head off and put it on a nude body, trying to make people think it was her. She had never given her permission to do this and certainty not to print it. This set off a bell in John's mind so loud you could hear it for miles.

"That's what happened! That's it! It's got to be that!" John shouted out. He was one hundred-percent sure now. After all, Katie would not ever pose for an ad like that. She was simply too high-class. She was too much of a lady. She didn't need the money; she didn't need the attention. Katie had no large ego like other celebrities. There was no reason for her to do this. That was the answer. It just was not her. Well, not her body anyway. He was sure. But now, what to do about it? Should he write her? Send her a copy? Call her on the phone? E-mail her maybe? John had too many thoughts going through his mind. He has always been good at reasoning things out. This time he wanted so much to do exactly the right thing. He didn't know her. He knew what she looked like, what she sounded like, but he really didn't know her.

Having a gut feeling about Katie, he believed in his heart that whoever had the obligation had to let her know. If he was right, and he believed he was, this would be the right thing to do. She should know about this, and she should know now! He took the ad and placed it inside an envelope, then put that one inside another larger envelope with a note. He addressed it to the AHS mailing address in Landover, and he saw on TV the real Katie Richard. That being the case, he marked it 'personal' to reach Katie Richard's attention."

Dear Katie,

I came across this ad. I thought you should see it. You might want to open it in private.

The small envelope was sealed and marked *Katie Richard, personal.* The note read,

Katie, I found a publication the other day while eating lunch in Dallas. This was a bad neighborhood. I was only there on business. The magazine was lying in the seat next to me, left by the last person. I have never seen a magazine like this before. One could find anything he or she might want. Then there it was, the ad that you are looking at. Katie, I don't think it's you. I do think you should see it before anyone else does.

PS: If you would like to call or e-mail me, my address and e-mail are below.

John drove straight to the post office. His first thought was to send it as a priority mail. Then he thought, *It's Friday. She wouldn't get it till next week anyway.* So he mailed it as a first-class mail, saving him money, and that's always a good thing in John's mind. John did make one mistake. He did not send it as a certified mail. Now he would be wondering if she received it or not.

The past two years, Katie was sent to Italy to do her show from the AHS studios in Rome. This year was no exception.

Morgan wished her a good trip and promised to take care of things while she was gone. The network picked her up in the limousine. It was important that she get to the airport on time. Morgan was on her way to Atlanta for the day when she saw the limousine pull off the road. She stopped to see what was wrong. Morgan immediately insisted that she take them to the airport herself. Katie got to Rome on time and without any other incidents. The show was good as usual. Katie saw some old friends and, of course, made some new ones.

She arrived back in Landover on Thursday of the next week. Morgan was glad to see her. She told Katie that all of her mail was on her desk. Customer service had checked her e-mail and replied for her. Katie did not like that. She felt it was her duty to address each one herself. As time-consuming as it may be, these were people who wanted to hear from her, not someone in customer service. But there was nothing she could do about it this time. She must have had over a thousand e-mails. There was no way she could get to all of them.

The next day, both of them had the day off. It was a good time for good friends to catch up on what's happening. Katie told Morgan all about her trip to Rome. Now she wanted to hear about home.

"I was lucky you were there when the limo broke down. I would have missed my flight, and the trip would have been cancelled for sure."

"You know, Katie?" She put her drink down, looked her in the eye, and pointed with that little finger (that was her trademark) at her, and she said, "Someone put sugar in the gas tank."

"No!" Katie answered. "The gates are always locked. Only the mechanic and drivers could get in there."

"I know, I know, but they are investigating it now," Morgan continued to tell her. "Bobby took a ride with Mike the day before you left. The limo was locked up when they got back."

"Wait a minute, Morgan. Bobby, the handyman, was riding with Mike? Why?"

"It seems as if they have become friends," Morgan explained.

"Bobby is up to something. No one likes him," Katie said while putting her drink down.

"I don't know about that. Nicky thinks he's is so cute," Morgan said while laughing.

"Cute, my you-know-what. There's nothing cute about him. You can't trust him. He must be up to something. Gary better watch his back." (Gary was the chauffer.)

"You're right about that, Katie. You know he was hitting on me?" Morgan was smiling when she said that.

"He hits on everyone," Katie remarked.

"Thanks a lot."

"You know what I meant. He doesn't care if you are married or not," she explained to Morgan.

"Speaking of that. Jim, the ladies' man (the new program manager), patted my rear the other day. Said it was an accident," Morgan said while taking another sip of her Pepsi.

"It probably was an accident," Katie replied.

"Well, here's an accident for you," Morgan said, now pointing her little finger right at Katie. "Mr. Accident, himself, has been saying how beautiful he thought you are, how sexy you are, and how he can't wait for you to get home. He even went into his office the whole three hours you were on, locked the door, and took no phone calls. God is the only one who knows what he was doing in there."

"You've got to be kidding! I only met the man one time since he's been here. He acted as if I was nothing to him. Just another hostess. That's all, nothing more or less. He seems to like Nicky or Kim more than me. He's always talking to them. I don't think that's anything to be concerned about," Katie told Morgan while looking around the cafe.

"Well, you…," Morgan started to say when Anne, a small but very attractive blond who was a hostess on ASH for serval years until she got sick and had to quit but now a waitress and owner of the café (Ann's Café), came up and said, "Hi, Morgan. Hi, Katie."

Both Katie and Morgan said at the same time, "Hi, Anne."

"Katie, I saw your show while you were in Rome. You were great. That evening gown was so beautiful. Did you get to keep it?" Looking over at Morgan, she said, "And, Morgan, your show was great too."

"That's all right, Anne. Katie did have a great show. Although I don't know why they didn't send me," Morgan added.

"They sent me because I speak Italian. Maybe next year they will send you."

"Maybe, but I'm not holding my breath on that one," Morgan responded.

Looking back at Katie, Anne said, "I don't know if I should tell you this or not."

"Tell me what, Anne?"

"Maybe I'd…better not say anything," Anne said as she turned to walk away.

Katie reached out and grabbed her arm, telling her, "No, you're not going to say that and then walk off. We won't say anything to anyone. It won't go any farther than the three of us. Now sit down, girl, and tell us."

"Well, right after you left for Rome, that new program manager and Bobby came in."

"Wait a minute!" Morgan demanded. "Bobby and Jim were together? They were here for lunch? Are you sure?"

"Jim? Is that his name?" Anne asked.

"Yes, that is his name," Katie told her.

"Go on! Go on!" Morgan added.

"I overheard them talking about you, Katie."

"What about me?"

"Maybe I better be quiet."

"Not on your life, girl. Not now," Morgan said to Anne with an excited tone. "I want to hear everything."

Katie, looking over at Morgan with a smile, told Anne to go ahead.

"Well, Jim was saying how beautiful you are and how sexy you are."

Looking at Katie, Morgan pointed and said, "I told you! Didn't I tell you?"

Looking back at Morgan with a friendly smile on her face, Katie told Anne to go on with the story.

"Have you heard this?" Anne asked.

"No, no. Go on, girl," Morgan insisted.

"Well, he said how he would be bedding you soon. Only he used the other word. He said he couldn't wait to you get back. He also said he just knew you would be hell in bed. But wait, Katie. Bobby said, 'You're right. Katie is great in bed, and I should know.' Katie, I didn't know you had slept with Bobby."

"I didn't know that either, Katie. Why didn't you tell me?" Morgan asked, laughing hard while asking.

"If you had slept with Bobby Greenwood, would you have told anyone?" Raising her voice a little, Katie state, "Of course I've never and never will sleep with Bobby Greenwood. That makes me darned mad!"

"You promised you two would not say anything," Anne reminded them.

"We won't say anything," Katie assured her.

"We gave you our word. Sure wish we hadn't, though," Morgan confessed as Anne was leaving.

Anne bent over to Katie and pleaded with her. "Watch your back, Katie. I don't trust them."

Katie, reaching out and holding Anne's hand, told her in a soft voice, "Thanks, Anne, I will."

Morgan, looking Katie in the eyes and pointing that little finger again in her face, exclaimed, "That was what we were talking about."

"Yeah, you are right," Katie agreed.

After leaving Anne's place, they continued to talk about Bobby and Jim on the way home. Katie was mad that what Bobby had said, but she wasn't that concerned about Jim and his dirty thoughts. She believed it was all talk and nothing more. Morgan, on the other hand, believed she should be concerned about Jim as well.

4

They Came Home

Knowing he wouldn't hear anything from Katie until she returned home, John decided to take a few days off and see both his and Patty's mother in Richmond. The next week, both Katie and John had returned home, and John checked his e-mail every day, looking for an e-mail from Katie. He was sure she would e-mail him back. He knew Katie would personally answer all her mail—he was sure. It would just take some time for her to get to his. He was continuously walking back and forth to his computer, waiting to receive that one important message from Katie, a girl he didn't know and one who didn't know him either. By now John could not wait any longer. He decided to e-mail her again.

Dear Katie,

While you were in Rome, I sent you a letter and an ad I found on a table one day at lunch. I thought this girl looked a lot like you. I sincerely hope I did not offend you. As I stated in my letter, I was concerned about someone using your looks to make money. That was all I wanted to do, just to let you know. I was not judging you or making a judgment call.

John returned to work on Monday. He had to tell someone what he had done. He was in serious desperate need of approval. John knew he would not get it from his wife.

Judy, who worked Mondays, was there. He saw her across the room and yelled, "Good morning, Judy." He started walking faster to get to her. John could not hold this news back. As much as he needed approval, he knew Judy was the one to give it.

"Good morning, John," Judy replied. "Did you have a good trip?" she inquired.

"Yes, I did. It was very good. Mom was okay. Got to see a lot of the family. Missed seeing one of my old friends. He was taking his vacation at the same time. He went to California this year. Judy, let me ask you something, you being a woman and everything, okay?" John asked with a wired look on his face.

"What did you do now?" Judy asked.

"Nothing. What makes you think I did something? I just want to get your opinion on something, all right?"

"Well, you got that wired look on your face," Judy explained.

"I don't have a wired look!"

"Yes, you do, John. This should be good. Go on, tell me or ask me."

"Well, Judy, let's say you were a TV personally on a family show. Nationwide that is. Women, men, and children watch you every week. You are a very wholesome person. Very down-to-earth."

"What did you do?" Judy asked again.

"I e-mailed her."

"Did you say something bad in the e-mail?"

"No, of course not. You know me better than that, Judy."

"Well, what did you said to her? And whom are we talking about anyway?"

"Her name is Katie," he told her.

"Does this Katie have a last name?" Judy wanted to know.

"Katie Richard."

"Never heard of her. What show is she on?"

"She's one of the hostesses on AHS, you know, one of those shopping shows."

"I never watched that show.

"what did you say to her?" Judy insisted.

"Well, suppose someone was using a photo of your head in a negative way. Wouldn't you want to know about it?"

"Using my head, nothing but my head? What are they doing with my head? What are you talking about, John?"

"Hum…let me tell you the whole story."

"Please."

"All right, it started before I went to Richmond. I got a lead on a new customer. This lead was in Dallas. When I got there, I had to wait, so I decided to go get some lunch. I drove over to Harry Hines Boulevard."

"You drove to Harry Hines to get something to eat? What were you planning on eating?"

"Lunch…a burger or something."

"Or something I am sure."

"What are you talking about? I was hungry. That was all," he explained.

"Are you trying to tell me you don't know what's on Harry Hines?" Judy asked.

"Well, of course, I've heard. Didn't know if it was true or not," John said, once again with that look.

"Okay, go ahead with the story. I only have five more hours left today."

"All right, quit interrupting me so much," John pleaded with her. "I found this magazine on the table in this restaurant on Harry Hanne. I picked it up and started to look through it."

"Looking at all the pictures."

"No, yeah, some, anyway. This ad came up—a very beautiful girl dressed in a very little bikini, selling condoms. I didn't know who she was at first…I just couldn't a name to her. I only knew that she looked familiar. Then it came to me who she was. When I got home, I turned on the TV, and there she was on right then. I matched her face to that ad. It was Katie Richard. She has a one-of-a-kind face."

"Let me see if I got it right. You have a copy of an ad from a sex-oriented source. The girl looks like another girl whom you don't know but believe to be very 'wholesome' and can be seen on a family show nationwide? And you sent her a copy of this ad thinking she will be ever so thankful for what you did. What happens if her boss gets the ad and not her? Maybe he would fire her. Did you ever think of that? If this ad is not her and she gets fired, how are you going to feel?"

"It wasn't like that, Judy. I addressed it to her, marked *personal* on it, put the ad in another envelope, and marked it personal," John was explaining.

"That's a big place. Suppose someone was opening her mail, screening it for her. Maybe that person didn't like her. Maybe she never got it. Someone else did. She now thinks you are a joke. She wouldn't even e-mail you about this."

"No. I…e-mailed her again."

"You e-mailed her twice? Has she ever e-mailed back, once?"

"Well…no."

"If she e-mailed you, and that's a big if, it would be a form letter, thanking you for writing and telling you to never do it again."

"I know you're right, but you know, it's kind of neat to talk to someone on TV—even if I don't know her. I know what she looks like, sounds like. I know she's too busy to talk with me, but if she did, wouldn't it be great?" John asked.

"Great? I don't know. I wouldn't waste my time talking to someone on TV that I don't know. You know, John, maybe you have got too much time on your hands," Judy told him as she walked off to wait on a customer.

Thursday morning, John checked his e-mail again as he has done three times a day since he got home. Today would be different, a special day, for this day he received an e-mail from AHS. He knew it was from Katie. His heart was beating faster now. The wired look on John's face was nothing to the silly look he has now. John clicked on the Read button. There it was, an e-mail from Katie Richard. She didn't let him down. It was signed by her. John was so excited he could hardly read it. As he started reading it, he realized that this is no more than a nice, polite, formal letter customized for his ad letter.

Dear John,

Thanks for e-mailing me. I never got that ad. Thanks for being concerned about me, and you have a good day. Oh, by the way, John, of course, you did not offend me. Thanks again. Bye-bye.

Katie

Bye-bye was Katie's trademark.

John sat back in his chair, looking at the e-mail, reading it over and over, as if it would change to something more than a nice note.

John walked around the apartment, going back to the computer monitor and reading it once again. It did not change. He would have to live with this being the end. *You can't just keep e-mailing people you don't know*, he thought. John closed the computer down.

He decided to move on to doing something more productive. *You got an e-mail from the Katie Richard, and that was a good thing, a great thing*, he thought, but John could not help but to think that she maybe in some kind of trouble. John had never had a feeling like this before. If Katie didn't get the ad, then who did? What are they going to do with it, and why didn't they give it to her? It just didn't feel right. Katie should have had that ad by now. He convinced himself that Katie must be made aware of the serious nature of this ad.

Confused and very concerned about Katie, John went back to his computer and once again e-mailed Katie the next morning. This time, he would make it clear just what was in this ad. Katie must know what's going on behind her back. He felt guilty about her not getting the ad. He would have to make it up to her somehow.

John couldn't just leave that ad out there. That ad was with someone, and it was not Katie. He felt very strongly about her not receiving it. It was his doing that might get her fired or something. John believed she must know what's going on with an image of her body out there. That's all there was to it. She must know.

John started the e-mail with

Dear Katie,

I appreciate you e-mailing back, but, Katie, I am very concerned about you not getting my letter and the ad. I can only hope no one opened it. I sent it to the network and your attention, marked it personal. It was a large tan envelope.

I don't think you understand why I'm so concerned and why I feel so strongly about this matter. Katie, I have watched you for years on TV. I know which school you went to, what jobs you had in the past. I know when you are happy and when you're not in a real good mood. The point I am trying to make, Katie, is this kind of ad and its publication in which it was found is so far out of character for you. I don't believe this woman is you. But I cannot get over the resemblance between you and her. *Fox & Friends* had a tennis player on a while back whose face showed up in one of the men's magazines with another body under it. Some other celebrities made photos while in school. Today's technology, it's not hard to change a head from one body to another.

Katie, you did not get the ad, so you did not see what I saw. I don't believe you really understand what I am concerned about. I don't know how to say what I want to say. Katie, I want to be very respectful of you in what I may say. Let me put it this way. You are a very successful TV hostess of a national family show. This ad is not associated with a family of any kind, especially AHS. The lady in this ad is not selling baby food. However, Katie, one might say after seeing this ad, "Oh baby." But I assure you there is no infant in this ad. If I am correct in my thinking, you might have a lawsuit on your hands. I really believe you should see the ad before you dismiss this.

About now you're probably leaning back in your chair looking at the monitor, asking yourself, what the heck is he talking about? Is this guy for real? Why I'm wasting my time with this? I imagine you think I'm some kind of weirdo. I may be, but I'm a good kind of weirdo. When I see a friend in trouble, someone that might be heading for trouble, I can't just sit here and do nothing about it. I know we don't know each other, but I feel as if I do know you somewhat, and I don't want bad things to happen to you. I hope you understand where I am coming from on this. Katie, if I'm right, and I did help you, I would feel good about it. And, Katie, if I'm wrong, I'll apologize to you now. I will try to find another copy of that ad and mail it to you if you would give me an address that you know you will get it. Do not give your home address. A post office box or another AHS address will not be okay. I want to make sure you get it so you can be the judge. Thanks for not deleting me. Take care, Katie.

John Garfield

John, leaning back, feeling good about the e-mail, knew there was no way she could ignore this e-mail. Katie would definitely have to address it. He reached and pushed the Send button. It was on its way. Katie now had it. She will read it and write back to thank him. After all, he was helping her. These were some of the thoughts going through his head.

5

Katie Goes to See Aunt Annie

Katie had another day off. She had made plans to go to Macon, Georgia, where her Aunt Annie lived. Aunt Annie had no children of her own. She thought of Katie as her own. Katie adopted her as her second mother, sending Mother's Day cards and looking out for her. Aunt Annie had a heart attack a few years ago and had to quit her job. The social security money would not be enough to allow her to keep her house. Katie bought her house and paid for a full-time housekeeper to help her out. Katie was always doing something nice for her. It was out of love.

Aunt Annie would come to see Katie when she was in college. She would have not missed the Miss National Female Journalist Pageant for anything. She was there with both Katie's parents. Aunt Annie could not have been any more proud of Katie than Katie's own parents. She loved Katie so much. She had tapes of all of her airtime. Katie would call and let her know when she would be on the air next.

Morgan had gone with Katie on several trips to see Aunt Annie. Like Katie, Morgan fell in love with her as well. The feeling was mutual. Aunt Annie loved Morgan so much. Morgan would call just to talk to her sometimes. Aunt Annie would always watch Morgan's show too. She would sometimes brag about her having two girls on AHS.

Katie had made plans to go see Aunt Annie. Morgan often went with her. This time Morgan could not get off in time. Katie went alone. After being there for a few hours, the phone rang. "Hi, Aunt Annie. How are you doing?" Morgan asked.

"Doing fine, honey. Why didn't you come with Katie today? I would love to have seen you," Aunt Annie asked.

"You know what? If I could have got off and caught up on these other things, I would have come for sure. Tell you what, Aunt Annie. I will come to see you next week, okay?"

"Okay, Morgan. I'm looking forward to seeing you. I saw you this morning. You were diamanté. Jean next door, I think you know her, she brought one of those rings, one of those two-thousand-dollar ones. I would never spend that much for a ring. But I did love it," Aunt Annie told Morgan.

"Yeah, I do remember meeting her one day. The real tall lady with a loud voice? You know, Aunt Annie, maybe Santa Clause will get you one for Christmas. You never know!" Morgan told Aunt Annie while laughing. "Maybe."

"Don't you girls go getting me anything that expensive. You hear? Morgan, I mean it."

"Well…we'll see. You never know what Clause will do, but you have to be a good girl. You hear now?" Morgan told her. "Aunt Annie, is Katie there?"

"Yeah, she's right here. You be sure and come see me next week. I'm looking forward to it you hear, girl? Here's Katie. Good-bye." Aunt Annie turned to hand the phone to Katie

"Hi, Morgan. What's up?" Katie asked.

"Hi, Katie. Jim has been looking for you. He thinks you were supposed to have taken Beth's place today. He was pretty mad about it. I told him I would fill in for Beth. Then you know what he said?"

"No, what?"

"He said that Nicky would take your place today, and listen to this! He said Beth told me, and I said I would tell you. Can you believe that? She never told me she wasn't going to be here today. You know I would have told you. Oh, another thing. He wanted me to call you on your cell phone. I told him no. Then Nicky said she found it by your computer."

"By my computer? I never took it out of my purse. I didn't use it while I was on the computer. I didn't even know it was missing, and what was Nicky doing at my computer?" Katie asked with that low wondering and confused voice.

"I do not know, Katie, but Jim wanted you to come back today. I told him you were out of town, that you couldn't possibly be back tonight, and don't you dare show up here today. You hear?" Morgan demanded of Katie.

"No, I'm not coming back today. I'll deal with this tomorrow. It's just a big misunderstanding, I am sure. I will take care of it tomorrow," Katie said, reassuring her that everything was okay.

"Okay. I didn't mean to mess up your visit with Aunt Annie. I will see you tomorrow. Give Aunt Annie a big hug and kiss for me."

"I sure will. And, Morgan, don't worry about this."

"You know, Katie, my intuitions are almost always right. I've got one bad feeling that something is going to happen. You be careful driving home tomorrow, you hear? Good-bye, Katie."

"It's okay, Morgan. Don't worry," Katie was telling her. "Don't worry. I'll see you tomorrow. Bye-bye." Hanging up the phone, she turned to see Aunt Annie looking her in the face.

"What?"

"Everything okay, dear?" she asked with a concerned voice.

"Yes, everything is fine. They thought I was going to fill in for Beth today. I didn't know anything about it," Katie explained to Aunt Annie. "Beth said she told Morgan that she needed me to cover for her one o'clock show today. Morgan doesn't remember talking with her about that."

"If Morgan said Beth never told her, then Beth never told her, the end. I'm sure it's more to this than that," Aunt Annie informed Katie.

Trying to change the subject, Katie asked, "Have you been to that new restaurant yet?"

"You mean that one on Main Street?"

"Yeah, that one. What they call it?" Katie asked.

"The New York Restaurant. Why they called it that, I don't know. Little Billy Smart owns it. Billy Smart has never left Macon in his life. He has never even been to Atlanta yet. But he can cook. The food is great," she announced.

"Then what do you say if we get ready and go see Little Billy Smart and have lunch?"

"Okay, Katie. But you know he likes you. I mean he really likes you. You sure you want to go anyhow?"

"Yes, I'm sure. I always thought he was cute."

"Well, don't let him know that."

The next morning, Katie was all packed and ready to go. Standing by the car, Aunt Annie was telling Katie she would miss her. "Katie, you listen to me. If that new guy gives you or Morgan any trouble—I mean any trouble at all—he will have to deal with me. No one picks on my girls, you hear?" she told her while looking Katie straight in the eyes.

"I will tell him that. Believe me, he doesn't want to mess with you," Katie told her while laughing and pulling Aunt Annie closer to her, giving her a big hug.

"I love you, Aunt Annie. I love you. You are the greatest." Katie hugged her again and kissed her on the neck.

"That hug and kiss was from Morgan," she informed her.

"Will you give her a big hug for me?" Aunt Annie asked of Katie. Katie got in the car and started the engine. Aunt Annie walked by the car as she pulled toward to the street. "You call me when you get home, you hear? You call me," she hollered to Katie while waving good-bye.

6

Katie, Back at Work

Katie arrived at the studio safely, and as usual, she was there two hours ahead of showtime. That gave her the time she needed to go over the products for her show. Morgan was on the air when Katie walked inside. Katie was on next, so there wouldn't be much time to talk. She did find time to call and let Aunt Annie know she was all right. Aunt Annie told her that she was watching Morgan now and would be watching her show too. After letting Aunt Annie know she was safe, Katie went into the control room.

"Is this Katie's mic?" she asked the director.

"Yes," he answered.

Picking up the mic, Katie said to Morgan, "I'm back. I'm going to tell Linda (the vendor setting next to Morgan) to do the talking for a few minutes so I can talk to you. Okay?"

Morgan nodded yes. Katie then switched to Linda's mic and told her to keep talking. She wanted to talk with Morgan. The director took the camera off Morgan. Morgan then ran to the side where she hugged Katie.

Katie asked, "Any changes?"

"No, nothing. But that juke Jim is not here today. He had a meeting in Atlanta," Morgan told her.

"Be nice now. He's the only one who wants to rub your butt," Katie said while laughing.

"There are a lot of guys wanting to rub my butt, and don't you forget!"

"Okay, if you say so. You know I didn't really want to talk with him anyway." Looking at Morgan, Katie exclaimed, "Girl, you look fabulous."

Morgan did indeed look fabulous—dressed in a short straight black leather skirt, with a white slick blouse. She indeed did look fabulous.

"Thank you, thank you," Morgan said while turning around.

"Oh, by the way, Morgan. This is the key to my new car."

Morgan and Katie always traded keys, both for the house and car.

"Thank you. I love that new car. If it's okay with you, I will drive it after the show today. I've been wanting to drive it so bad," Morgan said excitedly.

"Okay, but be careful, you hear? It's brand-new!"

Morgan, turning to look at the director, said to Katie, "I've got to go. Linda can't talk as much as I can. See you later."

Laughingly, Katie said while walking away, "No one can talk that much."

"I can hear you," Morgan announced to Katie.

A few hours after Morgan left and just before Katie's show started, Katie was walking back to her stage. One of the stagehands came in carrying a new computer.

"Hey, Katie, this is the new computer for your show today. I'm going to take it upstairs for you," he told her.

"Okay. Thank you," she replied politely, turning back to what she was doing. Shortly after he left, she heard a noise behind her. Katie jumped and turned around fast. The staircase had collapse. The stagehand was trapped under it. The computer he was carrying blocked the fall and saved him from being seriously hurt. Katie and the other stagehands ran to help.

"Are you all right? Are you all right?" Katie asked nervously.

"Yeah, yeah, I am all right," he told everyone while getting up.

Katie grabbed him and hugged him so tight. "God, I'm glad you are all right," she told him with a very sincere tone. "God, I'm glad you're all right," she repeated and hugged him even tighter.

"If I had known I could have gotten that kind of hug, I would have fallen before now," he told Katie while holding her tightly.

"Well, I'm glad you're okay," Katie said while trying to pull away from his hugging her.

She looked at him and said, "What the heck," and hugged him again and, this time, kissing him on the lips. He had thought maybe he had died and gone to heaven. Like all the stagehands, he too loved Katie.

The show started on time. Katie just moved to another stage, and another computer was set up for her. After the show, she went back to her office to catch up on some e-mail. While she was there, Jerry Ford walked in.

"Katie, I've got a favor to ask of you."

"Sure, what is it, Jerry?"

"My wife was going to pick me up today, but her car broke down. Can I borrow your car? I know it's a lot to ask. Your car is brand-new. I wouldn't ask, but she has no way of getting home," he explained to her.

"That's all right, Jerry. You would do the same for me. I don't mind. I don't mind at all. It's back in my spot," Katie informed him.

"Thank you so much. I really appreciate this."

"I know. Hey, Jerry. If the car's not there, call Morgan and tell her you need it. She was driving it a while ago. She will help. Okay?"

"Okay. You're great."

"Go on, Jerry. Your wife is waiting. Tell her I said hi!" Katie said as she started back with her e-mail.

A few minutes later, Jim walked in. "Oh, you're back. Did you make your show today?" he asked very coarsely.

Pulling herself out of her desk, she told Jim, "Yes, I did my show today. About Beth's show, I'm sorrow, Jim. I didn't know."

56

"That's all right, Katie. I think we can get over that. Maybe even becoming very good friends."

"I thought we were friends, are we not?" she asked of him.

"Yeah, of course, we are. We are working friends. I was hoping after our little meeting today that we could be really close. You know what I mean?"

"Yeah."

She knew exactly what he meant, but she would let that remark go by for now.

"Come on back to my office so we can talk."

"Okay."

Katie and Jim walked to his office. Upon entering the office, Jim offered her a drink.

"No, thanks. What's this about, Jim?"

"Well, Katie, this is about two things, or should I say two people? You and Morgan."

"What are you talking about?"

"It's seems as though your good friend may not be such a good friend after all."

"Go on," she asked.

"Your good friend didn't tell you about trading places with Beth, did she? You know, Katie, Beth told her, and she promised Beth she would tell you."

"Beth never said anything of the kind to her."

"Oh…Beth was lying?" he asked with a stronger voice.

"No, I don't believe she's lying."

"Then you believe Morgan is lying?"

"No! I didn't say that either. What I am saying is that's a misunderstanding of some kind," she explained.

"How well do you know Katie Morgan?"

"I know her well enough to know she's no liar, if that's what you meant!" She spoke with a strong voice of her own.

"Don't go raising your voice at me. Remember whom you work for!" he reminded her.

Katie sat back in her chair, looking him in the eye, and told him in a firm voice, "I don't appreciate you trying to make her out to be something she's not. Katie would not lie to you or me. She's not a liar. She's a good friend and a good person."

"Let me tell you something about your good friend and that good person. She took your cell phone from your purse while you were at the computer."

"Why would she take my phone? She has her own phone, and how do you know that anyway?"

"Linda saw her coming out of your office that day."

"That doesn't mean anything. Other people were in there the same day too."

"So now you're saying Linda is lying?" he asked with a smirk on his face.

"You don't get it, do you? Morgan did nothing wrong, and she is welcome in my office anytime she wants. I trust her so much that I gave her a key to it. She also has a key to my house and my car. She knows my password, and I know hers. We trust each other one-hundred-percent," she said, raising her voice in anger to Jim.

"You don't think she didn't tell you so she could get more airtime for herself? You know, Katie, more airtime, more money. Money has broken up good friendships before."

"You idiot, she gat more money than you or I. She doesn't have to do anything for money. She is here because she loves what she is doing, sir!"

"Before you get so upset with me, let me tell you Katie Morgan was in that limo the day before it took you to the airport."

"Of course she was. Gary drove her to Atlanta to learn about that brand of jewel she introduced while I was in Italia. She had something to do with that?" she told Jim with a sarcastic tone.

"You had better clam down, and I mean now. I could fire you any time I want to," he informed her.

"No, you can't! I've just signed a new four-year contract. This meeting is over," Katie announced and got up to walk out.

"That contract has a moral clause in it. You have already violated it. I can dismiss you whenever I want. Don't think so, try me, Katie," he shouted at her.

That statesman got her attention. Turning around and walking up to his face, she said with angry in her voice, "If you have something on me, show it! Use it, or shut up forever."

Anger in her voice was something that only a few people had ever heard. She did not like to get so angry at anything, but enough is enough.

He pulled a tan envelope out of his disk and handed it to her.

"What's this?" she asked while taking it from him.

"That's my reason to fire you," he answered while resting on the back of his chair. Katie pulled out an ad and unfolded it. Looking at it, she asked again, "What's this?"

"It's you in your birthday suit. Looking real good. Great tits."

"That's not me!" she hollered to him.

"Are you telling me that's not you in the flesh?'" he asked with that same smirk on his face.

"This is not me! Where did it come from?"

"Your good friend. You know that good person with all those keys."

"You're a liar."

"Well, she did. Your very own best friend."

"Katie walked in here and gave you this ad and told you this was me. Is that what you are saying?" she demanded to know.

"Not exactly."

"Then exactly how did you get this?"

"Morgan slipped it under my door yesterday."

"If it came under the door, what makes you so sure Morgan did it. Did you see her or get fingerprints, or maybe she was stupid enough to be in the hall to make sure you find it. What makes you so sure?"

"I saw it coming in and ran to the door. The only person in the hall was Morgan. Who do you think it came from? Which one of your other friends might have done it besides her?"

"I don't care if you thought Morgan had personally handed it to you. I would say she was a look-alike, or you are lying."

"Katie, I like you. I really do."

"You got a heck of a way of showing it."

"I like you and Morgan too. Katie…I could fire her and not worry about it. But you I really like. That picture really makes me hot for you."

"Go to hell," Katie shouted as she once again walked to the door.

"Katie, all of this could go away if you would be a more friendly," Jim said in a low smooth voice.

"If I go to bed with you, then you leave both of us alone?" she asked with an anguished look on her face and an extremely hostile voice as she headed for his disk.

"Well…maybe a little fun with Morgan too. She has a cute ass."

She clenched her hands to the disk. "Mr. Jim, you're new here, and I'm going to do you a big favor. I'm going to pretend this conversation never happened, and that's a good thing for you, Mr. Jim. You don't know me or Morgan very well. So I'm going to tell you the way it is around here. If there are two women you don't want to mess with in this company, they would be Katie Morgan and myself. Now I'm leaving. I suggest you think about what I said and what you said," she told Jim in a very stern tone—a tone that he knew that she was serious about what she had said.

Katie thought as she was leaving, *What's with that guy? He thinks I will. No way in hell with him, and what's with everyone and Morgan's rear anyway? No one has commented on my butt, and it's a great one.*

She was so furious at Jim that she thought she may not be thinking straight. She had been mad before but never this mad at anyone except that time with Morgan a few years back. While opening the door to leave, the phone rang. Jim picked up the phone and asked with a mad voice, "What? Yes, she's here. What cops? Okay, I'll tell her," laying the phone back in its cradle. Rising from his chair, he asked Katie, "What have you done now? There two cops in the lobby asking to see you."

Katie, not responding to that question, left the room and headed down the long corridor to the newly decorate lobby. As she walked, she put the ad in her pocket and still wondering where this ad came from.

She was also hoping this ad was the only one. She knew there may be more copies somewhere.

She thought while walking, *Who could be doing this to me?* The only thing she knew for sure was that girl was not her and it did not come from her best friend, Katie Morgan. Katie could not think of any way that ad could have gotten into Jim's hands.

Katie was not worried about why the police wanted to see her. They had asked her to be a speaker at one of their police get-togethers two years ago. She also sang there too. *Yes, that is probably what they want*, she thought.

As she walked into the lobby, an officer of the Landover police department got up when he saw Katie. He walked straight to her.

"Miss Katie Richard?" he asked very respectfully.

"Yes, I'm Katie Richard," she replied. "May I help you?"

"Miss Richard, do you own a new two-door Chrysler Sebring, a blue one?"

"Yes. Why do you ask?"

"I'm sorry to have to tell you, Miss Richard. This car was involved in a serious accident a while ago. Did you know your car was missing?"

"Missing? No, it's not missing. I told Jerry Ford he could drive it today. How's Jerry? He's all right, isn't he? He is okay, isn't he? Please tell me he's okay," she pleaded with the officer.

"Mr. Ford is alive, and he had your permission to be driving your car?"

"Yes, of course. Thank God," Katie said with a sincere voice. "Thank God!"

"Mr. Ford is in the hospital. He was knocked out and has some broken bones. He will be okay," Katie was told.

"How could this have happened? Jerry was a stunt driver from Hollywood before coming here. He jumps over cars. If there's anyone who knows how to drive, it's Jerry."

"His stunt driving experience was probably what saved his life."

"What happened? Someone ran into him?" she asked.

"No, Miss Richard, the brakes on your car failed."

"The brakes failed? That car only had nine hundred miles on it. The brakes were working well this morning when I drove to work. I don't understand. It's a new car for God's sake!" Katie added. "Anyway, how is he now?"

"He was taken to Landover General."

"Will someone call me a cab, please?" she asked of them.

Kim Peterson—another beautiful blonde hostess and a very close friend of Morgan and Katie's who had just finished her show—overhearing the conversation, told Katie, "You don't need a cab. I'll take you there, Katie."

"Thank you, Kim. Thank you."

Kim, looking at Jim who had walked in with Katie, asked him, "Are you going to the hospital too?"

"No. I can't go now. I'll go later. Tell him I hope he's okay."

Katie and Kim never addressed him. They were disappointed in him, but he was not surprised. Several other people said they were going to see Jerry too. Katie looked at the officer and asked if Jerry's wife knew.

"No, we cannot get in touch with her," Katie was told.

"I will take of care of this myself. I know where she is."

"Walking to the car, Katie pulled her cell phone out and called Morgan. "Morgan," she said, "I have some bad news to tell you. Jerry Ford was driving my car. The brakes failed, and he had an accident. Jerry is at Landover General. Could you please go by Brown's Auto Repair Shop and pick up his wife, take her to the hospital? Thank you so much…Yes, I'm all right. I'm with Kim. She's driving me to the hospital. Thanks again, Morgan."

They got to the hospital and walked in together. Katie ran to Jerry's side.

"I'm so sorry about the brakes being bad. I'll make it up to you, Jerry. I'm so sorry, Jerry. I didn't know."

"It's all right, Katie. Really, it's all right. I know you would not ever put me or anyone in harm's way. It's not your fault. You know, Katie, what I'm really glad I was driving."

"What?"

"It wasn't you driving."

"Jerry, I wish it was me there instead of you," Katie said with a tremble in her voice. "I wish it was me."

"Katie, stop that now. Had it been you or Morgan, one of you may be dead now. It was my training as a stunt driver that kept me from getting killed. So you see, Katie, it's okay. I'll recover, and I will be fine. You will see."

"Jerry, if this costs you any money, let me know. I will take care of it for you," Katie told Jerry with a very sincere tone.

"Katie, you are a good friend. But you don't own me anything. The insurance will take care of all this and get you another new car."

With tears in her eyes, Katie hugged Jerry.

At the door, Morgan and Mrs. Ford came in. Mrs. Ford, a very attractive woman in her right, felt a little bit jealous of Katie. She left Hollywood thinking there would no more completion for her. She believed Jerry was having an affair with one of the hostesses at AHS. The fact that her husband was driving Katie's brand-new car didn't make her feel good about Katie.

Entering Jerry's room, Mrs. Ford ran to her husband's side, hugging and asking him. In a very concerned manner, "What happened, Jerry? Morgan said the car you were driving had no brakes on it."

Turning and looking toward Katie with a rather mad look on her face, she inquired, "You are that Katie Richard woman, aren't you? I've seen you on TV. Why did you let him drive your car knowing it had bad brakes?"

Morgan walked between them and told Mrs. Ford in a stern voice, "Let's get one thing straight, Mrs. Ford. Katie would never let anyone be in danger if she knew it. She would rather it be her instead of Jerry. I know you are upset now, but don't take it out on her."

"It's okay, Morgan. She has every right to be upset."

"No," Jerry said, "she has no right to talk to you like that. I asked to borrow her car to go pick you up. She was only doing me a favor. She knew nothing about the brakes."

Katie walked up to Mrs. Ford and looked her in the eye. "I'm so sorry about this. I really am sorry. I would give anything if it had never happened."

Mrs. Ford looked Katie in the eyes, said nothing, and walked back to the bedside. Thinking how it might looked, she turned back to Katie and, in a low apologetic voice, said, "You're right. I'm sorry. I know you wouldn't hurt him." Morgan joined them in the hugging.

"I'm sorry too. I shouldn't have said that."

Jerry, lying on the bed, asked, "Katie, have you met my wife, Jenny?"

Everyone started to laugh and hugged again. Others from AHS were starting to come in.

Katie said, "I'm going home," then went over and hugged Jerry, then turned to Jenny Ford and hugged her too.

Morgan said, "I'm going too, Katie. I'll give you a ride."

Katie asked Morgan to come by for breakfast in the morning. Morgan accepted the offer. She had a night show and knew they could not catch up on everything till morning, and she knew Katie was a very good cook. Besides that, Morgan wanted to get caught up on what was happening with Jim. She knew Katie was not in the mood to talk tonight.

Morgan drove into Katie's driveway. Turning and looking at Katie, she asked, "Will you be all right?"

"Yeah, I will be all right. I'm going to take a long bubble bath and go to bed. You go home. I'll be okay. But be here about eight in the morning, hear?"

"Okay," she said, reaching over to hug Katie.

"You're welcome to come home with me, or I'll stay with you tonight."

"Thanks, that's sweet of you. But I will be okay. Go on home. You have a husband at home waiting for you."

"Oh yea, I do have one them at home. This week so far, he says."

7

The Next Morning

At 8:00 a.m. the next morning, Katie Morgan was walking through the door.

"There better be some bacon cooking," she announced as she walked to the kitchen, where Katie had already started cooking the bacon.

Morgan hugged Katie and asked, "How are you, girl?"

"I'm okay now…Now I know Jerry will be all right."

Morgan sat at the wooden table Katie made herself. She leaned toward Katie and pointed that little finger at her, saying, "You know it could have been either one of us."

"That was the second time yesterday I almost got hurt."

"Hurt? You could have been killed! What do you mean, the second time? What else happened?"

"It's probably nothing."

"Well, tell me anyway."

"You know that staircase in studio three?"

"Yeah, the one going to the computer room."

"Yes, that one. Anyway, Paul, that cute stagehand, was carrying my new computer upstairs. The stairs collapsed on him. He's okay. But that computer was supposed to have been there early yesterday morning. I would have been the next one to go up those stairs."

"Now that's creepy, just plain creepy," Morgan said as her voice trailed off.

"You don't suppose, do you?"

"No!" Katie nodded. "No…No…no, I don't."

"It could be."

"No. Don't even go there."

"Oh, let me tell you about Jim Bob."

"Jim Bob. You mean?"

"Yes, Mr. Delightful himself."

"This should be good. What, when, how, and how good was it?"

"How good was it? What kind of question is that?"

"Never mind. Now go on. I want to hear this. Every single word."

"He started talking about you."

"Me?" Morgan asked with a stunned look. "What about me?"

"Jim thinks you are not a good friend to me."

"Why? Because I didn't tell you about Beth trading places with you? You know she never told me. I would have told you."

"Of course, you would. But that's not the best part."

"There's more?"

"Ho, yeah. There's a lot more."

Morgan got up from the table and asked if Katie wanted another cup of coffee. After pouring the coffee, Morgan sat back down at the table.

"All right, I'm ready now."

"You were involved with the limo breaking down."

"I was? How?"

"You were using the limo the night before."

"That's ridiculous."

"Oh, it gets better."

"Jim really doesn't like me, does he?" Morgan asked while swallowing another sip of coffee.

"I'll tell you about that later. Here take a look at this," Katie told Morgan while handing her the ad she taken from Jim the day before.

"Wow, when did you do this?" she asked.

"That's not me, you fool!"

"Who is this then?"

"I don't know."

"She looks just like you. That's your face. But she got a better body than you," Morgan remarked while laughing.

"What are you talking about? My body is a lot better than that."

"She has more of all the right parts in all the right places."

"That's nowhere near as good as my body, and I have everything in their right places."

Changing the subject, Morgan asked, "Where did you get this from? And who is she?"

"I don't know who she is, and it came from you, of course."

"Me, of course? That jerk told you I gave this to him? What a jerk! You know I didn't."

"Okay, okay, Morgan, don't get too upset with Jim. He wants to go to bed with both of us. He said, and I quote, 'She's got a cute ass,' unquote. Personally, I don't see anything to it," Katie told Morgan while drinking more coffee and smiling.

"Okay, we're even now. But you know, Katie," she said as she pointed that little finger at her, "a clock that doesn't run is right twice a day…He told you I gave this to him?"

Smiling at what Morgan had just said, Katie answered her, "No, what he said was, it was slipped under his office door yesterday. He ran to the door, and guess who he saw in the hall?"

"Me, of course. I walk down that hall every day."

"Did you see anyone else in the hall yesterday?"

"Nicky was ahead of me and walking fast. She said, 'Hi. I'm in a hurry. I'm late for a luncheon.' It wouldn't be her anyway. Then Jim came out about that time and said hi to me. He didn't mention this to me."

Morgan started to say something else when Katie's doorbell rang. Looking though the breakfast room into the hall, Morgan asked, "Who's at the door?"

Katie got up and headed to the door. It rang again. Katie reached to open the door only to see two very big men there.

"Hi, may I help you?" she asked.

"Katie Richard?" one of them asked.

"Yes, I'm Katie Richard, and you are?"

"I'm sorry." Showing her his badge, he said, "I'm Detective Barker of the Landover Police Department, homicide, and this is my partner, Detective Parks. May we come in?"

"Yes, of course. Come on in. You said homicide? Jerry is okay. I talked to him this morning," she said with heavy concern in her eyes.

"Yes, he is okay. We're here to talk to you about your car."

"What about my car?"

"The brakes. The brake line was cut, Miss Richard."

"Call me, Katie. How? You mean someone deliberately cut the brake line?"

"Why?" Morgan, walking into the room, asked.

Looking at Morgan, Detective Barker said, "You are Katie Morgan. My wife loves you. Watches your show every day." Then, thinking what he had just said, he turned to Katie and said, "She loves you too."

"Thank you. But what about the brakes?" she inquired.

"Katie, is there anyone who wants to hurt you?"

"No. You think someone was trying to hurt me?"

"No, I think someone was trying to kill you."

"Don't be ridiculous. Katie doesn't have an enemy in the world. No one wants her dead!" Morgan snapped back at the detective.

"I hate to disagree with you, Morgan, but brake lines are cut for a reason," Detective Barker informed her.

"Katie, can you think of anyone who might want to harm you?" Detective Parks asked again.

"No…no one. Everyone one has been nice to me."

"What about your fans?"

"No, they're about the same. Some wanting to marry me, some wanting just the honeymoon, but nothing out of the ordinary."

"Old boyfriends?"

"No, they are all happily married now."

"Have you noticed anything, Miss Morgan?" Detective Barker asked Morgan as he turned toward the door.

"No, sir…nothing."

"Here's my card. If y'alls think of anything…anything at all, you let me know."

Katie assured him that they would let him know. Nodding his head to the two of them, he said very respectfully, "Be careful. I don't want anything to happen to you."

"Me neither," she replied.

Morgan, closing the door behind them, turned back to Katie with that little finger in the air and remarked, "Boy, you must have ticked somebody off, big time, any ideas?"

"You know, Morgan, I've never been known to do things halfway, but, no, Morgan, I don't have any ideas. Not one. But you know, I'm not going to hide. I'm not going to live in fear," she said in a voice that was tranquil.

Katie started to the kitchen and grabbed Morgan by the hand. "Help me clean up this mess, and then let's go buy me a new car."

"Okay. But, Katie, I don't want to drive it," Morgan said, laughing.

"I am thinking about one of those new T-Birds. Maybe a red one."

Morgan, pointing that little finger at Katie, told her, "I hear you can't cut their brake lines."

"Are you going to let me drive it sometime, Morgan?"

"Sometime, maybe. Oh, by the way, Katie, have you told Aunt Annie about this?"

"She knows of the staircase and Jerry's accident. I don't know if I'm going to tell her about it not being an accident," Katie said in a low voice.

"You have to tell her. She will be so mad if you don't," Morgan let Katie know.

"I just don't want to worry her."

"Katie, I think you're wrong."

"You really think I should tell her everything?"

"If it were your niece, wouldn't you want to know?"

"Yeah, you're right. I'll call her today and tell her. When are you going there?"

"After my eleven o'clock show Tuesday. I will be spending the night there and be back in time for my night show on Thursday. Can you trade with someone and come with me?"

"No, I want to be here right now."

"Maybe I should come back Wednesday instead of Thursday."

"No, Aunt Annie is looking forward to seeing you. Don't disappoint her on my behalf."

"You be sure to take your cell phone so I can call if something happens," Katie asked of Morgan. "Oh yeah, that's another thing Jim told me, you took my cell out of my purse. That's why I didn't have it."

"Me again? I guess I cut the staircase too."

"I feel safe already with you being out of town."

"Funny, if I wanted to hurt you, it would have already happen and you would be there instead of Jerry."

"Morgan, you couldn't hurt a fly. And if you try, I would catch you so fast it wouldn't be funny. Well, you let me know everything that's going on."

"Okay, Mom, but nothing is going to happen. Tell Aunt Annie what's happening. I am not going to tell her over the phone."

"Okay, that's a good idea."

8

The Orange Juice

Tuesday morning, after Morgan had left for Macon, Katie walked into the break room. Morgan and Katie loved orange juice. Almost every day, they would have a jar. Morgan had brought the last of a six-pack from home. She thought since she would be away the next two days that it would be nice to give it to Katie. She had noticed that Katie had ran out. Katie was grateful for her thoughtful gesture.

Katie arrived an hour or two after Morgan had left, so she didn't get a chance to see her this morning. She did talk to her on the phone earlier.

Remembering the orange juice Morgan had left for her, Katie opened the refrigerator door and grabbed it. It was marked *KR*. As she unscrewed the top and started to take a sip, a mouse ran across the floor. Katie jumped and dropped the jar. The juice ran everywhere, and so did Katie. She had always been afraid of mice, and this was no exception. She left the room to get help. George, an older man working as a janitor there, was more than glad to help Katie. He too was a big fan of hers.

"Katie," he said with a surprised tone, "look!"

She walked over and looked down at the mess she had just made. The mess wasn't what George was referring to. It was the dead mouse on the floor next to the orange juice it drank. Katie was backing up, looking pale and weak. George grabbed her and helped Katie to a seat. "Are you all right, Katie?" he asked with real concern for her.

"No, I'm not," she said with a trembling voice. "That juice was meant for me! Not that mouse, but me!"

"What can I do to help you, Katie?'

"Call security, please."

"Okay."

George pulled his two-way radio out and called security. It was only a few seconds before they arrived.

"Are you all right, Katie?" they asked of her.

"Someone is trying to kill me. They tried to poison me with this juice," she explained with a lump in her throat. "Here," she said to them while handing them Detective Barker's card. "Call him, and don't clean this up. I want to know what was in it."

Detective Barker was there in less than twenty minutes. He brought with him the CSI unit. They cleaned the mess and took samples of the juice back to the lab for testing.

"Call me when you know what was in it," Barker told the CSI unit.

"Where did this juice come from?" Barker asked.

"It was in the refrigerator."

"Did you buy it?"

"Yes. No, it was here when I got here this morning."

"Who put it there?"

"Morgan called and said she had one left and I could have it."

"Why would she be giving you her juice?"

"She was going out of town today. She saw I was out, so she was just being kind. We often do this for each other."

"You knew this juice was yours because it had *KR* on the cap?"

"No, Morgan and I only drank one brand. That brand is not sold in the vending machines here. We never put our names on the caps. We don't have to. Nobody here has ever messed with it."

"So you don't think Morgan had anything to do with this?"

"No! Certainly not. What's the…are you thinking?"

"Sorry, Katie. I have to look at every possibility. You can understand that, can't you?" the Detective asked very respectfully.

"No, I can't. Morgan is my best friend. She's like a sister to me, and I to her. She wouldn't hurt me any more than I would hurt her. You're wasting your time on her. She's not the one!" Katie hollered in an argumentative tone.

"Where is she now?"

"She is visiting my aunt today and tomorrow. Why?"

"I'd just like to talk with her and clear up some things. That's all."

"I'll clear them up for you now. She doesn't know anything about this."

"I'm sure you're right. But I still need to talk with her. Tell her when she gets back to call me, okay, Katie?"

"Okay, but you're wasting your time, and maybe my life."

"I would like to talk with everyone. Can you arrange that for me?" Barker asked of Jim, who had just walked into the break room.

"Sure. You can use my office."

"Don't worry, Katie. We wouldn't let anything happen to you, and don't forget to tell Ms. Morgan to call me when you see her."

"I would like to talk with you first, Jim."

"Okay, that's fine," Jim asked his secretary to arrange for the interviews. Both detectives, so as to save time, would conduct them.

"You're new here, aren't you?" the detective asked Jim.

"Yeah, I've only been here a couple of months."

"How well to you know Miss Katie...Do you think she is pretty?"

"Of course. Don't you?"

"Yeah, you're right. Do you get along with her well?"

"Yes, we have a good relationship."

"You and her had an argument the day of the accident?"

"Oh, that! It was nothing. She missed a show. I was little upset with her. It's all over now."

"Okay."

The phone rang. It was Jim's secretary telling him that Beth was here to talk with Detective Barker. Looking at the detective, Jim asked if he was finished with him and told him Beth was waiting.

"Yeah, that's all for now. I will talk with Beth next."

Beth walked in. "I'm Beth." She was trying to introduce herself when Barker interrupted her. Standing up, he extended his hand to her. Barker had known this woman well. He had watched on local TV. He watched her go to NBC national. He had been watching her for over ten years now on AHS. Like many others, he had nothing but respect and love for her.

"Yes, I know. I have been watching you for about twenty years now. I feel as if I know you," he told her while they were shaking hands.

"I haven't been on AHS that long. Thanks anyway."

"No, I first saw you on Kart TV when I was in college. Then I saw you again on the NBC networks," he said very excitedly.

"Well, I didn't think anyone would remember me from those days."

"I did. I sure did."

"Detective Barker, is that correct?"

"Yes. I'm sorry. I'm Larry Barker."

"What was it you wanted to talk with me about?" she asked politely.

"I'm so sorry. It's just an honor to meet you in person," he apologized to her.

"Thank you so very much, Larry. I don't mean to be rude, but I have a show in twenty minutes."

"Yeah…yeah, you're right. Have you heard anyone say or sound like they may be upset with Katie Richard?"

"No, nothing. Everyone likes her a lot. She gets along with everyone."

"What about the vendors, you know, the salespeople she works with sometimes?"

"Yes, I know the vendors. No, the same with them."

"Have you ever heard Katie Morgan get upset with Katie?"

"No, of course not. They're like sisters."

"What about Jim. Has he ever said anything about Katie?"

"Not to me. He seems to like her okay."

"That's all for now, Beth. It was so nice to meet you," Barker told her as he reached out for her hand.

"Thank you so much. It was a pleasure to have met you too."

Kim, one of the prettiest hostesses, was on her way in to talk with Detective Parks. "Hi. I'm Kim Peterson," she said, reaching her hand to shake with his.

"I know. You are my favorite. When I'm at home and you are on TV, I watch your whole show," he told her with a great deal of excitement in his voice.

"Thank you so much for that. How can I help you?" she asked while pulling her hand back from him holding it so long. Then she sat herself down in front of Parks, crossing her long legs, with that short skirt sliding up just far enough to make it difficult for Detective Parks to concentrate on his work.

"Kim, do you know anyone who might want to harm Katie Richard?"

"No, I really don't."

"What about Jim. Do they get along?"

"Jim is new here. He's a little different from Chad."

"Chad. Who's that?"

"Oh, I'm sorry. Chad was the program manager before Jim. He's the vice president now."

"How was Chad different from Jim?"

"Chad was just one of us. He would buy lunch for all. We could talk with him about anything."

"What about Jim?"

"Jim, well, he is no Chad. Jim likes to come on to all the girls. He really believes himself to be a ladies' man."

"Does he get too personal or close to all?"

"Well, let me put it this way. He has not crossed that line with me, but he has come right to the line."

"Do you think he would harm any of you girls if they say no to him?"

"I hope not. I have said no to him many times, and the girls tell me they have too. I think he thinks if he keeps on hitting, one of us one might go out with him. We have the advantage. If we get out of control, all we have to do is to call Chad. Chad would not put up with any kind of disrespecting of one of us."

"Chad got along with Katie okay?"

"Yeah, they had a lot of respect for each other."

"Were they involved?"

"No, Chad is married. They just admired each other."

"Do Jim and Katie have that same respect?"

"No, I don't think so."

"Why?"

"He was upset with Katie and Morgan both for missing a show. He made some remarks about it to some of the hostesses."

"Did he say anything to you?"

"No, not to me, but he thought Morgan was lying about not telling Katie to trade spots with Beth. He thought maybe she had told Katie and Katie went out of town anyway."

"Do you think that's what happened?"

"No, I don't believe Morgan ever heard Beth asking her to tell Katie. Katie would not have ever just left town when a friend needed her, and Morgan would not have not told her on purpose."

"How do you like cops? Jim...I mean, is he okay with you?" Parks asked with a low voice.

"I don't like the way he looks at the girls. I suppose he's okay."

"Do you think he might do anything to harm any of them?"

"Well, if anything, Jim would be too nice to them."

"What do you mean?"

"Jim fancies himself to be a big-time ladies' man."

"Has he ever come on to you, Kim?"

"Jim has come on to every woman here so far, but no one takes him serious."

"So you think Jim's okay?"

"Yeah, he's okay."

"Well, that's all I have to ask now. I may want to talk with you later."

"That's okay. Hope I have helped you," she said as she started for the door. Detective Parks watched her every little move. It was beauty in motion. She looked as good going as she did coming, in Park's eyes.

"Yes, I do," Kim said while turning her head halfway around fast enough so only half of her face was showing, with the other half hidden by her blond hair. She looked toward Parks with that sissy, sexy look on her face.

Parks, with a lump in his throat, asked, "You do what?"

"I like cops."

"You do?"

"Yes, I really like cops."

"Any one cop or all cops?" Parks asked with a trembling voice.

"I like you," she told him with that same sexy, naughty look.

"Call me some time," Kim told the detective in her low breathy voice.

"Call you? Yeah, I...I will...maybe we can go out sometime?"

"Why don't you call me and find out for sure?" Kim said again in that same low sexy voice as she closed the door behind her. With the door now closed, Kim said to herself, "He is all mine now. Darn, I am good."

The good detective was on cloud nine. The beautiful blond television celebrity, the very one whom he likes the most, had just asked him to call her. Maybe she would go out with him. Maybe it would lead to something. He was finding it hard to believe what just happened.

While he was still thinking about Kim's offer, the door opened, and Judy, another lovely hostess, entered the room. She was small in size but a bundle of energy—a very attractive lady.

"Hi, I'm Judy."

"Hi, I'm Detective Parks," he answered, with Kim still on his mind.

"Please, have a seat. Is Kim seeing anyone now?" was his first question. It just came out.

"Kim? No, I don't believe so. Are we talking about Kim?"

"No, Judy. I'm sorry," Parks said, looking and feeling like an imbecile. "We are talking about Katie Richard. Do you know anyone who might want to hurt her?"

"No."

"What about the new people here? Do they all like Katie?"

"Yes."

"Have any of them said anything bad about her?"

"No. Well…Nicky did say one time, 'Katie Richard really thinks she hot,' but she was kind of laughing when she said that."

"You think she might be jealous?"

"Nicky, jealous? No, I don't think so. Nicky is hot herself, and she knows it. I don't think she is capable of being jealous of any of us here."

"How does she like Katie Morgan?"

"I think she likes Morgan. She's either with her or close by a lot. I've never heard her say anything bad about her."

"Well, that's all, Judy. Thanks for coming by."

"I'm glad to help," she said, turning and walking to the door. "Would you like for me to find out for sure?"

"Find out what?"

"If Kim is seeing someone now."

Looking embarrassed, Parks said in a low voice, "Oh no, that's all right. Thank you, though."

That was Parks' last interview for the day. Everyone was not there at that time. They would have to talk with the others later. Barker's next interview was with Nicky.

Nicky walked in with a dress that looked as if it was made on her. Every string of her hair was in its place. The good detective couldn't help but to notice how beautiful she was, standing there with her hand out to meet his.

"How you do, Detective? I'm Nicky," she added with a sexy anxious tone.

Barker, obviously impressed with her beauty and charm, invited her to have a seat. After taking his eyes off of her legs he started off by asking her.

"Do you know anyone who might want to hurt Katie Richard?"

"No, everyone loves her."

"Have you never heard anything bad about her?"

"No…well, only good things. It's as if she couldn't do anything wrong."

"Nothing bad?"

"No."

"Have you ever heard her arguing with anyone?"

"No…Well…it was nothing."

"What?"

"Well, she and Morgan were hollering about something a few days ago. I don't know what. It's none of my business."

"You couldn't hear what they were fighting about?"

"No. I'm not even sure they were fighting. Anyway they seemed okay later."

"How do you like Morgan?"

"Morgan is a charming, funny girl to be with. We have gone out a couple of times. I like her a lot."

"Do you think she could have anything to do with what's happening?"

"No…Well, it does look bad for her."

"What do you mean?"

"Well, she was carrying a chain saw to studio three the morning before the staircase collapsed. She was using the limo the day before it broke down. She was the last one to drive Katie's car before Jerry's accident, and she gave Katie the orange juice. Now don't misunderstand me. I love Morgan. She's a dear friend. I don't think she could hurt anything. I think someone is trying to frame her."

"Who would do that?"

"I don't know. I just believe in my heart that she couldn't possibly do all that. I don't think she is smart enough pull all that off."

"Have you heard anyone say anything about either of them?"

"No. That's why I don't know. Everyone really seems to like them a lot."

"Well, someone wants Katie dead. That's for sure, Nicky. That will be all for now. Thanks for coming by," Detective Barker said while reaching his hand out to hers.

"You know, you have the most beautiful blue eyes, Detective. If I hear anything, I'll let you know," Nicky said as she left the room.

"Yeah, you do that. Thank you." He thanked her again while watching every move she made toward the door close behind her.

Walking in with his notes in his hand, Detective Parks asked, "Did you get anything helpful?"

"Not really. Did you?"

"Everybody loves Katie Richard."

"Everybody but one," Parks added.

"Did you get anything, Parks?"

"I gat Kim's phone number and was asked to call sometime."

"Kim's phone number. Anything useful?"

"Yeah, she might go out with me soon."

Parks was told to shut up about Kim and concentrate on this case.

The two detectives grabbed their notes and books. They were headed for their car when they heard Katie shouting to them.

"Detective Barker, please wait."

They turned around to know what she wanted.

"Detective Barker, what's going on in my and Morgan's case? They are going through our personal e-mail," Katie demanded an explanation.

"It's routine. They are computer experts, Katie. They are looking for a fan that might be mad at you," Barker explained.

"Why Morgan's computer?"

"Someone might be mad at both of you. He might be madder at Morgan than you. The truth is, Miss Katie, at this point, we don't know who we are looking for or why."

"Well, that certainly makes me feel safe," Katie said with a tranquil voice.

"Don't worry. We will be watching you and your home. We will get him," Barker assured her.

The two detectives went back to the station to discuss their notes. Morgan had left immediately after her 9:00 a.m. show was over. She never went back to the break room. She had a two-hour drive ahead of her. She wanted to grab a breakfast burger and a cup of coffee on the road.

9

Morgan Goes to Macon

Morgan arrived at Aunt Annie's house about 11:20 a.m. Aunt Annie was so glad to see her. She hugged Morgan at the car and told her how happy she was that she would be spending a couple of days with her.

"I wish Katie could have come with you," Aunt Annie told Morgan.

"Yeah, I wish she could have too."

"Tell me about the car wreck, girl."

"Well, Aunt Annie, Katie didn't want to tell you over the phone, but it was no accident. The brake line was cut."

"The brake line was cut? Was that what you said?" Aunt Annie asked.

"Yes, Ma, that was exactly what I said."

"You were driving the car just before that guy drove it. Thank God, you are all right. And that guy too, of course."

"His name is Jerry, but that's not all, Aunt Annie."

"Okay, Jerry. I am glad he is okay. Now tell me the rest."

"The police think I did it."

"What?" Aunt Annie shouted.

"Yeah, they think I did it because the car was all right while I was driving it."

"Anybody could have done it at anytime. The car was in the parking lot. Anybody could have done it," Aunt Annie told Morgan.

"Well…here's more, Aunt Annie."

"More?"

"The staircase collapsed on one of the stagehands. The staircase that Katie was supposed to be the next one up. That staircase."

"Is he okay?"

"Yes, he's okay."

"Did they blame you for that too?" Aunt Annie asked.

"Yes, little old me of course."

"Why?"

"Bobby had called me and asked if I would pick up the chain saw and bring it to him on studio three. Only thing was, he wasn't there when I got there and some people saw me with the saw."

"Will Bobby back you up? Didn't he?" she asked.

"No, he said he never called me."

"Why, that lying piece…"

"Aunt Annie," Morgan interrupted, "that's the same Bobby I told you was hitting on Katie and me."

I will show him what hitting is, and he had better tell the truth before I get to him."

Smiling, Morgan told Aunt Annie in a low soft voice. "It's all right. We have everything under control. It's okay."

"Morgan, do you think someone is trying to kill Katie and deliberately trying to make it look like you're doing it? Do you?" she asked Morgan with an anxious voice.

"Yes, Ma, it surely does look like that."

"Why does anyone want to hurt you two?" she asked with a very concerned motherly tone.

"I don't know. I just don't know."

"Can you think of anyone who might want to do this?"

"No, no one comes to mind."

"Why didn't Katie tell me?" she asked with an angry voice.

"Don't be mad at Katie. She was only trying to protect you. We talked about it before I came down, and we decided that it would be best for me to tell you face-to-face. Katie didn't want to upset you on the phone, and I agree. It was better for you that one of us would be here with you when you found out," Morgan said, trying to be comforting to her aunt Annie.

Reaching over, hugging Morgan, and holding her so tightly, she said in a tranquil tone, "I'm not mad at Katie or you, honey. You all did the right thing. You two always will do the right thing. I just don't want anyone to hurt my girls. I love you and Katie so much. The thought of anyone wanting to hurt you two makes me crazy." Her voice was rising.

"I know, Aunt Annie. Katie and I both love you so very much too. Don't worry. We'll both be here for a very long time," Morgan said, trying to reassure her once again.

"I know…I know, Morgan, but I can't help but worry some."

"Worry some is good, but don't go crazy on us. We need your sharp mind."

Hugging Morgan again, Aunt Annie repeated herself, "I love you and Katie."

"We love you too. Let's put this aside for now. I'm only here two days. Let's do something fun. What do you say, Aunt Annie?"

"What about Katie? Is she okay?"

"It's eleven. She should be on now. Let's look and see."

Aunt Annie turned on the TV set. She was so very much relieved that she saw Katie, and she was looking as if she had no worries in the world.

Aunt Annie said with relief, "Thank God she is okay."

"I told you she was okay. I'm with you. She is okay when I'm gone. Don't you know?" Morgan said while laughing.

"That's not funny, Morgan. That means that I'm in danger now, not Katie."

"Now, that's funny, Aunt Annie. That was funny. Come on, let's go somewhere."

"Oh, Morgan, Mary from across the street has wanted to meet you. She has met Katie, said she talked with you one day while you were on the air."

"I don't remember a Mary, but let's go see her," Morgan said, trying to get Aunt Annie's mind off Katie and her trouble. They walked across the street to Mary's house. A sweet small older woman opened the door, and with excitement in her voice, she invited them in. Aunt Annie introduced Morgan to Mary.

Mary, looking at Morgan, said, "I know, I know you're Katie Morgan. I watch you on that PPS channel, NBC, and now AHS. I called and talked with you one day but didn't tell you I knew Annie or Katie. It was that day you were selling that westward jewelry, and that salesgirl was on with you."

"Oh yea, I think I remember talking with you," Morgan said politely. "That was the day Susan was on with me."

"Yes, that day," Mary said with excitement.

"You know, Morgan, the show I remember was the one Katie did in the Miss National Journalist Pageant." Aunt Annie announced to them, "Katie was Miss National Journalist one year.

Turning to look at Morgan, Mary asked with a curious tone, "When? What year? Tell me all about it, Morgan."

Morgan, sitting up straight, replied, "No, it wasn't me. She was obviously talking about Katie Richard." Looking at Aunt Annie, Morgan said, "I didn't know Katie was Miss National Journalist. What year was that?" she asked.

"Well, she didn't really win Miss National Journalist. But she was the third runner-up to her. Then she became Miss National when that other Miss National dropped out and the first runner-up had her accident and couldn't do it. I shouldn't have said she won the Miss National Journalist title. That's what I meant to say," Aunt Annie explained.

"What year was it?" Morgan asked again.

"Let me see. It was 1990. Yes, it was 1990. That was the year I did the big ten cook-off."

"In 1990, I covered that pageant. It was the Miss National Journalist Pageant. I don't remember her name. Miss National was Nicole something, and the first runner-up was a Susan something. They both had an accident or something and Kathryn, yeah...What's her name? Turner! Yes, Kathryn Turner. Are you sure it was 1990, Aunt Annie?" Morgan asked.

"Yes, Katie was called Kathryn Turner. Some stupid reporter reported Turner as her name instead of Katie," Aunt Annie explained to them. Then, looking at Morgan, she put her hand on Morgan's hand. "I'm sorry, dear. I didn't mean all reporters were stupid. I was referring to that reporter only."

"I knew what you meant. As a matter of fact, I knew a few stupid reporters myself. Anyway, Katie was then the third runner-up, and she won by default. How did they get the name Turner, and why didn't Katie correct them?" Morgan asked while getting more comfortable in her seat.

"She tried, dear, but they kept on calling her Turner. Turner is her middle name, and her mother's maiden name. All they did was drop the last name."

"You know, I remember interviewing her. It was only one time, but I sure don't remember Katie being a Turner," she added. "It was my last year out of college, and I was working for that small station in that small town…Amazing, Texas don't ask where the name came from. There was nothing amazing about it. Anyway, they sent me to Jersey City to cover that pageant. No one else wanted to go. They were all in Dallas, something about the school board corruption I think."

"I was there the whole week with Katie's parents. I was so proud of her that week," Aunt Annie added with a look of pride all over her face—a look that could come from any proud mother.

Morgan, with that curious look on her beautiful face, was thinking. "That was the year that the first Miss National quit and the second runner-up was in an accident. She would not let me or any reporter talk with her after that. She was a beautiful girl with a great voice, as I remember. That's how Katie got to be Miss National Journalist."

"You're right, Morgan, and she made a big deal about not winning," Aunt Annie added.

Mary spoke up and asked, "Wasn't it something about the judges sleeping with the girls?"

"Yeah…I did a report on that," Morgan said.

"Katie wasn't doing anything like that," Aunt Annie said, defending Katie.

"Of course not! In my report I couldn't find anything to be true about that. There was one judge that was acting very suspicious when I try to talk with him. I can't think of his name right now."

"Ranges…Jeff Ranges," Mary told them.

"Yeah, Mary…I remember. I spelled his name wrong. I called him Ranger, not Ranges. Now I remember. He left a few days after the pageant. They never found him or heard from him…," Morgan said as her voice trailed off.

"I can't believe you and Katie didn't remember each other. You two were meant to be friends. That's all it is to it," Aunt Annie informed Morgan.

"I know I can't believe I didn't remember her."

"Well, I know one thing. You're sure lucky to have these two nice girls to come see you and look out for you, Annie. They would make any woman proud to be their mother," Mary said with respect.

Hugging Morgan, Aunt Annie said, "You're right about that. I couldn't love these two girls any more if they were my very own."

"And we love you so much too, Aunt Annie," Morgan replied.

"I've got a great idea. I'm going to take you two out for supper at that new fancy steak house," Mary announced.

"No, I can't let you do that. It's my treat," Morgan offered.

"It's okay, Morgan. She can well afford it, and she will not take no for an answer, believe me," Aunt Annie told Morgan.

"Then let's go. I'm hungry," Mary, said while getting out of her chair.

"Me too, I'm starving," Morgan told them.

10

The Tiding Together
of Morgan and Garfield

Detectives Barker and Parks were getting an update on the e-mails, both Katie's and Morgan's. Sergeant Pat Moore joined them in the briefing room with the e-mail information.

"Boy, do they get a lot of e-mails. It took ten of us go through it," she told the detectives.

"Did you find anything?" Barker asked.

"Yes, one name kept popping up on both e-mails. A John Garfield, from Plano, Texas, just north of Dallas. It seems as if he found a dirty ad in which Katie was posing in a small bikini and selling some naughty things. He e-mailed her with a copy of that ad, and she thanked him and told him she never got the ad. He wrote back not once, but twice. One real nice, the other still nice but disappointed she hadn't e-mailed him back. What he got when he did receive the e-mail was a very impersonal e-mail, not from Katie Richard, but from someone in customer service. No signature. It said, 'Katie was too busy to bother with you. She thanks you for writing.' Garfield's response was e-mail not Katie but customer service. One word, *okay*, and he signed his name. Neither Katie nor customer service had a response. But in all of his e-mails, he talked about Katie Morgan. Sound as if he had the hots for Morgan and not Katie. Katie probably got mad or jealous and didn't want to e-mail him. Now Morgan, on the other hand, did e-mail him and he did her. They sound like they were old friends. I did some checking. Morgan came from Texas. She spent some time in the Dallas area, attended school, and was born in Texas," Moore said as she handed the report to the detectives to look over.

"Thanks, Pat," Barker said with a confused look on his face. "Let's compare notes," Barker said to Parks.

"Morgan seems to be in all the wrong places at the all wrong time. One, she was in the limo the night before Katie had it. Two, she was seen taking a chain saw to studio three just before the stairs were cut. Three, she was the last one to drive Katie's car before the accident from the brakes being cut, and number four, she gave Katie the orange juice that had poison in it," Barker pointed out to Parks. "Either Morgan is not a very skillful murderer, or Katie has nine lives."

"Does Morgan seem that stupid to you? I mean, everything points to her," Parks asked Barker.

"No, Katie Morgan is a very smart and intelligent woman. If she was calling the moves, I think Katie would be dead by now. Morgan is not doing this or not doing this by herself. Who's helping her, I don't know, and what's the connection with Garfield anyway? Are they old lovers or old friends or what?" Barker was thinking out loud.

Parks added, "What was that ad about? No one said anything to me about an ad that was sent from Garfield."

"No, no one told me neither. I'm going to run a background check on him. We need to know the connection between them two," Parks said as he turned to his computer for that information.

"And Katie Richard never seems to get hurt. It's almost as if she knows what's going to happen next," Barker remarked.

"Katie, staging her own murder?"

"Yeah, and framing Morgan for it."

"Or they may be working together."

"A publicity trick or something? Hay, they are on TV."

"Maybe…but I don't think so," Barker remarked.

"What's the motive? Both of them have everything— looks, intelligence, wealth, and fame. What else is there to want?" Parks asked.

"I think we need to talk with Morgan and Katie again. See what you can find out about Garfield. Let's make a connection with Morgan and Garfield. She's not doing it by herself. That,

I'm sure of, and Katie, I'm not too sure what's she doing," Barker said as he started reading the e-mails.

Later, the information on Garfield came in. Parks pulled it from his printer. "It looks like Garfield and the girls are about the same age. There's nothing bad on his records. Oh, look here. He was a US marshal. After leaving the air force as a lieutenant, he was a delivery boy, salesman, sales manager, and vice president in an advertising company. He was a news producer in Dallas. He worked with Wards as an advisor to the CEO. He ran his own business. A news business, not a reporter but as an informer. Made big money, then lost it all. Now he works for one of those big-box companies. He's not in management, though. You would think with his background he would at least be a store manager," Parks reported to Barker.

"You couldn't find any connection between him and the girls?"

"No. Three different states they lived in, three different schools. Neither girl was ever in the air force nor a US marshal. Look here. Morgan was born in Texas. Garfield lives in Texas. Morgan worked in Oklahoma City with Katie. Oklahoma City is an hour drive or two to Dallas. They could have met during that time," Barker said.

Garfield had accounts in Oklahoma City while they worked there, so, yes, they could have known each other," Parks replied sharply.

"They could have. Oh, look! Katie Richard used to call herself Kathryn Turner when she was Miss National Journalist in 1990."

"Maybe she was married at that time."

"Maybe, what's the name of that detective in Dallas? The one we helped last year on that murder case that ended up in our lap," Barker asked. Parks pulled a binder out with lots of business cards in it.

"When did you get that?"

"A few months ago. I saw it and thought it would be good to keep up with names. Look, I got Kim's card, her personal phone number on it, and her address on the back," Parks said with pride. "She told me to call her sometime, you know, for a date. Kim has always been my favorite anyway."

"Now you got her phone number, is she your number one now?"

"Well, she's always been at the top of my list."

"I thought you liked Katie."

"Oh, I love Katie, but we're working with her now, so I couldn't ask for her number, could I?"

"She turned you down, huh?"

"No...I just think we shouldn't get involved with the victim, that's all."

"What are you going to do if we find out that Kim is the killer?"

"That cannot happen. Who's your favorite?" Parks said, wanting to change subject.

"I don't have one. I'm married."

"All right, if you weren't married, who?" Parks insisted.

"Nicky, of course. She is all sex. One hell of a woman."

"I like Dan," a voice from back of the room was heard. Toni, a police lady, spoke up, "I think he's so cute. I'll tell you another thing. Kim is nice. She's probably the same off air as on air. But I tell you, Larry, don't trust that Nicky. She's too damned beautiful. A woman like that is used to getting her way, and when she doesn't, watch out, it will be hell to pay. Mark my words."

"Um, Toni, you are just jealous," Barker told her.

"Honey, there's not a woman out there that I'm jealous of, and don't you forget it," Toni said with authority as she walked back to her desk.

"I still like Nicky. But Kim is a good one too."

"Oh, here's his card. Detective Jeff Cook. He gave it to me. I will call him. He owes us one."

Barker reached for the card, punched the number, and the Dallas Police Department answered. He asked to speak with Detective Cook.

"Cook here," a voice came through the phone.

"Jeff, this is Detective Larry Barker from Landover Police," Barker introduced himself.

"Yeah, Larry. How are you?"

"Fine. Look, Jeff, I need some help on a case from Plano to here. Can you help me?" he asked.

"Plano? Why don't you call the Plano Police?"

"One thing, I don't know any of them, and I'm not sure this guy has done anything wrong. I'd appreciate it if you could ask him a few questions for me," Barker asked of the Dallas detective with a concerned tone.

"Sure, I'll help. It's a nice little drive up to Plano. What are the details?"

Barker filled Detective Cook in with what was going on in this case. Barker and Parks left for AHS. They knew it was about time for Katie's show to end, and they wanted to talk with her before she left.

Walking into the lobby of AHS, they asked to see Katie Richard. The detectives were told she *was* in her office for them to go on back. Knocking on the open door, Barker asked, "May we come in, Miss Katie?"

"Yes, of course. Please," she said while turning from her desk and reaching her hand out to greet them.

"Have you learned anything yet?" she asked with a cautious look on her face.

"Not really. We just want to ask you a few more questions," he explained.

"Okay, what you want to know?"

"You and Morgan worked in Oklahoma City before coming here?"

"Yes, that's where I met her."

"Did you know of her before?"

"No, I don't remember ever seeing her on TV."

"So Oklahoma City was the first time you ever saw her?"

"Yes. I thought we went over this before."

"Just trying to tie up some loose ends, Miss Katie. Have you ever been to Dallas?

"Yes, why?"

"Do you know a man named John Garfield?"

"No. Who is he?"

"Has Miss Morgan ever talked about him?"

"No, I never heard that name before. What does he have to do with this?" she asked.

"He e-mailed you several times."

"I'm sorry. I can't remember all the names from my e-mails. Some of them are not even the real names."

"This one sent you a copy of an ad, an embarrassing one."

"Yes...it was a very personal ad. A look-alike of me. But no one sent it to me."

"Did you ever see that ad?"

"Yes...no, not from him."

"When did you first see it?"

"Is this ad important?"

"Do you have a copy of it?"

"Yes. Why?"

"May I see it?"

"I don't carry that kind of thing around with me. It's at home. That ad is not important. I wasn't in it anyway. She looks a little bit like me. That's all."

"So you did see that ad. And you told Garfield you never saw it. Why did you tell him that? And why was customer service so rude to him when they returned his e-mail? How did you come of it if you didn't get it from Garfield?"

"Wait a minute. I got one e-mail from Garfield, and I only sent him one. No customer service e-mail for me unless I ask, and I did not ask. I like to do all e-mailing. Jim showed it to me."

"Jim, your boss."

"Yes, but the ad Jim showed me was not the one Garfield sent. The ad Garfield sent I had on a bikini and the ad Jim showed me nothing on but my birthday suit. This was not me. She looks a lot like me."

"How did he get it?"

"I don't recall."

"So Jim called you in one day and said, 'Look what I have.'"

"Yeah, somewhat like that."

"What was Jim's reaction to this ad?"

"It was nothing…Really it was nothing."

"So your new boss sees an ad of one of his girls in the nude, selling some naughty products, and it's nothing?"

"You said she was wearing a bikini?"

"Yes. A very small one, according to Garfield's e-mail."

"Damn!" Katie said with an angry look on her face. crap

"What's wrong?"

"The e-mail said she was wearing a bikini. The ad I saw she was in the nude."

"There are two ads!"

"Yes, but I never saw the other one."

"According to the e-mail, it got lost while you were in Italy."

"Yeah, I remember that e-mail now. It was so polite, as if he really did find it and was concerned about me. I e-mailed him back and never heard from him again. I never saw the ad either. I thought it was funny he never wrote back. He sounded serious about it. I thought he would write me again. Then I got busy and forgot it."

"Did you look for it?"

"Yes, I looked all over and asked everyone if they had seen the envelope, and no one had."

"Who took care of your mail while you were gone?"

"Morgan picked up some of my mail for me."

"Did she read any of them? Could she have opened the ad and gotten mad about it, possibly done something with it?"

"No, Morgan never opens my mail. I'm telling you, Morgan is not behind this."

"Did you know that Morgan and Garfield are e-mailing each other and talking about you?"

"No, as far as I know, Morgan doesn't even know Garfield."

"Garfield always mentioned Morgan in your e-mail. Could she have read it, or maybe you told her and she wanted to meet him?"

"No, I don't remember saying anything to her about him."

"Here, read it yourself." Barker handed her the e-mails.

After reading all the e-mails from Garfield and customer service, Katie handed them back to Barker with an anguished look on her face.

"I've never read them before. I never e-mailed him but once. I don't know who wrote him telling him I'm too busy. It wasn't me. I like to answerer all my mail myself. I can see how it would make him or anyone mad. I wouldn't do that. Certainly not on that kind of e-mail."

"Why is he e-mailing Morgan now?"

"I don't know."

"Has Morgan ever said anything to you about those e-mails?"

"No, never."

"Let's go back to Jim for a minute. He wasn't upset with the ad?"

"No. I told you he thought it was nothing."

"Don't you have a moral clause in your contract?"

"Yes, but it was not me. Jim knows that. That's why it was nothing."

"Where did he get the ad from?"

"I don't know."

"Does Morgan know about the ad?"

"Yes, I told her."

"What was her reaction?"

"She didn't think the girl looked like me either."

"She didn't have any idea where it came from, and Jim didn't know where it came from either. It just appeared one day. Nobody gave it to him," Barker asserted.

"I don't believe it, but Jim said it was slipped under his door that day."

"He didn't see anyone?"

"No, he didn't see the person putting it under the door."

"Who do you think it might be?"

"I don't know."

"Are you happy in your life? I mean, is everything going the way you would like for it to be?"

"Yes, of course."

"Happy here at AHS…your job, your love life?"

"Yes. Why are you asking these questions?" Katie was demanding an answer.

"Have you talked with Miss Morgan about the orange juice? When will she be back?"

"First, Detective, why are you asking this?" Katie said, still wanting to know.

"It may be a tide between Morgan and Garfield. I need to know if so."

"Morgan and Garfield have nothing to do with this."

"What about my question, Miss Katie?"

"Yes, I've talked with her. No, I didn't tell her about the juice. She will be back in time for her two o'clock show tomorrow."

"Why didn't you tell her about the juice that she was so nice to leave for you? Was she surprised to hear from you, being alive and anything?"

"No, she wasn't surprised that I am still alive. She's happy I am alive."

"But why not tell her?"

"She was with my aunt Annie, and I didn't want to worry Aunt Annie with this. I will tell Morgan about it when she gets back."

"You let her go and stay with your aunt Annie. Not her aunt Annie but yours. Why?"

"Why not? Morgan loves her as much as I do."

"Morgan is a possible suspect in this case, that's why."

"Morgan wouldn't hurt anyone! Why don't you go find the real suspect and get off her back?"

Parks walked to the door, with Barker beside him, looked Katie in the eye, and said, "I really hope you're right. I don't want anything to happen to you, and I like Morgan a lot. If anything comes up, you will call us?"

Barker and Parks headed down the long hall to Jim's office, walked in, and asked if they could see him. They were told he would be with them in just a few minutes. They thanked the secretary and began to wait. The office door soon opened, and Bobby Greenwood walked out, not saying anything to anyone. He appeared to be in a hurry.

"Well, Detectives. You're back. Come on in. What can I do for you today?" Jim asked with an anxious look on his face.

"Just a couple of things we need to clear up," Parks told him.

"Okay, what? Can I get you something? Coffee, Pepsi, or something?" he asked of the detectives.

"No, thanks. Why didn't you tell us about the ad?"

"What ad?"

"The one you showed Miss Katie."

"One of your hostesses posed in a nude ad, and it's nothing? Doesn't that violate her contract?"

"It wasn't her. It just looked like her, that's all."

"Why did you even show it to her then?"

"I thought she would get a kick out of it."

"Did she?"

"Yeah…she though it was funny. The girl didn't look as good as Katie."

"Where did you get it from?"

"Morgan."

"Morgan gave you this ad and told you it was Katie?"

"No…not exactly."

"What did she say?"

"She didn't say anything. She slipped it under my door."

"You saw her?"

"I ran to the door, and Morgan was the only one in the hall. It had to have been her."

"Did you ask her if it was her?"

"No, she turned around and smiled at me."

"Oh, Morgan usually doesn't smile or say hi to you when she sees you?"

"Look, there was no one else in the hall but her. What would you think?"

"Do you have any copies of the ad?"

"No…no, I didn't want to keep a copy of that," he told Barker and Parks with a big grind.

"So where's the ad now?"

"I gave it to Katie."

"Katie has the ad now?"

"I supposed…I don't know. I gave it to her."

"Has anyone ever said anything about that ad to you?"

"No."

"Did you tell anyone about the ad?"

"No."

"How did you feel, looking at her in the nude?"

"What do you mean? I didn't feel any way. What kind of question is that?"

"She is a beautiful woman, and there she is, in her birthday suit."

"I don't think of these girls in that manner," Jim answered with an anguished look on his face. "What does the ad have to do with anything?" he bellowed back at that question.

"Maybe nothing and maybe everything."

"Did you discuss letting her go because of the ad?"

"No, of course not."

"Why not?"

"It wasn't her in the ad," Jim said as he raised his voice a little.

"It looks enough like her for you to call her in and talk to her about it."

"I though it was funny. The girl did look somewhat like her."

"You didn't try to make any kind of agreement with her in order for her to keep her job?"

"No! I don't know what she told you, but nothing like that ever happened, and I resent your implying that," Jim said in a higher tone.

"You worked on the *Boy Jones Show* before coming here, didn't you?"

"Yes. If you are referring to Becky Snell, she dropped all her complaints, and I was never fired. I quit...I didn't want to work with her and the others anymore. But nothing happened. It was not true."

"So you, Katie, and Morgan are okay with each other?"

"I have nothing against either one of them."

"Wasn't that Bobby who just left your office?"

"Yes. He is one of the stagehands."

"That the same Bobby that Morgan said called her to take the chain saw to studio three the day it got cut?"

"Yes, but he never called her."

"How do you know that?"

"I asked him when I heard what she had said."

"So Bobby is more believable than Katie Morgan?"

"No, he's a junky. I generally don't believe anything he says, but this time I think he's telling the truth."

"Why this time?"

"He likes Morgan. He thinks she's sexy. He wouldn't do anything to push her further away from him."

"Morgan likes him, huh?"

"I don't know."

"Do you know of anything is going on between them?"

"I don't think so. I don't know."

"What about Katie. Does he like her too?"

"Bobby likes all the girls here, on camera and off. They are all sexy to him."

"Has he ever talked to you about Katie Richard?"

"No."

"Could you tell us where we can find Bobby? We'd like to talk with him."

"Yes, he's working on stage four. Turn to your right, and the first set, you come to will be number four."

"Thanks for talking with us," Barker said gracefully as they turned to the right and started walking down that long hall again, this time to stage four.

"I don't believe a word he said," Parks said to barker.

"Me neither. You notice there is a lot of doors and cross hall here?" Barker remarked.

"Yeah, and I'm thinking that someone could have been in front of Morgan and run into a room," Barker replied.

Walking into studio four, the detectives saw Bobby working on a new table.

"Bobby, I'm Detective Barker, and this is Detective Parks. We would like to ask you a few questions."

"Is this about Morgan trying to kill Katie?" he asked fast.

"You know Morgan is trying to kill Katie?"

"Well...I mean, it looks that way."

"You don't like Morgan?"

"Yeah...I like her a lot."

With a smile on his face, Detective Parks told Bobby, "She's kind of sexy, hot, you know, the way she walks, the way she dresses...I mean, she's hot! She's hotter than Katie. Don't you think so?"

"Yeah, she's hot."

"Have you and her...you know...you two?"

"No! The bitch thinks she's too good for me."

"What you mean, Bobby? I thought you really liked her."

"I do, but she thinks she is too good for me."

"Is that what she told you?"

"No, women like her never talks like that, at least not to your face. She says all the right things, like she wouldn't date any coworkers and she is married."

"Well, isn't that true, Bobby? Do you know of any coworkers she has gone out with, and she is married?"

"No, I don't know for sure. She goes to Texas a lot. There's a guy down there she's fooling around with, but he's a lot smarter than me. Got more money or something."

"You know what his name is?"

"I walked in one day when she was e-mailing him. I saw John on her computer. That's all I saw before she turned it off. She told me it was a fan. I don't think so. You see, Morgan would let me read some of her answers before, but not this one."

"It might have been a fan, for all you know."

"All I know is, after that, when she's on the computer, her door would be locked. It was never locked before."

"When was this?"

"A few weeks ago, when Katie was in Italy."

"How do you like Katie?"

"She's okay. She's cute and nice."

"Ever been with her, Bobby?"

"No…she had a drink with me once. That's all."

"What's your opinion of the attempts on her life?"

"It's bad. I hope they don't kill her. She's a nice girl."

"You think Morgan might have anything to do with it?"

"I don't know. I don't believe she would hurt anyone. Morgan is so mild. No, I don't think she's involved with this. She's too goody-goody."

"We will talk with you later, Bobby. If you see anything, you will let us know, right?" Barker asked of Bobby.

"Did you notice he said 'they'?" Barker asked.

"I think he might have something to do with this."

"Yeah, but he's not smart enough by himself."

The two detectives went back to the station so they could discuss what they had heard. Detective Cook should have gotten back with them by now. It has been long enough that they should have talked with Garfield.

11

Dallas Police Talks to Garfield

John Garfield had arrived early for work. Judy was there, and they were talking about almost everything but work. John got a page to come to the front. He arrived at the front, thinking it was a customer problem of some sort.

"John, those two guys over there want to talk to you. They wouldn't tell me why," Nancy, a very attractive and sweet lady of thirtysomething, told him with a very concerned look on her face.

Thanking Nancy, John walked to them. "I'm John. May I help you?" he asked.

"John Garfield?"

"Yes, I'm John Garfield."

"I'm Detective Cook with the Dallas Police, and this is Sergeant Rowe. We would like to ask you a few questions, if that's all right."

"Yeah…of course. What's this all about?" Garfield asked.

"Do you know Katie Morgan?"

"No."

"Do you know Katie Richard?"

"No. What's going on? Who are they?" Garfield asked.

"You don't you know either one of them, and you have never e-mailed or talked with them?"

"Are you talking about the girls on AHS?"

"Yes. Do you know them?"

"No…I know who they are and what they look like, but I don't know them personally."

"Have you ever met Katie Morgan?"

"No, wish I did know her, but I don't."

"Why? She turns you on?"

"No. She's seems like a nice person, and I like nice people."

"Is Katie Richard a nice person too?"

"All right, what is this about? Tell me, or I'm going back to work," Garfield demanded of them.

"You sent a couple of e-mails to them, didn't you?"

"No, I wrote to Katie Richard twice, and she asked me not to write back. That was all. I didn't say anything bad in my e-mails. Why are you asking about the e-mails?"

"Have you ever e-mailed Katie Morgan? Have you ever talked to her or seen her in person? Are you and her old friends or maybe old lovers? She's from Texas, you're from Texas. She worked in Oklahoma, you worked Oklahoma."

"No, I don't know either of them, and I only e-mailed Katie Richard. I have never e-mailed Katie Morgan. Why are you asking all these questions?"

"Well, Mr. Garfield, someone is trying to kill Katie Richard."

"Oh my God! Is she all right? How about Katie Morgan? Is she okay?" John asked with a concerned look.

They both looked at each other, wondering why he was so concerned about Morgan.

"They are both okay now. Someone has been sending e-mail to Katie Morgan from your computer. She has been returning it to him. The name is yours, Mr. Garfield," the detective explained.

"My name? Why my name?"

"We believe it has something to do with that ad you sent her."

"What about the ad?" he asked with a crispy tone.

"That ad found its way to her program manager's office."

"He didn't fire her, did he?"

"No, but an ad with one of his girls in the nude was somewhat startling."

"Nude? She was not in the nude! Not in the ad I sent her!"

"Do you have a copy of that ad?"

"Yeah, I might have a copy."

"Let's go see it."

"Well, I will have to let the boss know that I'm leaving. I will be right back."

"We will be waiting for you here."

"Okay," John said as he walked back inside. "Is Jim here?" he asked of Nancy (Jim being the day manager).

"Yes. There he is. Are they cops? What do they want with you? What did you do? Are they taking you to jail?" Nancy was asking.

"Yes, nothing, nothing. And, no, I'm not going jail," he told Nancy, then turning to face Jim.

"I've got to leave for about an hour or so. I'll take it off my lunch if that's okay with you?" he asked of Jim.

"That's okay, John, but what's happening?"

"They are cops. They are taking John downtown to book him," Nancy was telling Jim while laughing.

"Nancy, they are not going to book me for anything. They just want to see some papers I have at home."

"Let me know when you get back. Okay, John?" Jim asked of him.

Garfield took the detectives to his apartment and showed them the ad and the e-mails he had sent Katie Richard. They checked his computer to see if Katie Morgan had e-mailed him. They found nothing to be concerned about. The two detectives also checked with the apartment office and found that no one had seen Garfield using their computer. They returned John to work. After leaving John, Detective Cook called Detective Barker to tell him what they had found out.

"Hey, John, come here," Nancy was shouting. "Come here. What happened? Are you going to the big house?"

"Nancy, you would like to see that, wouldn't you?" John asked with a very sarcastic tone, which did not bother Nancy at all.

"Well, tell me. What happened?" she demanded.

"It was about some e-mails they thought I wrote and an ad which I found. That's all."

"That's all? Did this have to do with that girl on AHS?" Judy asked while walking up to John after seeing he was back.

"What girl? You know a girl on AHS? Which one?" Jill, another coworker, was asking.

"No, he doesn't know anyone on AHS. He would like to know them, though," Judy explained.

The phone rang, and Nancy had to leave for that call. Judy and John walked off to discuss it more.

"Why are they asking you about the e-mail? Did you tell them it was nothing? She never even found the ad, and I told you not to write anymore. You said okay. That was all, wasn't it?" Judy asked with a concerned look on her face.

"Yeah, that's all I did. They think Katie Morgan and I were e-mailing each other. They also think Katie Morgan and I knew each other. They asked if we were lovers."

"You wish."

"Anyway, someone is trying to kill Katie Richard. I think they think Katie Morgan and me have something to do with it. I don't understand the connection. There's more than they are not telling me. It has something to do with that ad. I knew it was not she in the ad, but how did they get another ad of her in the nude? I only sent one ad, and she was not in the nude—almost but not in the nude," John said with a confused look on his face.

"Where did the nude ad come from?" Judy asked.

"I don't know. I don't know what happened to the ad I sent her either."

"What do you know for sure?" Judy inquired.

"Well…I know her boss got an ad with her in the nude. I know he didn't fire her. I know somebody has been using my name to e-mail Katie Morgan. I know either Katie Morgan or someone using her name e-mailed me back. I know someone is trying to kill Katie Richard, and they think it maybe me or Katie Morgan, or both of us. What I don't know is why. Why would they pull me into this?" John asked Judy as he walked around talking.

"It doesn't make any sense. How do they think they can connect you with Katie Morgan or anyone else?"

"Yeah…How did they know about me anyway? Who's the person reading Katie Richard's e-mail, telling someone perhaps, or maybe she is involved in this?"

"Maybe you can call some of your old cop buddies," Judy suggested.

"I don't know any of them. It's been almost twenty years ago. I was undercover then Only a few people even knew I was one. I don't know how to find any of them. But you know,

Judy, you are right. I do need to find out more information on this," John replied to Judy.

"There must be some way. The Internet maybe. No, I don't think the Internet will not have this story yet, but I will definitely find out. I have to know now. Someone has involved me."

"John, don't worry about this. You are in Texas, not Georgia. There's nothing they can do to you."

"Judy, I may have started this whole thing with that stupid ad. God, I wish I had never sent it to her," John said with an anguished look on his face.

"John, listen to me," Judy demanded of John. "You did nothing. Both of them, well, are okay, and there's nothing you can do about it anyway. So, John, just forget it. It will be okay."

"You may be right. But you may be wrong also. Can I take that chance with someone's life?" he asked of her.

"John, it's nothing you can do. Believe me, there is nothing you can do," Judy repeated her thoughts to John.

"There must be something I can do."

"Just pray for both of them. That's all you can do."

"Well, I will certainly do that, of course, but I know I can help in some way. The ad I will find that girl in that ad. That would tell me a lot."

"How are you going to find her? There must be thousands of guys looking for her every day. You think they're going to just hand you her name and phone number?" Judy asked while laughing.

"No, of course not. But I will find her or her maker. She may not be real."

"I don't think you're real. You're wasting your time. Even if you find her, or it, there's still nothing you can do to help either one of them."

"No, if I find her, then I find the person behind the ad. That may be the killer."

"Oh, great! Now you're going to face the killer. Mr. Killer, are you the one who's trying to kill Katie, and what's your name, and will you please stop right now?"

"No...no, Judy, it won't be like that," John said in a low tone with a weird look on his face.

"Oh, no, John! You have that stupid weird look on your face again," Judy informed him.

"No, I don't."

"Yes, you do, and that means only one thing. You are about to do something really stupid, aren't you, John?" Judy said.

"No...not really stupid. I'm going to find the source of that ad."

"Then what?"

"I...don't know what."

"That's what I thought."

"It's okay, Judy. It will let me know what's going on. That's all."

"All, it's never 'that's all' with you. This will lead to something else and so on and so on, but it's never 'that's all'."

"Oh, Judy. You're worrying about nothing."

Some customers came up, and they had to postpone their conversation. John had the next two days off. This would be enough time, he thought, for him to get the information he so needed.

12

John Garfield's Plan

John could not get this off his mind. He started working on a plan. By the end of the day, he had developed that plan. It normally wouldn't take him that long; however, the store was very busy that day, not leaving him a lot of time to think.

The next morning, John got dressed like a businessman and drove to the store where that ad had been featured. John walked in and met a lovely young lady. He introduced himself to her as Jerry Moore and asked to see the manager or owner. He was introduced to a big, heavy, tall man of sixty-something who called himself Joe.

"How do you do, Joe? I'm Jerry Moore. I'm an attorney. I would like talk with you. It will only take a few minutes."

"I'm busy! What the hell you want from me?" Joe asked with an extremely hostile tone.

"Joe, it's about finding a girl."

"I don't run no whorehouses. If that's what you want, go down the street. You will find a lot them down there," Joe said roughly as he walked away.

"No, Joe hell, no! I don't need a girl for that. The girl I'm looking for, her father is dying, and he wants to see her and make things right between them."

"What's that got to do with me?"

"Well, Joe, she's been in one of your ads. Maybe you can tell me the ad agency."

"Hell, boy, I don't know anything about no ad agency."

"That's too bad, Joe. The family is willing to pay the people who help find her. Thanks anyway, Joe. You have a good day now," John told Joe as he turned and started walking to the door.

"Hey! What's your name?" Joe asked.

"Jerry, Jerry Moore. Have a good day, Joe."

"Jerry, how much money?"

"A few thousands maybe. You take care now, Joe."

"Damn it, man, quit walking away when I'm talking to you," Joe shouted.

"I don't want to take any more of your time."

"Well, it's my time. I may be able to help. Which ad?"

John opened his briefcase and showed him a copy of the ad that looks like Katie Richard.

"This girl, Joe. Seems she left home after having a big fight with her father. She never came home again. After she left, he became rich. Now he feels bad about what has happened. He wants to see her and make things right between them," John explained to Joe.

"Yeah...that's good and everything, but what do I get out of it?" Joe asked.

"If the information you give me helps and she is still alive or her father is still alive, you could possibly get up to ten thousand dollars."

"How soon will I get the money? Now?"

"Now, Joe, you're an intelligent man. You know I can't give you anything now. Heck, Joe, I can't even tell you for sure if it will be next month or whenever. You're a businessman. You know how these thing works. Look, Joe, you're a father. Wouldn't you want to make things right with your daughter before you die? I can look around and see you are very successful in this business. You know, Joe, some things in life are worth more than money. Do the right thing, Joe," John said in a sensitive voice. "You got a name, Joe?"

"Yeah...this is it. The Carter and Carter Agency." Joe handed the card to John.

"Joe, I thank you so much for helping him find his only daughter. You did the right thing. I'm proud of you, Joe," John said with a big smile on his face and his hand out.

"Thanks again, Joe. May God bless you and your business. I will be in touch with you if this helps. Thanks again, Joe."

"Yeah, that's good, all right. But I still want the money."

John said nothing to him, only waving his hand in the air and walking as fast has he could to get back to his car. He wanted to get out of that place fast and away from Joe.

John drove down the street and pulled over to read the address on the business card Joe had given him. The address was in downtown Dallas. John knew the address and how to get there. The drive would take about thirty minutes. That would give him enough time to think of another plan.

About thirty minutes later, he found the building and a parking space close by. Leaving his coat and tie in the car, he changed to an old shirt, massed his hair up, and headed for The Carter & Carter Agency. John walked into the lobby and asked if he could see Mr. Carter and get some information on one of their models and where she was at now. He was told no on both counts.

"Ma...ma, I...don't mean to be no trouble. I came here from North Dakota, and I...want to just find my daughter. I've not seen her in over fifteen years. Please help me. I... come a long way. I have a bad heart condition and want to see before I die. Please don't let it be for nothing. Wouldn't you help me, please?" John asked with a sad look on his face and voice that sounded like an uneducated old man who just want to see his daughter again.

"Let me see if I can find someone to talk with you. Would you like a cup of coffee or a soft drink?" she asked very politely.

"Yes, ma'am, the coffee will be good," John replied.

A few minutes later, a young man in his late twenties came out to talk with him. "Hi, my name is Bill Clark. How can I help you, sir?"

"Mr. Clark, I'm Jim Brown from North Dakota. The name means nothing to you, but you may know my baby, and that would help me a lot, you know."

"Mr. Brown, I don't know if I can help you or not, but I will try."

"Oh, thank you so much, Mr. Clark. You know, I have not seen her since she was seventeen."

"Come on in, Mr. Brown. Do you have a picture or the name she is using?"

"Her name was Lisa Brown. She had red hair and a big beautiful smile."

"That's good," Clark said with a smile of his own.

"I think this is her." John pulled the ad out of his back pocket and handed it to him.

"She is beautiful, Mr. Brown, but I don't know her."

"This is your ad, isn't it, Mr. Clark?" John asked.

"Yes, but I don't know that girl," he told John again while picking up the phone and asking for Mary to come in. "Mary is in charge of picking the right model for the right job. She knows most the girls. Mary travels from Dallas to New York. We do most of our ads up there. What makes you think this is her if you haven't seen her since she was seventeen?" Jim Clark asked.

"I received this picture of her when she was fifteen. A friend of mine down the road from me, Jimmy Bob Myers, made me one of those updated pictures of what she might look like today. He used his computer to do that. The girl in your ad and this picture are the same one," John explained with an excited tone.

"Mr. Brown," Mary said as she was walking back into the room, "this girl is a computer-generated person. She doesn't exist, Mr. Brown."

"Don't exist? She's my little girl. Is she dead? What you mean she don't exist?" John asked as he stood up and walked toward Mary. "She's my little girl. She exists! I know she do."

Mary reached out her arms to hold him and comfort him. She was holding him so tight and so sweetly that John almost forgot that he was Jim Brown from North Dakota. John was enjoying this so much and was holding her so tightly himself. After all, Mary was a very beautiful woman, every bit as beautiful as either of the Katies. He wanted to hold her much longer, but Mary was now pulling away from him. She took his hand in hers and led him to the sofa, where John continued to hold her hand. John looked up at Mary and asked, "Are you sure this girl is not real?"

"No, Mr. Brown, I'm not. It is possible to take a head from one person and place it on another body. That's not hard to do. It is illegal to do this without the permission of both parties. Sometimes they want a celebrity to look good and make one up. I can give you the name of the company that I got that photo from, but I doubt if they will tell you anything. If your girl is a professional model or someone famous and they didn't ask for permission, then they are not going to tell you. I'm so sorry, Mr. Brown. I can't tell you any more than that. This is more than I would have told most people. I do wish you all the luck in the world in finding your daughter."

Mary reached over and held John in her arms again. John was in no hurry to leave now. This felt so good, but he was running out of things to say, so he backed off and thanked both of them for their help. He assured Mary he would let her know if he found his daughter. Standing up and walking toward the door, John held Mary's hand again as they walked. At the door, he hugged Mary once again and told her, "I thank you so much for helping me. You are so sweet." Looking into her blue eyes, John told her, "You know, Mary, I wish you were my daughter too." Mary was so touched by what he had said that, again, she held John so tightly and so long. When they finally pulled away from each other, she kissed John on the cheek, and they said good-bye to each other. It was as if they were old friends parting on their way somewhere.

John walked to the door, holding Mary's hand all the way. Looking into her baby blue eyes, again John thanked her, turned, and walked away. He walked down the street to his car, opened the door, and slammed it, placing his hands on the steering wheel and resting his head on the head rest. John was thinking about what has just happened. But he wasn't thinking about the information he received. He was thinking about Mary. John wanted to savor the moment, remembering only holding Mary in his arm and Mary holding him in her arms. It made no difference that Mary was holding Jim Brown, not John Garfield. John had always thought Shakespeare was right when he said, "A rose by any other name is still a rose." He didn't care who Mary thought he was; it still felt so good.

Sitting up and starting the engine, John started his drive back to Plano. John turned his thoughts to the information he had just collected. He had always believed the ad was a computer-generated person. He also believed that the head was Katie's. He didn't know where the ad originated. Now he knew. New York City. How would he get to New York City to talk with them? He hardly had enough money to go Dallas and back.

John knew that this agency, The McCann & Tate Agency, had the answer to his questions. John's problem was that McCann & Tate was in New York City and he was in Plano, Texas. John drove his car to a parking lot outside of the Higgins department store, a large chain of stores in this area. They had about twenty-five stores in Dallas, Fort Worth. He was familiar with this small chain. He knew who ran it and more in five other states. The chain was up for sale.

After looking at the store in front of him for a short period of time, John reached for his cell phone and the paper that Mary had given him with the phone number of McCann & Tate agency written down for him. John called that number and asked to speak with someone about advertising. A voice came on introducing himself as Larry Tate, the vice president.

"Mr. Tate, I'm John Goodman of the J. W. Patterson Investment Co. in Dallas, Texas. "How are you today, sir?" John asked.

"I'm fine, Mr. Goodman. What can I help you with today?"

"You've probably read that the Higgins stores were for sale. Well, we are buying them. They have had some bad times in the past, and I'm hoping to change that with a lot of advertising. This is where you come in, Mr. Tate. I saw an ad that you did for a local store here. The girl in the ad is everything I'm looking for in a spokesperson. I would love to use her for all my ads," John explained.

"We use computer-generated models only."

"Can she be made to talk?"

"We have been successful in that. Come in, and let's talk about it."

"I'm very familiar with your agency and its reputation for doing quality work. I also know that this agency could use a real person's head and computer-made body or someone else's body. What I'm hoping is that the face is real. I would like for her to do personal appearances at the stores. Money is not a problem. My bosses want this girl."

"Okay…okay…she is a real person," John was told.

"I need something to tell them now. They love the way she looks. People would feel comfortable doing business with her. I have the code number from her ads, if that would help."

"What's that number? I will run it though fast, and we will see who she is."

"Thank you. The number is lr2348."

"Good. Then we can do some business. You have her name and address where you can get in touch with her?"

"Let's see…Kathryn Turner…that's funny. I don't have her address or phone number…The code reads that the head only was used, not the body. The agent who signed off on this was NP. I don't know her. Let me pull her files up…That's funny too. She's not working here now. And her files are empty. I don't understand that. We always keep a complete record on all our agents and what they do. This one is gone. Tell you what, Mr. Goodman, give me your phone number, and I will find this Kathryn Turner for you. She must be under contract with us now or before. I'll find her and call you back," Mr. Tate said with a concerned tone.

"Yes, this is my number, 214-555-34—. That's my cell phone, so call me anytime. I do thank you so much for helping. If you can sign her up in the next couple weeks, I will be in the city, and we can close this deal. Thanks again. I will be waiting for your call. We need her as soon as she can get down here. Thanks again, Mr. Tate," John said as he turned his phone off and looked up at the Higgins store with a big look of success on his face.

John knew now that the girl in the ad was real. The body may be that of Kathryn Turner, or the face may be Kathryn Turner. The question now was, *who is Kathryn Turner?* If she's the face, then it is another girl who looks just like Katie. *If she's the body, who is the face?* John has to get more information.

Since it was the wrong name, it must belong to the body and not the face. John knew he needed to put a name to that face. Whether it was Katie Richard, Kathryn Turner, or Mary Smith, the face must have a name.

Larry Tate said he would find her and call him back, but how long would it take? Could Larry Tate even find this girl? The file was empty; the agent working with her was gone. Tate didn't even know the name of his agent. John could not afford to wait on Tate. He needed to know now. Two weeks maybe too late for Katie Richard.

John once again started driving back to Plano. He knew he needed to get to New York City to ask the right questions. John had two connections in the big apple. One was a very successful newswoman. Her name was a household name; today almost everyone knows her. She and John were very close at one time. They had both helped each other get ahead. She had worked for John; he made her a partner and helped her go to national. John paid for her college degree and got her a job on a local station and, later on, a cable news show. Although she didn't last long and was told she could not do this can of work, she knew in her heart she could. Being told time after time she couldn't make it in this business, she went to work for a small reporting job where she became best-loved newswoman on TV. She helped John build his business. And when she left, she promised John she would not ever ask for help again, even if she didn't make it. John promised the same. They never called each other. They never kept in touch at all. John could have called her at any time, and she would have come running to help. He would have done the same for her, but neither call was ever made. He could not ask her for help. She never asked him, and he too would keep his word. John knew someday he would see her again. He thought that when that day comes, he wants to be as successful as she is now. He had one other girl he knew in New York City. He too helped her, although she was not as famous as Karen Carter. She never promised John anything. He had seen her on TV from time to time and felt sure she would help. He just hated to ask for help from old friends he hadn't seen in a while. But this time it wasn't about helping him. It was about helping Katie Richard.

The next day, John started to find Lisa King, another of his friend in the Big Apple. He had to make several phone calls before he could locate her.

"Lisa…Lisa King," he asked the person who answered the phone.

"John, is that you, John Garfield?" she asked excitedly.

"Lisa. Yes, it's me. How are you?"

"I'm fine. How are you? Are you here, in the city now?"

"No, I'm still in Dallas. Sure wish I was there with you.

"You sound so good and happy."

"Yes, John, I'm so very happy. I'm so glad you called. Why did you call?"

"I miss you and was thinking of you."

"Really? You are so sweet. Now tell me why you really called."

"I do miss you, Lisa, and I do think of you every day. I always wonder how you are doing. I see you on TV every now and then."

"Oh, I miss you so very much, John. I'm coming home this fall sometime, and I want to see you. Okay?"

"You better call and come by when you get to Dallas. Oh, by the way, I saw your mother a few days ago. She's so proud of you. She got you on prints and tape. She put your pictures all over the walls."

"I know. I told her not to do that. She's going to make everyone hate me."

"I doubt that, Lisa. She loves you so much."

"And you?"

"You know I love you, Lisa."

"Then come see me."

"I don't have the money, Lisa."

"Well, if you are too cheap, then I will pay your way. I want to see you."

"I know. I really want to see you too."

"Then come on up."

"I will soon."

"Are you're still married to Patty?"

"Yes. Lisa, I have a favor to ask of you."

"So you are, and that's why you called."

"No, Lisa, this has nothing to do with Patty. We never said we wouldn't be calling each other after you left. But I've really do missed you so much, Lisa, and I do need this favor."

"So you are still married, aren't you?"

"Yes."

"You know that doesn't make any difference to me, John. Of course I will help you, but when I get home, I do want to see you. Okay, John?"

"I wouldn't have it any other way."

"Okay, what do you need?"

"I need to know about an employee of the McCann and Tate Ad Agency."

"I know them. They do computer-generated models, not real ones. The union is raising hell with them. They want them to use some live models. What's your interest in them?"

"So you know this agency? I'm looking for a girl named Kathryn Turner or Katie Richard, an employee with the initial NP, and I wanna know where they are now."

"Katie Richard and Kathryn Turner sound familiar. Who are they? Wait a minute—that Katie…Isn't she on the American Home-Shopping Channel? And that Kathryn Turner is a movie star."

"Cute Lisa. Yeah, that's her. I don't know who Kathryn Turner is yet."

"How did you meet her? What's the connection between them?"

"It's a long story, Lisa. I can't tell you everything now. I don't know everything yet."

"Come on, John. This is Lisa you're talking to. Now tell me the whole story."

"Well, I think McCann and Tate may be using Katie Richard's face on Kathryn Turner's body."

"Why would they want to do that? Katie Richard has a great body of her own. Why not use her totally. Besides that's illegal. Do you know for sure they're doing this?"

"No. I think that NP person is behind it. She left the agency and closed her files out. They don't know where she is now. They don't know where Kathryn Turner is either. I need to find Kathryn Turner and talk with her, face-to-face."

"Okay, but it will take a few days. I'm going to Boston tomorrow. I will be back in two days. Give me your cell number, and I will call you when I find something."

"Lisa, I don't mean to hurry you, but I need this ASAP."

"There's more to this, isn't there, John?"

"All right, I'll tell you, Lisa my friend, not Lisa the reporter, okay?"

"That's not fair. I'm a reporter. What's the rest of the story, John?"

"Someone may be trying to kill Katie Richard. AHS is keeping it quiet for now."

"I can't promise you, John, but I will find this information for you. Remember you owe me one, you hear?" Lisa said while laughing.

They exchanged cell numbers and said good-bye to each other. Both of them sat back and started thinking about old times in Texas. It was a good feeling for each of them.

13

The Road to Georgia

John spent the next day working on a plan that would get him to Georgia. He had several thoughts on this subject, but only one was needed to find the most productive way of getting there from Plano. He came up with an old plan that he had been putting off for some time now. It was a good plan; it would cost some money to activate it. This could, if it worked right, be the end of his money problems as well.

John had always believed in this plan. The only holdup was his confidence to sell it. The plan involved a company in West Texas that makes Mexican food, chips, salsa, and so on. This company would put John's private label on their product and drop-ship it anywhere in the US. The markup was very good. The initial holdup was always the upfront money. John had none.

John called the company and talked about AHS paying them directly, and the company taking his cut out and mailing it to him. This was like being a commission salesperson for a company. They agreed to this. Now John needed to cover the cost of his labels, which was a thousand dollars. Feeling good about himself, he said, "No problem. I will make the deal with AHS, and they will send you the check."

The deal was sealed. The next move was up to John. He had to sell it to AHS in a fast manner. He also had to cover that thousand-dollar check he promised. John ordered some samples to be sent to AHS with his labels on them. Then he called AHS and talked to them about his new product line. They were very interested in what he had. John promised to send the samples to them. John knew they would get back with him when the samples arrived. John was very pleased with the results of his two-days-off-from-work plans.

The next day, John couldn't wait to tell Judy what had happened.

"Good morning, Judy," John said as he walked closer to her.

"Good morning to you, John. They let you out of jail?" she asked while laughing.

"Very funny. I found out who that girl was in the ad. And I'm going to Georgia to help out."

"Who was she? That girl on TV, Katie something? I told you it would be her."

"No, no, Miss Know-it-all. It was not Katie Richard. Well, not all of her anyway."

"Not all of her?"

"I don't really know. The name I got was Kathryn Turner. I don't know if it's her face or the body."

"So you don't know any more now than you did before, do you?"

"Yes…I know a lot now," John remarked with an angry tone.

"So what do you know?"

"I know this girl is real. I know it may be Katie's face. I know this ad is two girls, not just one."

"Big deal. That's what you always thought. So how's that helping you?" Judy asked.

"Listen, Judy, I know that the girl in the ad is not Katie. It may be her head. It may be her body. But the total girl is not her. That means I was right about someone trying to use her looks," John explained to Judy.

"What does that have to do with someone trying to kill her? If they want her dead, why do all this?"

John stood there and thought for a moment. "I don't know. Maybe they just wanted to harm her in the beginning, and for some reason, they changed their mind and now want to kill her. I don't know, but I'll bet you it's the same person doing all this."

"All right, let's say you are right. What are you going to do when you get there?"

"I am the only hope for her. Without me helping, one girl will go to jail and the other will go to her grave. It's my fault. Don't you get it?"

"No, I don't, and you're stupid if you believe this is your fault. It would have happened even if you hadn't sent the ad. Speaking of the ad, she never got your ad. The ad she got puts her in the nude. Your ad had her in a bikini."

"Nude or in a bikini, it makes no difference."

"The Dallas cops never saw the ad. They don't really know."

"I know...I know...I really do, Judy. There's some reason that I'm involved now."

"Yeah, you're stupid. That's the reason."

"Things happen for a reason. You just don't understand, do you?" John said in a low voice. "You just don't understand."

"I understand that you want to save two girls who don't know you and never asked for your help. John, as far as you know, her friend might be the one trying to kill her, and if you get in the middle of that, then you may be killed also."

"I don't think so."

"Why? Because they are so beautiful, sexy, and so, so sweet on TV that they can do no wrong?"

"Well, you're right. They are beautiful and sexy, but they are not killers."

"I don't know what else to say, John. But you are making a major mistake."

John started to reply, when he saw Mike coming toward them. Mike was a close friend of John's. They had helped each other on occasion, mostly Mike helping John. Mike, like John, loved a good adventure himself.

"I thought you were going to get the chair. What are you doing here?" Mike asked.

"Very funny, old sparkly couldn't do me. I was too tough for sparkly, so they told me I could go."

"Everything okay now?"

"Yeah, it's okay."

"Okay, nothing," Judy interrupted, looking Mike in the eyes. "He's going to Georgia and probably will not be returning."

"You're transferring to Georgia?" Mike asked.

"No, you idiot! He's going there to die," Judy said in a mad tone.

"Die? What's wrong?"

"Nothing is wrong. I'm going there to help some girls. That's all."

"Are they beautiful?"

"They are real beautiful and real sexy."

"As if you will ever find out how sexy they are," Judy added.

"What are y'alls talking about?"

"A girl in Georgia. Someone is trying to kill her."

"Her friend is the one trying to kill her, and John wants to save one and keep the other one out of jail. Fat chance of that happening," Judy told Mike.

"It sounds like fun. Can I go with you?" Mike asked.

Judy turned and walked away, partly because she didn't want to hear anymore and partly because she saw a customer walk in looking for some help. That was the only help she thought John needed to be giving, not trying to save a life that he doesn't know.

Mike and John talked about the trip for the next two days. Mike was beginning to get serious about going with John. A little excitement sounded good about now. It sure seems as if it would be more fun than running up cows and baling hay. They went out to lunch a few days later, and John wanted him to go with him.

"Mike, I've been thinking about you going with me."

"I was just kidding. I don't want to go and get killed."

"Nobody is going to get killed if we handle it right."

"Handle it right? John, we have trouble putting a lawn mower together. We are not in the lifesaving business."

"Who's going to pay our medical bills? When we get hurt?"

"We're not going to get hurt."

"Oh, we are not going to get killed."

"No, Mike. I will come up with a plan. Don't worry."

"Wasn't that what Custer told his troops?"

"I'm not Custer."

"No, that's what worries me. He was a professional, and he died."

"Mike, I've been through tougher things than this before."

"Yes, but you were in your twenties and well trained, not to mention you had a backup to help. You don't have a backup this time."

"We will find the killer and stop him before he kills anyone."

"That should take about one day, yeah."

"No, it will take longer than that. Probably a week or two."

"I've only got two weeks. That's all. Two weeks," he repeated himself.

"Okay, then. You're coming with me?"

"Okay, I'm crazy anyway."

There's one thing I need to ask of you, Mike."

"What?"

"I need five thousand dollars to make the trip."

"Where are you going to get it?" Mike asked.

"Can you loan me the money?"

"No! Hell, no!" Mike made it clear to John. "No."

"Mike, I will pay you back."

"With what? You don't have anything worth anything, do you?"

"I've got that car."

"That old Ford?"

"Yes."

"Wasn't that the car that the apartment people gave you a free garage if you would keep that car in it?"

"They just didn't want anything to happen to it."

"Yeah, like being seen."

"Mike, AHS is buying three hundred thousand dollars in their first order. That's thirty thousand for me."

"You're making thirty thousand and asking for five from me?"

"I won't get the money for a few weeks."

"Wait a minute! That's ten per cent. I thought you told me you were making forty-five per cent. What happened to the other thirty-five?"

"I had to make them an offer they couldn't refuse."

"All right, but I want eight thousand back. And I want it within the next month. If something happens to us, I want your wife to pay mine. Okay? Do we have a deal?"

John reached out his hand to meet Mike's. "Yes, we've got a deal."

John wasn't making as much money as he could have, but this trip was not about money. It was about saving lives. John would make the big money later. He wasn't worrying about that now. He wanted enough money to make the trip and not hurt his family. They finished their lunch, and Mike made sure John was paying. They walked in together and saw Judy.

"Well, if it's not the Hardy boys. Did you save any lives while you were out?" she asked.

"Three, but one didn't count," John told her.

"Yeah, that one would not pay, so we left him."

"Judy, we're going to Georgia together as soon as we can get the vacation time approved."

"Are y'all really going?"

"Yes, we are," John said.

"You two are going to save two girls from halfway across the country, whom neither one of you know anything whatsoever about. All you know is they are cute and sexy. Well, that and a dollar will buy you a cup of coffee. And why are you going, Mike? You haven't even seen them on TV yet and still you're going too."

"Judy," Mike said with a low voice. "You will see me on TV. I'll be the salesman for his products. Watch me on TV, and let me know how I did," Mike asked Judy.

"His products. You didn't tell me they were buying from you. Now that makes sense. They're buying from the man who might be killing one of their best hostesses. Yeah. I can see them doing that," Judy remarked.

"She's got a point. They wouldn't buy from you if they knew it was you," Mike said with a concerned look.

"What! You think I'm stupid? Of course they don't know about me. They think you are the president."

I only told him of the sales and the new company that I and Mike had started. The manager was willing to let them go. He told them that he would tape the show and play it back during the next store meeting.

Everything was now set—everything except John explaining to his wife why he is going to Georgia and how he's paying for it.

"Yes, you are, both of you," Judy shouted as she walked toward another customer.

John and Mike went to see the manager about the vacation time. They did not tell him about the girls or the attempted killing. They just asked for vacation time.

14

The Wife's Approval

John knew he couldn't tell her about the girls. He couldn't tell her about the attempted killing. He could tell her all about the company finally making some money for them. John decided to talk with her after supper tonight. Then he thought, *Maybe the best time would be when she first gets home.* Talking about the money would be his strategy. While he was still thinking about what he would say, the door opened. His wife (Patty) walked into the room.

"Honey, I've got some great news to tell you," John said with excitement written all over his face.

"What is it?" she asked.

"I made a sale."

"That's good. How much?" she asked while hanging up her jacket.

"It was a small one, only three hundred…thousand!" John shouted.

"Did you say three hundred thousand, as in dollars?"

"Yes, yes, three hundred thousand of those dollars," John answered her, jumping at the same time. "Three—not one, but three—hundred thousand dollars."

"Okay, now tell me the truth."

"That is the truth. Three hundred thousand dollars."

"Who's stupid enough to spend that much money with you?"

"What? You will be surprise when I tell you who was smart enough to buy from me."

"All right, I give up. Who was smart enough to buy anything from you?"

"Your old friends, that's who."

"My old friends? John, my old friends wouldn't buy the time of day from you. Now tell me who is buying this and why."

"Your friends at the American Home Shopping Network. That's who."

"Wait, you are telling me AHS is buying from you? Why?"

"Why not?"

"It's food, dear, food, Mexican food."

"What in the world are you talking about, food? We don't sell food!"

"Oh, now it's 'we'?"

"If any money is involved, it's *we*. Now tell me the whole story. No more kidding around."

"Well, I made a deal with the National Mexican Food Company in West Texas. They are putting my name on their food. AHS will send them a check for three hundred thousand dollars, and NMF will send me a check for a hundred thousand. The three hundred thousand is only a committed amount. That number was only an introductory offer, and they have ninety days to order more at that price. Then the prices well go twenty-five per cent for me," John explained with a great big smile.

"Us."

"Yeah, of course us."

"So what you are saying is while you are away I will receive a hundred-thousand-dollar check, is that right?" she asked with a gleam in her eyes.

"No! That's not what I'm saying," John told her.

"Well, let's see. The check will be made out to your company, which I'm a signer on that checking account. So that means I can deposit it and write checks on that account, right?"

"Well, you can, but you not going to."

"You are in Georgia. I'm in Texas. Okay, I won't."

"I don't…I feel you really don't mean that."

"Think about it. You are up there with your girlfriend, having a good time, and I'm here at home, the good little Maxwell housewife, just having fun and a hundred thousand of my best friends over."

"This time, it's only thirty thousand."

"Okay, thirty thousand of best friends."

Shaking his head, he asked, "What girlfriend?"

"You telling me you didn't pick AHS because of Katie Morgan?"

"I picked it because I knew that show was the best."

"Yeah, you are glued to the TV every time she's on, and she had nothing to do with your decision?"

"It was about money, nothing but money…big money."

"So you will not see her or any other hostesses while you're there?"

"Why are you so concerned about her? It's the money, thirty thousand dollars. That's reason enough to go."

Reading the contract that AHS and John had agreed to, she asked, "If she's not on your list of people to meet, then why is her and Katie Richard's names on this contract? It states that Katie Morgan will do two three-hour shows on your products, not to mention Beth, Kim, and of course Katie Richard."

"They get paid on commission. I was only trying to help them get a little more money. Besides, they will sell more food. They are the best. What's wrong with that?"

"That's okay. I was just kidding. But I wasn't kidding about the check coming here. Oh, and another thing, it said that Mike Gross would be on the show. Why not you? It would be a good way to meet Morgan. Who the heck is Mike Gross?"

"Mike Gross is the sales manager of this company. I don't do well on camera."

"You do fine on camera. I suppose having Mike sell for you will cost us. How much? If Mike is selling and Mike is meeting your girlfriend, then why are you going?"

"She's not my girlfriend. I think Mike could do a better job than I."

"How much?"

"How much what?" John asked as if he didn't know what she was talking about.

"How much are you paying Mike?"

"Eight thousand."

"Eight thousand? Did you say eight thousand? You meant eight hundred, of course," she shouted.

"Yeah…thousand is right," John corrected her in a very low voice.

"Why?'

"Well, I borrowed five thousand from him to help finance this operation."

"That leaves three thousand. You're paying him three thousand for a five-thousand-dollar loan? He must be a hell of a good friend. What is this trip costing you anyway, your life?" she asked with a concerned look.

John answered with a look of guilt all over his face. "God, I sincerely hope not."

"Why did you say it like that?"

"Well, I…want a safe trip up there and back for both of us."

Changing the subject to money, John told her, "I don't know exactly how much, but I'm sure it will be some leftover for us."

"They are sending that hundred-thirty-dollar check here to me while you're away?" she asked.

Reluctantly, he said, "Yes."

"Good. You boys have a good time in Georgia," she remarked with laughter.

"Maybe I had better stay here."

"No, no. Go ahead. Don't worry about me. I will have thirty thousand reasons to be happy while you're gone," she told John while walking into the kitchen.

"I will hug Katie Morgan and Katie Richard for you."

"Don't hug them for me. You can hug Dan or Bob, and be sure, and give them a big wet one just for me."

"Any wet ones will be on Morgan or Katie. Darn sure not on anybody named Bob or Dan."

They laughed, joked, and planned how they would spend the new money. They talked more about the trip, the new company, and its future.

The trip was now set. John had gotten the added information he wanted, the deal he wanted, the money he wanted, his product was on its way to AHS, and the approval of his wife. Mike was also ready. The only thing left was to wait for Sunday to come.

15

Katie Morgan Comes Home

Katie and Aunt Annie returned home after having a most entertaining dinner with Mary.

"You know, Aunt Annie, Miss Mary is so much fun," Morgan told her while hanging up hers and Aunt Annie's jackets.

"She sure is, and she never misses watching you and Katie on TV. She always calls me and says, 'She's on. Are you watching?' Morgan, I've got the scrapbook on Katie and the pageant, if you would like to see it."

"I would love to see to it. It's not too much trouble, is it?" Morgan asked with an excited tone.

"No, of course not. It's right here. I sometimes look at it. I've clippings of you too," Aunt Annie told Morgan.

"What clippings?"

"I have clippings of you and Katie when y'all worked together. I have clippings of your shows and the commercials you made. I save everything about you and Katie. You're my children. That's the way I look at you and her."

"You're just a clipping fool, aren't you, Mom? You know, Aunt Annie, I couldn't love you and Katie any more if you and she were my blood family. I love you so much, Aunt Annie," Morgan told her has she reached out to hug her.

"I feel the same way, honey. I love you so much," she told Morgan with a big hug. "Here's the book."

Morgan, taking the scrapbook from her, walked back to the sofa and started looking at the pictures.

"Look, Aunt Annie! That's me."

"Where?"

"Right there, to the right."

"Lord, honey, you had short hair then."

"Yeah, what was I thinking with that hair? That's Katie. You know, I always thought I knew her from somewhere. I thought maybe I had seen one of her shows."

"That's funny, because she said the same thing about you."

"I wonder why she never told me she was Miss National."

"Don't be angry with her, dear. She never talks about it. I don't really know why. I think it may have something to do with the girl who had that bad accident the day after the pageant. Katie was never close to her, but for some reason, she felt really bad about her accident."

"An accident…yeah…She was the first Miss National, and the first runner-up was also in an accident. Then Katie moved into that spot. I did an interview with the first Miss National after her accident. Then she left town, and I never saw her again. The second runner-up was so mad and angry with me for even trying to talk to her. It was something about someone was sleeping with the judges and cheated her out of the first place or something like that. I can't remember all the details. Do you have anything about the accidents in here?"

"No, I only kept things about Katie. But I remember Katie being upset about winning the way she did."

"Yeah, Katie likes to win on her own. She doesn't like to have it given to her."

"You got that right."

"Wasn't there something about the second runner-up and that car wreck? Oh yeah! She had traded cars the night of the accident, and that girl ended up in the wreck. What was her name?" Morgan was trying to think about that night as she talked.

"I don't know, Morgan, but Katie was supposed to be with Miss National, and she couldn't make it because of me. She thought I was having what they thought was a stroke and wanted to be with me. Of course, I was okay, and she went in another limo. She was also the one who wanted to trade cars that night with that other girl."

"Maybe that's why she doesn't like to talk about it."

"I don't know, dear. The cars were all limos. Katie liked the white one. It was the only white one they had. That's why she asked for that car, and no one objected."

"She shouldn't feel bad about that."

"The three girls had a limo assigned to them. None of them had the white one. Katie just asked for that car. That's all."

"I recalled something about that girl and the limo. Wasn't her name, Nicole? Anyway, she was supposed to have asked for the white limo, and instead she got one of the black ones. I think she was drunk that night and didn't realize what color the car was. She kept blaming everyone for what happened. And you know what? She didn't like me at all. She cussed me out. Told me to not ever talk to her again. Said I was the worst reporter in the world. You know, I may not have been the best, but I'm sure somewhere in this world there had to have been someone worse than me," Morgan said while laughing and walking to the kitchen to get some of Aunt Annie's famous pecan pie. "I have to have a slice of that pie, Aunt Annie. Can I get you a slice?" she asked as she pulled the pie from the refrigerator and started cutting.

"Yes, Morgan, please, and I will take a glass of milk too," she told Morgan as she continued looking at the scrapbook.

"Okay, I think I will have a glass of milk too."

"Oh, look, Morgan. That's you again."

"Yeah, that's me. The girl to the right of me is Donna. She's now on NBC. She called and told me she could help me get back on at NBC. I decided to stay here and do the home-shopping thing. You know, I really like what I do. Oh, look! There's Katie, and that's the girl Nicole…I believe that is her name, and the first Miss National, Susan something. She was so nice to all the reporters and me. I wonder where she is now. When I get home, I'm going to pull out all my reports from that time. There's something bothering me about that pageant and Nicole. I can't put my finger on it right now, but something is really bothering me. I've got a feeling it is something important. Why, I don't know," Morgan explained while taking another bite of her pecan pie.

"Let's go to breakfast in the morning. Okay?"

"Yeah, of course. How about Tony's? It was really good food the last time we went there."

"Tony's is very good food, but I was thinking about Mickey's Pancake House," Aunt Annie said as she picked up the pie plates and started walking to the kitchen.

Morgan, grabbing the glasses and following Aunt Annie, said, "Mickey's is okay if it's where you want to go, but we'll have to leave here an hour earlier so I can bring you back and be on time for my show."

"You don't have to bring me back, dear."

"Well, we're not taking two cars, and I'm not putting you on a bus. We will just get up a little bit earlier. That's all." Morgan reached over and kissed her on the cheek.

"You don't understand, dear. I'm coming home with you. I'll stay with Katie and keep an eye on her."

"That's good and all, but really, you don't have to do that. She will be all right."

"No, someone is trying to hurt both my girls, and I'm going to be with her and you too. The end."

"Okay, you're welcome to stay with me, and I'm sure Katie would love to have you too."

"Thanks. I will stay with Katie."

"Are you going to call her tonight and tell her you're coming?"

"No, let's surprise her, okay?

"Okay, let's do that. She will definitely be surprised. But she will love having you with her."

The next few hours, they looked at and talked about the scrapbook. Morgan was trying to keep Aunt Annie's mind off the trouble back home. She was also trying to think what she would tell Katie about Aunt Annie coming back with her. Aunt Annie was a person whose mind was almost impossible to change when she makes up her mind to do something, and Morgan knew that. She also knew that she would be running the risk of hurting Aunt Annie's feelings. Neither Morgan nor Katie would ever take that risk. The respect and love they had for her would forbid them from doing so.

The trip home was a very pleasant one. The weather was great, and driving conditions were good, and when Morgan and Aunt Annie arrived at Mickey's House of Pancakes, Morgan was recognized immediately. People gathered around her as if she were a movie star. Morgan was, as usual, so graceful and so delightful to talk to that they all fell in love with her all over again. The old, the young, the girls, and of course all the boys and men loved her as well.

Two hours later, they left Mickey's and headed straight for the studio. Morgan had an afternoon show, and Katie would be ending her show about the time they would be arriving.

They walked in at the last ten minutes of Katie's show. The two of them stood by the camera so as to let Katie know they were home. That is, Morgan and Aunt Annie both were home. Katie looked up and saw them. You could read the thought on her face. *What is she doing here?* Morgan gave her the sign that she couldn't help it. Katie got off the phone from talking with one of her customers and fan. Looking directly at Aunt Annie, she said, "I see my Aunt Annie is here. Come on over, Aunt Annie. I want to introduce you to the nation." Aunt Annie, looking embarrassed, walked slowly toward Katie with the help of Morgan nudging her.

"Come on, Aunt Annie. They want to see you. I have told them about you." Katie said, not being able to wait any longer, she started walking to Aunt Annie, reaching out her arms and hugging her on camera.

"This is my aunt Annie, from Macon, Georgia. She is going to spend some time with me. She's my best fan. Say hello, Aunt Annie," Katie insisted. "Isn't she fabulous, folks?"

"Hello…hello…everybody. I'm going to let you get back to work, dear," she said as she waved good-bye to the cameras and walked off the stage, walking a little faster off than going on the stage.

"She doesn't have to worry about you getting her, Morgan. I'm going to get her myself, and did you know she was going to do that, didn't you? Now you are on my list too," Aunt Annie said with a sarcastic tone.

Morgan, watching and laughing as hard as she could, said to Aunt Annie, "I didn't know she was going to do that."

Some of the others working there came up to meet Aunt Annie. They all talked with her and began begging her to tell them some good stories about Katie and Morgan too.

"I will tell you all the bad stories about her and this one too," she said as she looked at Morgan.

"Aunt Annie, come on over and help me get ready for my show. Okay? Please," Morgan begged of her while pulling her by her arm toward her. Seeing them startling to walk to Morgan's set when they heard Katie hollering to them.

"Wait, wait," she shouted. They turned around and waited for Katie to catch up.

"You're okay, Aunt Annie? Remember, I love you."

"Yeah…I'm all right," Aunt Annie said while reaching out to hug her. "But don't you ever do that again, you hear?"

"I promise, okay? Morgan, I have a few things I need to do, and then we can go home, okay? You don't mind if we leave now, do you, Morgan? They are going to work on my car if I can get there by eleven thirty," Katie said.

"No, that's okay. You just be careful now. You hear, girl?" Morgan said as she reached out and hugged Katie.

"Morgan, there's a lot of things I need to tell you, so you come over for supper tonight, okay? If Wayne doesn't mind."

"He is out of town again. Okay, I will pick up some chicken if that's all right with you two."

"That's fine. See you about six."

"Yeah, that's fine," Morgan replied.

Beth walked up to them and hugged both Morgan and Aunt Annie.

"What are you doing here today? I thought you were off today," Morgan asked.

"Jim called me in. He wasn't sure if you would be here today, Morgan."

"I told him I would be here today. I've never missed a show yet. What is he thinking?" Morgan answered with a sarcastic tone.

"Beth, bring Morgan up to date on what's happening."

"Morgan, I don't have the time to tell you myself. She will fill you in on what has happened the last few days."

"Okay."

"What did happen?" Aunt Annie asked.

"Come on, Aunt Annie. I will tell you on the way. Bye-bye, see you at supper."

"Thanks, Beth, and of course, you are always invited," Katie said while waving good-bye to them.

"Now tell me what has happened and why you are really here," Morgan demanded of Beth.

"The police are looking for you. Katie would not tell them where you went. Jim thinks they are going to arrest you today."

"Why? They know I don't have anything to do with what's happening to Katie," Morgan said with a troubled voice.

"It's the orange juice, Morgan. They think you put the poison in Katie's drink. Only she didn't drink it."

"What poison? What orange juice? What are you talking about?" Morgan asked with an upset tone. "I don't understand what you are talking about."

"The day you left, you left Katie a cup of orange juice. That juice had poison in it. Had she drunk it, she would be dead now."

"Wait…wait a minute, Katie tested the juice I gave her? She didn't trust me, is that what you are trying to say?"

"No, of course not. Katie trusts you with her life. She has always, and she will always trust you. You should know better than that," Beth told Morgan with a hurt tone. "You should know better. She loves you. She would never think anything bad about you."

"You're right. I knew better. I'm sorry I said that. She wouldn't not trust me any more than I not trust her. Don't say anything to her about what I said. I didn't mean it. I'm just upset with everything going on here. So how did she know it had poison in that juice?"

"She went to open it, and a small mouse run across her feet, and of course she dropped it. The mice lipped it and died. She called the police then, and they tested the juice."

Before Morgan and Beth could finish talking, Detectives Barker and Parks walked up.

"Well, it looks like my ride downtown is here now," Morgan said with a look of trouble on her face.

"Katie Morgan, I'm sorry, but you are under arrest for the attempted murder of Katie Richard. You have the right to keep silent. You have the right to an attorney. If you cannot afford one, one will be appointed for you. You have the right to remain silent. Anything you say can and will be used against you in a court of law. Do you understand this?" Detective Barker asked as he was putting the handcuffs on her.

"Yes, I understand. But do you understand I had nothing to do with any of this?" Morgan shouted back at the detective.

"I'm sorry, Ms. Morgan, I have no choice. I could have put out an all-points search for you while you were away. I didn't do that. You're my favorite, and my wife is going to kill me when she finds out that I arrested you. The evidence points too much to you for me not to arrest you," Barker explained to her with a look of sorrow.

Beth came over and hugged Morgan. She told Morgan, "I know you didn't have anything to do with this. I will be down to bail you out."

"Thanks, but I have the money for bail. You stay here and do my show. Do a real good one today, you hear?"

"I will, Morgan. I will see you later today, love you."

"I love you too. Call Katie, and tell her what has happened, okay?" Morgan asked of Beth as the detective escorted her to the car.

"I will, and don't you worry. Everything will be okay. I will call Katie for you," Beth promised her.

"You want to call Katie Richard? Why? She's the one you are accused of trying to murder. What makes you think she will help you?" Detective Barker asked, knowing why she wanted Katie to know.

"She's my best friend. She's like a sister to me. She doesn't believe I would ever do anything to harm her," Morgan explained.

When they arrived at police headquarters, she was fingerprinted and put in an interrogation room for almost haft an hour before anyone came in to talk with her. The two detectives came in and started talking to her.

"Tell me about the orange juice," Barker demanded of her.

"I didn't know anything about the juice until Beth told me. That was about five minutes before you came in. That's all I know about it. I never put anything in it."

"Was the juice ever opened?"

"No, it was new. Katie and I drank only that brand of orange juice. I had two left. I drank one myself and put the other one in the refrigerator for her. It was never opened."

"Did anyone see you put the juice in the refrigerator?"

"Yes."

"Who?"

"Judy, Jill, Patty, and Nicky."

"Anyone know you had saved it for Katie?"

"Yes, all of them knew that I was leaving it for her. Maybe Nicky didn't know she is new here, but everyone else knew. We have often done this. We have always done things like that for each other, and I have given food and drinks to others, and they have me."

"So four other people knew you had put the drink there for Katie?"

"Yes, sir."

"They knew it was left for Miss Richard because you wrote KR on the cap?"

"No, I never put anything on the cap. Everyone just knew that was our brand."

"Did any of them return to the break room after you left and before Miss Richard got there?"

"I don't know. People are in and out of the break room all day and night. I don't know. I left right after that."

"Did you see Bobby that morning?"

"No, sir."

"Do you trust those four girls?"

"Yes, of course. None of them could do something like that."

"Tell me about Patty. I haven't met her."

"Patty is one of the sweetest girls I have ever met. She loves everybody. Patty couldn't hurt anyone. She's too nice."

"What about Jill?"

"The pretty girl next door, as her fans refer to her. She hasn't been real happy lately. She gain some weight and can't get it off. That's bugging her. We go out to eat a lot. She's a good friend. She couldn't hurt Katie or me or anyone else, as far is that's concerned."

"Has Miss Richard ever kidded her about her weight?"

"No, of course not. Katie would not ever kid about that. She was overweight in high school, and she hated how they treated her. Beside that's not her style."

"It has been two hours, and Miss Richard has not shown."

"She will be here."

"She will."

"Tell me about Bobby, Ms. Morgan."

"Bobby? I don't know anything to tell you about him."

"Why do you think he lied about the chain saw?"

"I don't know."

"Why do you think he lied about the limo?"

"I don't know why. I only know that he is lying. That's all I know," she told the detectives with a look of disgust on her face.

They continued to question her for two hours. They asked the same questions many different ways. Morgan answered them all the same way. Her story never changed.

"Ms. Morgan, looks as if your good friend is leaving you here tonight."

"She will be here. May I make a call?" Morgan asked.

"Yes, of course you can."

Morgan called Katie. No answer. Then she called Beth. She answered.

"Beth, did you call Katie?"

"Yes, her cell battery was dead. I had to call around to find her. I talked with her about twenty minutes ago. She and Annie are on their way. Are you all right, honey?"

"Yeah…I'm fine. Thanks for getting Katie."

Looking out the glass door, she could see Katie and Aunt Annie coming in now. "I've got to go. They are here. Thanks again," she said to Beth with an excited tone. Turning toward Detective Barker, she said, "I told you she would be here. She wouldn't let me down."

"Good. Actually, I was hoping she would show up for you," Barker said with a smile.

"You don't think I'm guilty, do you?" she asked with a sigh of relief.

"No, but I do think—" Before he could finish his sentence, Katie and Aunt Annie walked into the room.

"She's no damned killer, you idiot. Now come on, dear, let's go home," Aunt Annie said to Barker and Morgan.

"Not so fast, Mama. Who are you?" Barker asked Aunt Annie.

"I'm your worst nightmare if you don't let her go. That's who I am."

"I'm sorry, Detective. This is my Aunt Annie," Katie told Barker.

"And what's she to you, Ms. Morgan?"

"I'm her aunt too," Aunt Annie told Barker with a loud voice.

Katie pulled Aunt Annie to her and told her to be quiet.

John Gardner

"You're her aunt too? I didn't know you two were related. Are you cousins or something?" Barker asked with that surprised look.

"No, we're not related, not by blood anyway," Morgan explained.

"Is that Chucky Albright?" she asked, looking at the campaign poster hanging on the wall of the district attorney.

"It's Charles Albright. Do you know him?" Baker asked.

"Yeah, Chucky and I go a long way back when he was the assistant DA. In Georgetown, Kentucky."

"That was over twenty-five years ago."

"I met him in college. We went out a few times. He left town a few years later and then came back to be the new ADA. In Georgetown. My husband got a transfer to Macon, and I never saw him again," Aunt Annie told everyone.

"I remember him. I was only about fourteen the last time I saw him."

"He was a good friend with your mother and dad, especially your mother. He went out with her too—before she married your father, of course," Aunt Annie explained to everyone.

"Of course," Barker added.

"Well, I hate to tell you this, but he's the one who insisted on arresting her, and he's the only one to okay letting her go," Barker informed them.

"Call him. I want to talk to him," Aunt Annie demanded of barker.

Barker picked up the phone and called Albright. "Barker here. Let me talk to Charles, please. Yes, it's important."

"Okay."

"Give me that phone," Aunt Annie demanded of him.

"You tell Chucky I want to see him now! This is Annie Turner from Georgetown, Kentucky. I want to see him now, not in an hour, but now. Do you understand? Thank you." Aunt Annie handed the phone back to Barker and said, "He's on his way now. Thank you."

"Okay, I think," Barker remarked.

Through the glass door, Barker could see the DA and shouted, "Here's Chucky."

Katie and Morgan smiled at what he had said.

Aunt Annie saw Charles and ran with arms wide open. He too ran to her, picking her up and turning around several times. He put her down. "God, Annie, you haven't changed at all. You're still beautiful." He hugged her again. "What are you doing here, Annie?"

"I came to get my niece out of your jail. That's why I'm here. I didn't know you were the DA here, Chucky."

"Annie, they call me Charles now."

"Well, I will call you anything you want me to call you if you let Morgan go. I will call you a few other names you won't like if you don't let her go," Aunt Annie said while laughing.

"Now, Annie, that's beneath you to call me names. Which one is Morgan?"

"This one is the one you had us picked up."

"I don't remember her."

"Of course you don't. This is Katie Richard, Mary Ann's daughter."

"Oh my God! You have grown up, young lady," he said as he walked to Katie and hugged her also.

"I remember you, sir. You and dad went hunting together some."

"That's right. How are your parents?" he inquired.

"Okay, Charles. Everybody is okay except your new jailbird. Now tell the good detective that she can go home," Aunt Annie said with a stern look.

"Yeah...I can't do that, Annie," Albright said while backing away from her.

Aunt Annie, walking up to his face, asked with a mean tone, "What did you say?"

"There's too much evidence to let her go, Annie."

"Let's walk outside where I can talk to you alone," Aunt Annie said, grabbing his arm and opening the door as they walked outside.

"Do the paperwork, Detective Mogan," Katie told Barker.

Barker walked slowly back to his desk. After sitting down, he looked up at the two girls looking out the glass door, knowing that Aunt Annie would get her way. He didn't want to believe that Morgan had anything to do with what was happening to Katie, but the evidence was there, and he was a cop.

Addressing Katie, he asked, "Why would you want her out on the streets again? All the evidences point to her and only her."

Katie turned around and walked to Barker's desk. "You don't get it, do you? Morgan and I are like sisters. We are best friends. Sisters and best friends don't kill each other. As far as the evidence is concerned, you have had other cases where the evidence had shown one person to be guilty when they were not, haven't you, Detectives? It is so obvious that someone is trying to frame her. I don't know why you can't see it," Katie said to Barker in a somewhat polite tone.

Barker started to say something when Morgan interrupted him. "They are hugging now. Here they come," Morgan announced.

Albright opened the door for Annie. Walking in the room, he said to Morgan, "Ms. Morgan, I'm letting you go for now. I don't know your character any more than I know hers. She might be doing this to herself. The two of you might be working together for some kind of publicity. The point I'm trying to make is, I don't know either of you. What I do know is Annie. Her word is good enough for me. Annie will be reasonable for you. What this means, Ms. Morgan, is that if for any reason you leave town or not show up when we call you, it will cost her fifty thousand dollars. Do you understand this?" he asked in a very stern tone.

"Yes, sir, I understand."

"Aunt Annie has nothing to worry about. Morgan never ran from trouble in her life. She has always faced any problem head-on, and she won't run from this one either," Katie told the DA.

Barker, turning toward Albright, asked, "How are you going to do the fifty thousand? You can't do a bond?"

"I don't need to. Annie gave me her word," he explained to Barker.

"I don't understand you people. No one's word is that good today, and you, Miss Richard. Maybe Morgan doesn't have anything to do with it, but if someone is trying to frame her, as long as she is free, your life is in danger. When she was out of town for these few days, nothing happened to you."

Barker tried to finish his sentence when Morgan shouted out, "You're right, Detective. I'm not the one trying to kill her. But this person needs me to be out there for it to work. As long as I'm out, Katie is in danger. I want you to lock me up until you catch this person. I don't want her to die. I won't leave! Lock me up, Detective," Morgan demanded.

"I can't."

"You can. I'm guilty. I'm the one who has been trying to kill her. I put the poison in the juice. I'm the one, Detective, so do your duty and lock me up before I kill her," Morgan said with a nervous voice.

Katie walked over to Morgan and put her arms around her. "You are so sweet and so stupid, Morgan. You couldn't hurt anyone, and you're not going to stay in jail to protect me. This person will wait for you to get out. It may be years, Morgan. I'm not going to let you stay here another day. I will be okay. Remember, this killer is not very good at this. I am still alive," Katie told Morgan.

Morgan, looking at Katie with tears all over her beautiful face, said, "No, I can't leave. I can't let anything happen to you. Maybe it is me. Maybe I have other personalities I don't even know about. People like that don't know what they are doing. It may be me."

"I don't think so, Morgan. One personality is enough for you. Even if this is true, we will get help for you. But that's not the case. Someone else is trying. If you stay here, then they will be winning. I'm not going to let them win, and you're not either. You hear me, girl?" Katie told Morgan.

"I just don't want anything to happen to you because of me."

"Nothing is going to happen. Detective Barker will catch them before that."

"Now let's go home, Morgan."

"She's right. Everything will be okay, Morgan. You will stay with us until Wayne gets back in town," Aunt Annie told her.

Aunt Annie came over to Morgan and reached for her hand. "Come on, dear, let's go home." Looking back at the DA and the detectives, Aunt Annie said, "Thanks, they will be okay. They're with me."

The three of them went back to Katie's house, where she had three bedrooms. Morgan agreed to stay until her husband got back.

The short ride back was a quiet one. Katie was driving, Aunt Annie was beside her in the front seat, and Morgan was in the rear seat. Aunt Annie broke the silence when she told Katie to go to the chicken place and reminded Morgan she was buying supper. They all got a big laugh out of that, and for a few minutes, everyone's mind was taken off the trouble facing them. After supper, they helped each other in cleaning up the leftovers and throwing away the mess. Each one picked her favorite chair to sit in. No one was speaking. Katie had a look of deep thinking on her face. Aunt Annie recognized that something was going on in her head.

"What are you thinking so hard about, dear?" she addressed her.

"Oh, nothing, just thinking."

"Tell us, dear. What?"

"It was something that Nicky said the other day. It bothered me when she said it."

"What was it, Katie?" Morgan asked.

"It...it...was nothing. It just kind of bothers me."

"Tell us, dear," Aunt Annie requested.

"Okay...All she said was the same thing everyone is thinking. She said, 'What did you do to someone to make them hate you so much that they would want you dead?' That's all."

"That juke. Where does she get off talking to you like that? Wait until I see her. I'll straighten her...out. Who does she think she is anyway? I never really liked her whole lot anyway," Morgan told them.

"Well, it just bothered me that she would say that. I wouldn't say that to her."

"No, and I bet you no one else would have said anything like that to you, did they?" Morgan asked.

"No, everyone has been real nice to me. She probably didn't mean anything. I don't think she was trying to be mean, and don't say anything to her about this. Okay?"

"I won't say anything about this, but if she says anything to me about me, I'm not holding back. There's something about her. I can't get close to her."

"Girls, what's her name...? The truth is, and I don't want to hurt your feelings, but she was right," Aunt Annie told them.

"What?" Morgan asked with a criticizing tone.

"Calm down, dear. I don't think she should have said that to Katie either. What I'm saying is, she was right. What we need to do is figure out who that person is and stop him. No matter who he is. So let's do some thinking about this. Also, Morgan, they may hate you too, or they're maybe wanting to hurt Katie even more by harming you too," Aunt Annie explained.

The three of them talked all night about this. Most of it was repetition. As hard as they tried, they could not come up with a name. Katie thought of people who might not like her, but it did just not like her, certainly not hating her, and she wasn't even sure about that. They talked so long each of them fell asleep in their chair.

The east sun was rising and filling the once darkened room with new light, with new hope, letting everyone know this was a new day—a new beginning and another chance to find the murderer before he finds them.

The early morning sun awakened them one by one. Aunt Annie, being the first one to speak, said, "Did we all sleep here last night? Right here in this chair?"

Katie, standing up and walking to Aunt Annie, kissed her.

"Yes, you with Morgan and me," Katie said.

Urging as hard as she could, Morgan was trying to say, "Let's get dressed and go to breakfast. I'm starving. Katie will buy."

"No, you girls have spent enough money on me already. I'm going to cook breakfast for us. After that, we all get cleaned up and get dressed," Aunt Annie said with a smile.

After breakfast, Morgan went home to get a change of clothes and look for her old notes on the pageant. She didn't know why that was so important or if it was even important. What she knew was that it kept bothering her.

Morgan and Katie had talked about it the night before, but like Aunt Annie had said, "Katie did not like to talk about the pageant."

Katie had very little to say about the pageant. She was surprised to learn that Morgan was there and that was all she would talk about concerning that week. They laughed and joked about the pageant and some of the people who was there. Katie said she didn't recognize Morgan, and Morgan said the same about Katie.

The next several days were uneventful. There were no attempts made on Katie's life. No phone calls, no e-mail, no ads popping up. It was as if the killer had packed his bags and left town. The girls were somewhat at ease.

Jim had kept them busy doing things around the station. They had a new vendor coming from Texas, selling Mexican food in a gift package. He had sent some samples to AHS and to Morgan and Katie. He had also requested that both of them do a three-hour show on his products. The Mexican food was good and made Morgan a little bit homesick for Texas.

16

Here Comes the Marshal

John Garfield and Mike Gross were on their way to Landover, Georgia. They were the new vendor of the Mexican food, the same food that made Morgan homesick for Texas

No one at AHS knew that Garfield was the owner of that company. They only knew that Mike Gross would be introducing it. They knew that Mike was the sales manager, and that was whom they thought they had talked with on the phone. Actually, they spoke with Garfield himself.

Garfield, of course, was using Mike's name so as not to let them know he was coming.

It was an eight-hour trip to Landover. Mike still wasn't clear on what Garfield was going to do there. Garfield wasn't totally sure himself. All he knew for sure was that he had to be there for the two hostesses.

"Okay, let see here. I'm going to sell Mexican food with Katie and Katie. They don't know who you are, but you are the one to save them, right?" Mike asked.

"Yeah...pretty much so."

"You know that I have never sold anything on TV?"

"I know. It's all right."

"How are you going to save them, John?"

"I don't know, but I will," John assured Mike.

The initial trip was like that. John was thinking as hard as he could about saving Katie.

He knew that Lisa would find more information on that Tuner girl, and that might be a help to solving this case. He had to learn more about Katie. He was sure that this person was in her past somewhere. They arrived on time. Garfield rented a car. They checked into a rather nice hotel.

The next morning, they took that long walk to the other side of the hotel where the restaurant was located. The food was great, the service was superior, and the conversation was a serious one.

"Mike," Garfield said while buttering his biscuits, "you have a ten o'clock appointment with Fred Simon. He's the buyer. Remember, you have already talked with him. The deal is good for ninety days. The price goes back to fifty per cent for his company. The more he orders, the less he pays now."

"I don't understand all that," Mike told Garfield whiling reaching for more eggs.

"I thought you might have a problem remembering this, so I wrote it all out for you," he told Mike as he was pulling some paper from his briefcase.

"You got everything down I need to know?"

"Yeah…after breakfast, we will go over this. This is important for you to know. I sent AHS a list of things about the company and the food. Katie Morgan will be asking you about them. She will mention it on the air. You read over what I gave you a few days ago, didn't you?"

"Yeah…I remember most of it."

"Most of it is not good enough, Mike. We will do a rehearsal after breakfast."

Mike was a quick learner. He got it down perfect. It was almost showtime. Mike went to the studio and introduced himself. He soon met Katie Morgan. Later tonight, it would be the first of three three-hour shows and a lot of one-hour shows. She talked about Texas and how good the Mexican food tastes. She was so delightful and charming that she put Mike at ease. Morgan told him not to be nervous, she would carry the show. Mike had no problem with that. He now could understand how Garfield would want to help such a nice person as Katie Morgan. The show went very well. Morgan, as usual, sold a lot. She put Mike at total ease and made him look like a real pro. If Katie's sales were as good, then AHS may have to order more. This was the sale of the day. Every host and hostess would be selling it. The sales looked really good. Mike was very proud of himself and the sales. After meeting Morgan and then Katie, Mike now understood why Garfield did not want anything bad to happen to them. They were really nice girls. They acted the same off camera as they did on camera. Mike came to like and respect the both of them so much that he was giving them a lot of samples. He figured Garfield wouldn't mind after all. He gave it to Morgan and Katie.

By the time Morgan's second show came up, at 9:00 p.m., that night, Mike was a pro. He felt good about this new job. He called home. Everyone saw him and told Mike how good he looked on TV. Mike's wife taped everyone of his shows from midnight to midnight. The people back at work were watching and taping it also.

While Mike was on TV, Garfield was doing some investigating on his own. He went to the Epson Street Bar. He had heard that a lot of the crew hung out there.

"Hi, I'm Paul Johnson, a private detective from Little Rock, Arkansas. I'm looking for a girl who used to work for AHS." He showed them a picture of his wife. "Have you ever seen her?" he asked a couple of boys standing at the bar.

"No, but I sure would like to know her. She looks a little familiar, but I don't know her. That guy at the pool table may know. He has worked for AHS for a long time. He claimed to have had all the girls over there. You might want to talk with him. His name is Bobby," one of them told Garfield.

This was the same Bobby who said he had been with Katie Richard.

"Bobby," Garfield asked while holding out his hand to shake Bobby's, "I'm Paul Johnson from Little Rock. I'm a private detective looking for a girl who had worked here at AHS. Maybe you can help. You work there, don't you?"

"Yeah, I work there. Who is she?" he asked as he hit the cue ball again.

"Her name is Nancy Morgan."

"Nancy Morgan? You don't mean Katie Morgan, do you?"

"No, Nancy Morgan. She was born in Texas and moved to Arkansas and then here. Who's this Katie Morgan?"

"She's that cute little dark blond on the show. You don't mean her, do you?" he asked again.

"This girl is in her thirties and about five four. She has brown hair."

"Hey! That sounds like Morgan, but she's not that tall, more like five two or three."

"Can I buy you a beer and talk more?"

"Yeah, a beer sounds good about now."

They walked to Bobby's favorite booth and ordered a beer and a sandwich.

"You don't mind the sandwich, do you…Paul?" Bobby asked after ordering it.

"Paul, Paul Johnson. And, yes, the sandwich is okay."

"Now tell me more about this Katie Morgan."

"She's cute and sexy. Her husband is out of town a lot. She's a fun girl."

"I like to think so."

"But is she really?"

"I don't know. She kind of likes me."

"You like her?"

"Of course. I told you she was beautiful and sexy, didn't I?"

"You said cute and sexy. Now she is beautiful?"

"Yeah."

"Have you ever been with her? The truth now I don't care if you have or not, but I need you to tell me the truth, not some bragging. Okay, Bobby?"

"Okay…no…I've never been with her. Damn sure like to do her sometime," Bobby told John as he took a sip of his beer.

"Are you fooling around with any of the girls on the show? Remember, the truth, Bobby."

"Yeah, one…and that's the truth…Paul."

"Which one, Bobby?"

"She's new here. Been here less than a year. Now she gets all the hot e-mails. She is the prettiest and sexiest of all the girls."

"Even Morgan?" John asked with a big smile on his face.

"Hell, Paul, she's even sexier than the other Katie."

"Wait, there are two Katies on the show?"

"Yeah! You don't watch the show?"

"Man, I just don't have time for TV, and when I do watch, I watch murder mysteries."

"You like murder mysteries?" Bobby asked.

"Yeah. Tell me more about the other Katie."

"It's funny you asked, Paul. Someone is trying to kill one of them."

"For real?"

"Yeah, but I'm spending most of my time with Nicky nowadays."

"Nicky? Who is Nicky?"

"She's the one I told you was the prettiest and sexiest of all of them. Remember?"

"Yeah. Tell me about Nicky. Why is she with you so much?"

"What the hell do you mean? Pretty girls like me too," Bobby said with a mean look on his face.

"Of course, pretty girls like you. No, you're kidding, aren't you, Bobby?"

"No, man. Someone put poison in Katie orange juice one day, but she didn't drink it."

"You sound disappointed."

"Oh no. Don't get me wrong. I love her."

"Bobby, who are you talking about, Katie Morgan or the other Katie?"

"The other Katie, of course."

"I thought you love Morgan, and does this other Katie have a last name?"

"I do love Morgan, but Katie Richard and me are close."

"Richard, that's her last name? What do you mean you and her are close. Are y'all lovers?"

"No, but I think she wants to be."

"I don't look as good as you. You're tall and muscular. I'm not."

"Yeah, you are about the size of Morgan."

The waitress walked up again, and Bobby ordered another beer. This time he added a piece of apple pie.

"Tell me more about this Nicky girl."

"Well, she's got money. She works here because she likes doing this. She's real generous with her money. She brought me a new pickup."

"She asked any favors of you?"

"No…not really."

Robert, another worker at AHS, came over to remind Bobby it was time to go to work.

"Bobby, it was nice talking with you. And don't say anything about what we were talking about, okay, Bobby?"

"I could forget everything if I had a fifty spot to go back to work with. You know what I mean?"

"Yeah, I know, and that's okay, but you know we haven't finished talking. You won't forget it, will you, Bobby?" John asked of him as he handed him a twenty-dollar bill and told him, "You will get the balance when we talk again."

John didn't like paying fifty, but it was some good information. It might help. At the very least, it was another piece to the puzzle.

Garfield talked with several other people about Morgan and Katie. He learned that Nicky and Bobby were closer than

Bobby had said. He didn't know what the connection was, if any, with Nicky and Bobby. Nicky was a beautiful woman with money. John didn't know what she could see in Bobby. Bobby was a loser, a junky. You couldn't believe everything he said, so why was Nicky with him? Maybe this has nothing to do with what's happening. Garfield put those thoughts in the back of his mind. As he learned more, he would start fitting the pieces together.

17

Morgan Meets Garfield

A fter the midnight show, Morgan went home to get some rest. Mike took a nap at the studio. He was on again in only two hours. Morgan got up close to noon, and of course, she was hungry. Looking in the kitchen and not wanting to cook herself, she decided to go to Ann's Place, but first she made herself one cup of coffee and walked out to her patio. She loved having breakfast on the patio. The view was so great all year long. It faced a big beautiful lake of forty acres. Before she could sit down in that old wooden rocker, her dad made her over a decade ago. She could see a little girl walking close to the lake, this little girl she had seen before but never able to talk to. She would run away every time Morgan would try—always wearing the same dress.

After drinking her coffee and trying once again to talk to that little girl, she got dressed and walked to her car, which was parked inside her three-car garage, next to her husband's old pickup truck that he has been working on for years.

Opening the car door, she could see the papers she had pulled out the day before. She had read some of them. None of which made any sense to her. She thought maybe this was just a waste of time. Leaving the papers in the car, Morgan drove to Anne's Place for lunch. Ann's Place was owned by Anne Trucker, a former hostess on AHS. It was located close to the AHS studio. The food was always great, and the people in there were just as great as the food. She felt at home there.

John Garfield had heard that most of AHS employees eat at Anne's Place, especially Morgan and Katie. He thought maybe he could go there and talk with more people who knew them.

Morgan drove up and started to get out of her car, when she saw those papers again lying there. She thought, *What the heck? I will take them inside with me.* Grabbing the papers with one hand and opening the car door with the other, Morgan left her car and walked to the door of Anne's Place. Anne saw her as she was walking by the door. She ran to the door and yelled to Morgan to come in and have lunch. Morgan was glad to see a friendly face. She hugged her, and Anne showed Morgan to her favorite booth.

"Anything you want today, Katie. It's on me," Anne told Morgan.

"No, I can't let you do that, Anne. I appreciate the thought." Morgan thanked her.

"That's the least I can for you. Everything you've been through. Besides, if it weren't for you, I wouldn't even have this restaurant. So I owe you one."

Two years ago, Anne had left AHS because of poor health. She had some very hard times. Her health had recovered for the most. Morgan had cosigned a note for her—a fifty-thousand-dollar note, which opened the doors to Anne's Place.

"Okay, Anne. This time only. You hear? I don't want to have to pay that note. Anne, you haven't told anyone about that, have you?" Morgan asked.

"No, of course not. You asked me not to, so I haven't."

"Good. I've even forgotten about the note myself."

"Every payment has been made on time, just as I told you and the banker."

Anne left to get Morgan's lunch. Soon she returned with it. This was a big lunch, and Morgan would not be able eat it all.

"Here you go. A big lunch for a big friend. What's all that?" Anne asked as she served Morgan her oversized lunch, looking at the papers on the table next to Morgan's lunch.

"Anne, I can't eat that much!"

"Well, don't worry about that. I will finish it myself. What are those papers? You are doing some research or something?"

"No, this is some of my notes from when I was a reporter. I didn't know this, but I was one of the reporters covering the

Miss National Journalist pageant, the same pageant where Katie was the third runner-up and then became the Miss National Journalist. She didn't remember me, and I didn't remember her either, and now we are best friends. Didn't even know we had met earlier. Is that a hoot or what?"

"Katie Richard was Miss National Journalist? I didn't know that. She has never said a word about it to me."

"She doesn't like to talk about it. Why? I don't know. Don't say anything to her about this, okay, Anne?"

"Yeah, that's okay. I wonder why she never told us. I have to go now. I'll be back in a few minutes."

"Anne, if you can, tried to keep fans away from my booth today. I don't really feel like socializing today," Morgan asked of Anne.

"You got it."

Morgan had just finished eating and was looking at her notes when she got a phone call. Garfield walked in about the time she started talking on her cell phone. Anne walked up to Garfield.

"Welcome to Anne's Place. I'm Anne. May I show you to a table?"

Garfield looked at everything in Anne's Place. Then he spotted Katie Morgan sitting all by herself talking on her cell phone. He couldn't take his eyes off her. She was so much prettier in person than on TV. He had always thought she was so beautiful. Now he's seeing her in person.

"Sir?" Anne asked of Garfield. "May I show you to a table?"

"Isn't that Katie Morgan over there?" he asked with an excited voice.

"Yes, that's Katie Morgan, and she's not up to talking with anyone now. I've got this nice table on the other side sir," Anne told Garfield.

One of her waitresses came up and told Anne she was needed in the kitchen. Anne asked her to show Garfield to a table, a table on the other side. When she turned around to Garfield, he had gone to Morgan's table.

"Katie Morgan, I can't begin to tell you what an honor this is to meet you. I feel as if I know you. I watch your show every day," Garfield said as he mumbled his words. It was as if he was sixteen again and Katie was the most popular girl in school.

"Thank you so much for those kind words. I don't mean to be rude, but I would like to be alone. I've got a lot on my mind today, and I'm leaving in just a very few minutes," Morgan told Garfield in a polite tone.

"I know, Katie. You're worried about Katie Richard. I'm worried about the both of you," Garfield informed her.

Anne came running over to the booth where they were. "Morgan, I'm sorry. Sir, the table I told you about is over here," Anne said, pulling Garfield by his arm.

Pulling away from Anne, Garfield said, "Thank you, but I like this booth."

"What makes you think you know anything about me and Katie?" Morgan asked.

Garfield, sliding into the booth across from Morgan, said, "I know about the attempted threats on Katie's life."

"Who are you, and just what do you think you know about either of us?" Morgan asked with a sarcastic tone.

Before he could introduce himself, Detectives Barker and Parks walked up.

"Well, what do we have here? Two old lovers, two old friends from Texas, or just people who happen to meet for the very first time here in Anne's Place? Two people who don't know each other and never met before now, wow," Detective Barker asked of both of them.

"What are you talking about, Barker?" Morgan asked with a confused look on her face.

"You're trying to tell me you don't know each other?"

"Of course I don't know him. I just met him. I don't even know his name."

"Well, let me introduce you. His name, Ms. Morgan, is John Garfield, and he lives in Texas. The words e-mail means anything to you, Ms. Morgan?"

"Garfield," Morgan shouted as she turned to face Garfield. "You're John Garfield? Great, that's all I need, is for you to show up. And, no, I have never met him."

"Morgan, I was about to tell you when they came in. I wasn't going to keep it from you," he tried to explain.

"Just when I was trying to believe you, Ms. Morgan. Now I find you have been lying to me about Garfield all along. What else have you lied about?" Barker wanted to know.

"I never lied to you. I don't tell lies, and I didn't know who this guy is. I never met him or e-mailed him. I don't know him."

"She's right, Detective," Garfield said. "She doesn't know me. I've never met her."

"He's right. He didn't know Morgan before he walked in here. He asked me if that was Katie Morgan," Anne added.

"I was on my way out when he came over," Morgan said.

"Where were you going?"

"Patty called and said she had a package for me. She was going to the mall and wanted me to meet her there. I was about to leave when he came up."

"You girls shop at the mall?"

"Yes. We don't buy everything from AHS."

"Would you mind calling Patty and confirming this little get-together?" Barker asked of Morgan.

"Really, Detective! If Morgan said she called, she did," Anne told Barker.

Morgan picked up her cell phone and called Patty.

"Patty, it's Morgan...Yeah, I'm okay...Look, Patty, Detective Barker wants to talk to you, okay?" She handed the phone to Barker.

"Patty, this is Detective Barker. Did you call Ms. Morgan a little while ago? I see. You haven't called anyone for two days. Your battery was dead. So did you call Ms. Morgan from any phone today? Is that right? Thank you, Patty."

Handing the phone back to Morgan, Barker said, "You are just telling the truth all over the place, aren't you, Ms. Morgan? Maybe we had better go back downtown." Barker wanted to say more, but his cell phone rang.

"Barker. When? Seventy-five Ford pickup? Was anyone hurt? She got away. The truck, are you sure? Belongs to Morgan. No, she had nothing to do with that. She's been here for the last hour or more. Thank you."

"What was that about, Detective?" Morgan asked with a concerned look.

"Your old pickup with a lady who looks a lot like you tried to run Katie Richard and her aunt off the road about twenty minutes ago. Everyone is okay. They found the truck. The only fingerprints on it were yours and your husband's. I apologize, Ms. Morgan. I do believe you are telling me the truth."

"Thank you, Detective. I accept your apology. That is what that phone call was about. To get me out of sight. And that truck was in my garage this morning when I left to come here. Is Katie and Aunt Annie okay?"

"Yeah, it seems as if they didn't really want to hurt them. Maybe just frighten them a little. Didn't even mess up Ms. Katie's new car."

"Let me call them. I want to talk with them. To hear their voices, you know what I mean?" Morgan said while punching in Katie's number.

"Katie! Are you all right? Good. How's Aunt Annie? Good, she's okay. Your car is okay too? That is great, Katie.

I'm here at Anne's Place. Come on over. I'm so glad you all are all right. What happened to my truck? They found it near the lake. Okay, dear, I'll see you in a few minutes, good-bye."

"Oh, by the way. I forgot to tell you. Your old buddy Bobby ran in front of the police car, chasing your truck. The police ran into him," Katie told Morgan.

"Do you think Bobby had something to do with all this?" she asked Barker.

"He claimed the brakes failed. They took him downtown, and that's where I'm headed now. I'll keep you informed on what's happening, Ms. Morgan. Mr. Garfield, I want to talk with you later. Don't leave town yet," Barker told her as he and Detective Parks left to talk with Bobby.

"Thank you, Detective. Oh, one more thing. Was Bobby driving his new GMC?" Morgan asked.

"No, it was an old pickup. Why?"

"Just wondering if he would wrack that new truck?"

"So he has a new GMC pickup?"

"Yes, Nicky got it for him."

"Thanks, I will ask him about why he was driving an old truck today."

Turning back, looking Garfield in the eyes, and pointing that little finger right at him, she asked, "Why are you here? What's it to you, John?"

"I probably would not have been here had it not been for that ad," John tried to explain to Morgan when she interrupted him.

"So you saw an ad with a look-alike of Katie Richard in the nude, and it got you all excited. Thought you could come up here, and she would be so grateful that she would just throw herself at you, and say, 'Oh, my hero, let's go to bed.' That's all you are after, sex, isn't it?" Morgan said to John with a nasty tone.

"No, I didn't come here for sex with her or anyone else, and, Morgan, it wouldn't hurt for you to say, 'Thank you, John.' Had you left on time instead of talking with me, the detective would have arrested you then. As far as why I came up, it has to do with two cops coming to my job and asking questions about you and Katie Richard. Someone got me involved in this. I did feel as if I might have started the whole thing, and I just want to help keep you out of jail and Katie Richard alive. And I did send her an ad, but she was wearing a bikini," John explained to Morgan with a little attitude in his tone.

Morgan, who judged herself to be a good judge of character, accepted what he had said.

"You're right, John. Thank you. But I don't see how you can help. The cops don't even know anything yet. You might as well go home."

"Well, I know a few things, Morgan."

"What things?" Morgan asked.

"I know you are not trying to kill Katie. I know that Katie is not doing this to make you look bad. I know you and I have not been sending e-mails to each other, and I know where the ad came from. The ad was not Katie Richard's body, only her head. It was a computer-generated picture. I know it was made in New York City. The girl who did it no longer works for them. She took all her papers with her. They don't know her name or anything else. They just know that her initials are NP. I know you and Katie now know that a girl named Nicky and Bobby are very close—if you know what I mean. What I don't know is, what is a beautiful and rich girl like this Nicky doing with a loser like Bobby? I meet Bobby this morning. He didn't seem to be overloaded with brains. And where is the ad I sent?"

"We don't know. No ever saw it, and you're right about Bobby, he's not. But are you surely right about him and Nicky? They have nothing in common, you know, John?" Morgan sat up in her chair, pointed that finger again, and said, "Nicky's last name is Parson. That's NP, okay? Nicky and Bobby are doing this. Isn't that what you are saying?"

"I may be right, Morgan. However, Nicky has been here for a year now, and Bobby has been here over four years. Do you and Katie get along with them?"

"Nicky has always been nothing but nice to everyone. I don't really like her a lot. Maybe I'm jealous of her. As for Bobby, he has the hots for all the girls…but, you know, he seems to like Katie a lot more. He claimed to have slept with her. Then he would come on to me. Didn't make any difference to him if I was married or not. He has always been hitting on me, although he has not been hitting me as much lately."

"Maybe Nicky is taking care of him."

"She might be, but Bobby is not a one-woman man, and you know, John, that might be the way in. Bobby is the weak link. I bet I could get Bobby back on my side again," Morgan said with an excited look, and now holding her hands together, she was pointing two fingers at John.

"What are you thinking, Morgan?"

"Maybe I can…yes, I know I can make Bobby talk. It has been awhile since I came on to a guy, but I can still turn guys on, especially a guy like Bobby." Morgan was jumping in her seat while she was telling John about her thoughts.

John thought, *You sure can turn me on.* "Bobby is not too smart. He may fall in love with you. What are you going to do then?"

"You're right, John. I could take him away from Nicky or any other girl. I've still got it."

"Katie," John said as he put his hands on top of heirs, "I know you can turn on any guy. But you don't want to turn on Bobby. He might just use you and still be loyal to Nicky. We don't even know if they have anything to do with this."

"Right, we don't, but I am sure of it. Okay let's eliminate them so we can find the real killers. If it's not them, we go looking somewhere else. They will win."

"Katie, it's not a game."

"It is a game, and it's all about winning. I am not a loser, John, and I certainly don't want Katie dead. Maybe you can help, John. You will help me? Right?" she asked John while she was locking her fingers inside John's fingers. This was making it difficult for him to say no to anything Morgan might have asked of him. John also knew she was right. Nicky and Bobby might be the ones, and the sooner they found out for sure, the safer the girls would be. John squeezed her hands tighter and agreed to help.

"Thank you so much, John…John, don't say anything to Katie about this, okay? She wouldn't understand."

"You mean she wouldn't approve of this?" John corrected her.

"Yeah, whatever…whatever," Morgan said with a laugh, still holding John's hands.

"Look! There's Katie and Aunt Annie," Morgan told John as she waved to Katie and watch Aunt Annie walked to Morgan's booth. John stood up to greet them. Morgan also stood up and hugged both Katie and Aunt Annie.

"Who's this?" Katie asked Morgan.

"You will never guess."

"I don't know, Morgan. Probably that guy from Texas? Hi, I'm Katie Richard, and this is my aunt Annie. Everybody calls her Aunt Annie, and you are…?"

Seeing how beautiful she really was in person, John took a deep breath, then said, "I'm the guy from Texas, and I'm glad to meet you and your lovely aunt too. I see where you get your good looks," John said as he reached out to hold Aunt Annie's hand. "Yeah, the good looks are on your side of the family," John said to Aunt Annie with a big, friendly Texas smile.

"Okay! Aunt Annie, we are cute, and you are…?" Katie asked again. "No kidding, who are you? Don't tell me you are that jerk from Texas."

Morgan sat back down in the booth and laughed at Katie.

"He's John Garfield, but he is no jerk. He's here to help us," Morgan butted in to tell Katie.

"You have to forgive Katie today. She's never this rude," Aunt Annie told John.

"John, I'm sorry. I didn't mean to be rude to you. I read at least one of your e-mails. You sounded so sweet. You sounded like someone I might like to know. The thing is, John, I don't know which e-mail was yours. And why are you here anyway?"

Katie and Aunt Annie moved into the booth side by side. John seated himself next to Morgan. He would have been happy next to either of them, including Aunt Annie.

"He came to help us, and he is no jerk," Morgan told Katie again.

"I didn't mean to call you a jerk. I don't even you yet, but why are you here?" Katie asked.

"That's fine, Katie. I just felt this was something I had to do. I really feel as if I can help."

"I'm sorry, but I don't see how you can help. I don't even understand why you're here," Katie replied.

"He has already helped. He knows where the ad came from, and soon he will know who made it. John met Bobby this morning, thinks Bobby might know something about this," Morgan explained to them.

"That's fine, but how is this helping us? Bobby is not smart enough to do anything like this. Besides, he likes us. He likes us a whole lot. So why would he want to hurt us?"

"Did either of you make Bobby mad about not going out with him?" Aunt Annie asked.

"No, we were always nice to him, and he knows that I'm married. I think someone else is using him. I think Nicky is using him," Morgan said while taking another swallow of her Pepsi.

"Nicky? What's with you, Morgan? Nicky has never been anything but nice to both of us. Why do you dislike her so much? She didn't mean anything by saying that someone hated me so much that they wanted me dead. She was just talking. She's okay, Morgan," Katie said with a stern look on her face.

"All right, you two, knock it off. Morgan didn't mean to upset you, Katie. She just didn't like anyone talking to you like that. I don't like it either, Katie, but we are not to fight among us. Do you understand that?" Aunt Annie said as she turned her head from one to the other.

"As for you, Mr. Garfield, we welcome your help, but Katie is right. I don't understand why you are here either. It doesn't involve you, but thanks for your help."

"Thank you, Aunt Annie, and please call me John."

"Morgan, will you come to the restroom with me please? Y'all will excuse us?" Katie asked of Aunt Annie and John.

They said, "Yeah."

"We will be right back," Morgan said as she slid out from the booth.

"Morgan, I wanted to talk to you alone. You act as if you have known John for a long time. You told me and the police you didn't know him. What's going on, Morgan?" Katie asked.

"I don't know him. This is the first time I ever met him. I've got a good feeling about him. I think that he can help. Why would he come up here if he didn't want to help us?"

"Morgan, you know I believe in you and your judgment of people. When Barker finds out John is in town, you know what's will be thinking. I am going to give him the benefit of the doubt. Morgan, you and John might just end up in jail together. Be careful. Learn more about him."

"You are right. He might be with the killer. I really do have that good feeling that I can trust him."

"You're probably right. He seems really nice, and he's cute. But his charms and good looks may not keep you out jail and me alive. To be honest with you, Morgan…I think you may be right about him. The police are not any closer today than two weeks ago. I might be closer to the grave than we think," Katie said in a sad voice.

Morgan could see her watery eyes. Morgan reached out and hugged her.

"Nobody is going to kill you, Katie. The police are watching you, somewhat, but they are watching you, and they will catch this guy before he can do anything bad. Okay, honey?" Morgan said, comforting her.

Katie, pulling away and wiping her eyes, told Morgan, "I'm okay. I don't want Aunt Annie to see me like this."

Morgan held Katie again and helped to composed herself so Aunt Annie wouldn't know how worried she really was about this case.

Katie and Morgan went back to the booth and rejoined John and Aunt Annie.

Katie invited both John and Morgan to join them for dinner in Atlanta. Morgan couldn't go. She had that nine o'clock show, which meant that she had to be there about seven to get ready. John thought he might hang out with Morgan until work time and then see what else he could find out about this case.

John took Morgan to a fine restaurant in town. They talked about the case and about Texas. They agreed to meet again at Anne's Place before lunch, about eleven or so. Both Morgan and John were enjoying each other's company.

18

Morgan Still Has It

Morgan went home to change clothes. She wanted to look sexy. She had a blouse that was blue with gray stripes made of silk. It fit her perfect. The top button had a way of coming open by itself. Sometimes, Morgan didn't even know it was open. That is, some of the time she didn't know. None of the men would tell her, but the women were sure to tell her. She pulled out a dark navy blue leather skirt; only this one was not the conservative navy blue skirt she has been wearing to her knees. This one was about three or four inches above her knees. Navy blue high heels, with stockings that made her legs look worth a million dollars. Morgan was looking especially good tonight, and she felt especially good about herself, curling her hair and putting on the finishing touches, using only her best makeup. She was ready to go to work. She walked out through the kitchen door into the garage. Opening the car door and sliding into her car, the skirt went way up her legs. She felt a little funny about it but then thought it would be all right to wear. Walking into the studio, she had a lot of compliments on the way she looked. She was feeling really good about herself tonight.

"Don't you look beautiful tonight!" a voice came from behind her. She recognized the voice. It was Bobby—the reason she was looking like this. Morgan knew by his tone that he liked what he was seeing.

"Thanks, Bobby. That's real sweet of you to say that," Morgan said with a sexy smile.

"You know, Bobby, I really want to talk with you tonight. I know that person who called me wasn't you, and I told Detective Barker about your brakes on that old truck. I told him about the brake cylinder or whatever you call it. He seems to understand what I was talking about. I'm so glad you are out. I know you don't have anything to do with what's happening, Bobby. Call me when you got a break. I want to talk to you alone, you know what I mean?" Morgan said with that same sexy smile, rubbing his hand. "Call me at your break, okay, Bobby?" Bobby was standing there in shock. Katie Morgan, the most popular woman on the show, wanted to meet him alone tonight.

Confused and extremely excited and happy all at the same time, he said, "Yeah, hell yeah, I'll call you, Morgan…in about an hour." Morgan as she walked through the doors to her studio. The doors closed behind her, and Bobby was still standing there, looking at the doors. It was as if he could still see Morgan.

Soon Morgan's cell phone rang. It was Bobby. "I've got the time now, baby, if you have," Bobby said to Morgan.

Morgan took a deep breath and wondered if John might have been right. It made no difference now. Morgan knew she could handle Bobby. She did say a pray, "Oh Lord, help me."

Later and before her nine o'clock show, she met him outside the locker room. It was a small area that they could hide in and talk for a while.

Morgan walked to Bobby with her blouse somewhat open. He could see all most all her breast right to the beginning of her nipples. To make sure that button would open on time and two more, she opened them herself.

"Morgan, let's go over here, okay?" Bobby asked of her as he led her by the hand to a more secret area of that room. He knew there were no cameras or mics in this room.

He looked at her breast and waited for her to say something.

"Bobby, I meant what I said about believing you. I know you are a good man and wouldn't hurt Katie or me. That's why I need your help, Bobby," Morgan explained in a low and soft tone.

"You want me to help you and Katie? That's what this is about?'

"No, Bobby, I really wanted to be alone with you. I have for some time now. But I need your help please," she asked of Bobby as she walked closer and closer to him. "I think there are may be two people trying to kill Katie. You know everyone around here. If you could just keep your ears open and let me know if you see or hear anything. I know how smart you can be when you want to be. You know, Bobby, smart is sexy now," Morgan said a low sexy voice that Bobby had only dreamed of hearing.

"Yeah, I'm sexy. I mean I'm smart."

"You are Bobby. You really are." Morgan stilled using her low soft voice.

Bobby walked right up to Morgan's face, putting his hands on her waist, and asked, "What's in it for me, Morgan?"

"You mean besides you doing the right thing to help Katie and me?"

"Yeah...that's...what I mean."

"I know just what you meant, Bobby." Morgan moved closer into his arms, placed her hand under his T-shirt, and slowly moved it over his stomach. "Bobby, you know if Katie is alive and I'm not in jail, we could be so much fun to you. You know what I mean, Bobby?" she asked him while moving her hand farther up his shirt and then back down to his belt while kissing him.

"You...are saying you...and Katie will...with me?" Bobby asked in an excited voice.

"You know, Bobby, we have always thought you were so cute and sexy."

"Katie thinks I'm sexy, and you think so too?"

"All the girls here think that about you, Bobby. Will you help us, please, Bobby?" Morgan asked of him in that soft, low, sexy voice and with her hand just inside his pants, but she didn't go any farther.

"I don't know, Katie. I'm seeing someone now. You know?"

Morgan, still with her hand on his stomach, moved closer and hugged him lightly, turning her pretty face up to his and looking him right in the eyes. Then she gave him the kiss he had always wanted.

They exchanged a few more kisses, and then Morgan told Bobby, "Two playmates are better than just one. Don't you think so, Bobby?" She slowly started to move her hand down his stomach and past his belt. She had half her hand below his belt again. She was being careful not to go too far. Morgan kissed him ever so lightly on the lips and asked again, "Don't you agree two are better than one? It will be our little secret, Bobby. Just you, Katie, and me. Isn't that what you really want? Hum, Bobby?"

She moved her hand around some more, being careful not to touch anything that she shouldn't be touching but far enough to make him think she was going there.

"Okay, Katie, I will help you and Katie."

Morgan hugged him real tight and kissed him on the cheek. She pulled her hand away and turned in front of him. Bobby saw her blouse was open. Two buttons were open, and Bobby was looking as hard as any man would. Morgan knew the buttons were open. She made no attempt to close them right then. As she turned to walk away, Bobby put his hand on her shoulder, and they fell to her beast. Morgan then put her hand on his and slowly removed his hand.

"Bobby, I'll keep in touch with you, and you let me know everything you learn, Bobby, no matter how small you may think it is. Please let me know, okay?"

"Let's go somewhere after your show tonight, Morgan."

"I can't tonight. Wayne will be home when I get off tonight but another night maybe. Okay, Bobby?"

"Okay, but one more kiss now."

Morgan moved back in to his arm. The kiss was better than he had planned on it being, and Bobby had managed to slide his hand into her bra, touching her nipple. Morgan didn't seem to be a hurry to remove his hand. Thinking of what was happening, Morgan pulled away and buttoned both of her buttons.

"Morgan, let's have oral sex here before your show."

Bobby wanted some can of sex.

"No, Bobby, not here. Another place, another time," she explained to him and started wondering what she had done. "I really have to go now. Another place, another time."

She pulled away and walked very slowly down the hall. She knew Bobby was watching every move she made. She could almost feel his eyes and hands on her body. Morgan was feeling great, proud, and worried. She was feeling really good. She now had proved to herself that she could take any man away from the beautiful Nicky, and it felt so darn good.

Morgan was a little bit surprise that she allowed him to go so far. She thought, *What have I done? Every time, from here on, he will be trying to hold, kiss, and touch me. I cannot let this happen again, ever. Oh Lord, what I have done? Please help me. Thank you.*

Katie and Aunt Annie got home a bit after nine o'clock and turned the TV on to Morgan's show.

"That's her. I recognize her voice," Aunt Annie said.

Katie walked into the room with a couple of glasses of tea for Aunt Annie and herself.

Seeing Morgan on TV, Katie asked, "What is she doing? That skirt is almost up to her butt. And that blouse will not stay buttoned. She looks like she has a hot date after the show and Wayne is out of town."

"That's okay, Katie. Morgan is a beautiful woman, and she has great legs. I wish you would dress like that. I thought you don't like Wayne."

Katie just shook her head.

19

The Day After

The next morning, Morgan met John for breakfast at Anne's Place. John had some news to tell her and Morgan, who, of course, had something to tell him.

"Last night I learned about how Nicky got her job. It seems like a girl named Lyn Tucker had the job. Then Nicky talked with the program manager, and next thing you know Nicky got the job. Lynn came to AHS because her mother was sick and she lived close by. Lynn had experience working for another shopping network. Nicky had no experience at all, but she got the job. Do you know anything about Lynn Tucker, Morgan?" John asked.

"I heard she turned the job down. She's working for cable news now."

"Didn't you work for them too?"

"Yes, a while ago. Why?"

"I thought we could go and talk with Lynn. Can you still get in over there?"

"Yeah, I still have connections. Let's go now. She's on the morning show. I found something else, John. Bobby called me on my cell phone. How did he get that number? I never gave it to him, but I did give it to Nicky."

"Good thinking! Oh, by the way. How did it go last night? Did you have that little sexy talk with Bobby?"

"Yeah…he's mine now. In actuality, it went pretty good. He didn't say anything last night, but I think he will come around. He did say he was seeing someone special. Well, baby, she's not special anymore." Morgan leaned back in the booth and gave a very sexy smile at John. "He didn't have a chance.

"The poor fool did not have a chance," John remarked to Morgan.

"Not a chance, baby. Not with me there. Not a chance," Morgan repeated.

They decided to go to Atlanta now.

While walking out the door of Anne's Place, Joe—another worker at AHS with whom John, as Paul Johnson, talked to look for Nancy Morgan—walked in.

"Hi, Paul, I see you have met Katie Morgan."

Morgan turned her head to face John's and said, "Yes, I met Paul this morning. You and old Paul are friends?" Morgan asked with a curious look on her face.

"Oh no, I just met him yesterday. Were you able to help him find Nancy Morgan?"

"Nancy Morgan?" she asked while turning to look at John.

John spoke up before she could say anything else. "No, she had never heard of her. It was nice seeing you again, Joe," John told Joe, rushing Morgan out at the same time.

"Morgan, you looked great last night," Joe told her as the door was closing on them.

"Thanks."

Smiling and turning back to John, she said, "No, I didn't know Nancy either."

John and Morgan walked to the car in silence. John opened the door for her. She started in and then stopped.

"Paul, Nancy Morgan? Who are you? John Paul Jones?" she asked.

John closed the door for her and walked to the other side of the car before he got in. Morgan was asking again, "Who are you?"

"I'm John Garfield. John Paul Jones? The name I used was Paul Johnson. I told him I was a private investigator looking for Nancy Morgan to tell her that her father was dying and wanted to see her."

"Are you a private investigator?"

"No, of course not. I was a US marshal once."

"US marshal too. You just make up things. I need to know I was right about you, John. I need to trust you."

"Morgan, I am John Garfield. I'm here only to help you and Katie to take the spotlight off you two. I really want to help keep you out of jail and Katie alive."

Looking embarrassed, she apologized, "I'm sorry, John. I didn't mean that. Of course, you're here to help, and I appreciate your being here." Apologizing to John, she reached over and held his hand and smiled at him as if to say, *I trust you, John*.

"That's okay, Morgan. I understand. I know where you are coming from. I would think the same thing if the tables were turned, so we are okay?"

"If you are okay with me, I am okay with you."

The rest of the one-hour trip was full of fun and games. The weather was hot enough to run on the air conditioner. John had an FM station with soft music while they talked. They joked about the show and talked about some of the people whom Paul had met. She told him of some of the funny things that has happened to her on live TV. You would have thought these two had known each other for twenty years.

Walking into the lobby of cable news, Morgan was recognized immediately.

"Hi, I'm—" Morgan started to say.

"Katie Morgan! I watch your show all the time. You are so funny. I'd rather watch you than some of the other shows on now. They told me you worked here once. I'm so glad to meet you in person. You know, my mother loves you too. She will be so happy to hear I met you, Katie," the lady behind the desk said excitedly. "This must be your husband. He's so cute. Y'alls make a good-looking couple. Oh, I'm sorry. I'm Mary Jean Smith. May I help you?"

"Thank you so much for all those beautiful thoughts. I will try to live up to them. Tell your mother I said hi. You and your mother call me sometime and talk with me on the air. I would love to hear from you both. What we're here for is to see Lynn Trucker."

"She just got off the air. Let me call her." Mary Jean punched in Lynn's number and said, "Lynn honey, you won't believe who's here to see you. Take a guess. No, no…no…it's the Morgans. You know, Katie Morgan, AHS. They want to see you, okay? Katie and her husband…Yes, Lynn…I'll tell them." She looked back at John and said, "He's so cute. It's no wonder you picked him. Lynn will be right out."

John started to correct her on him being Morgan's husband, but Morgan stopped him.

"No, dear, she's right. We do make a cute couple. Besides, you are so cute," Morgan said with a big fringy smile.

Lynn Tucker, a thin, very attractive lady of thirtysomething, walked through the double doors.

"Hi, I'm Lynn Tucker."

"I'm Katie Morgan, and this is John. May we talk with you?"

"Yes. About what?"

As Lynn walked away from Mary Jean, Morgan asked, "Why did you turn down the job at AHS and come to work here?"

"I didn't turn that job down. I wanted it a lot more than I wanted this one. It would let me spend more time with my mother, and it paid more. No, I would have never turned down that job."

"I'm confused, Lynn. I was told you called and said you didn't want that job. That's not correct?"

"No! What's her name…Jane called and told me I didn't have the job."

"Jane called you? You didn't call her?"

"No. What's this all about? It's been over a year now. Why are we talking about this now?"

"Well, I thought something was funny about you not taking the job. What I heard was that you had the job. Then you didn't have it, and it was your choice not to take it."

"No, I still would love to work with you, Katie. You know I did this for ten years after I left broadcast news. That's what I love. I don't really like this job. It pays the bills, and I'm closer to Mom, but…"

"I can't promise you anything, Lynn, but don't be surprised if you get a call from Jim or me telling you to come to work with us. I think maybe we can get you there. Please don't say anything to anyone about what we have talked about, okay? This is my doing. Only Jim and AHS don't know I'm here. I will keep in touch with you, Lynn. I've seen your show. You're a natural at this."

"Thanks for coming by today. I've been praying that I could get on at AHS. I only live ten minutes from there, and this is about an hour drive to work every day. Think again, Katie. It is so good to have met you and John. I won't say a word to anyone. I will wait for your call. This is my cell phone number. Call me here. Morgan hugged Lynn, and Lynn hugged John.

Morgan felt good about Lynn. She really wanted her to be one of the hostesses on AHS. They were walking out when a voice came from back of the hall. "John, John Garfield. What the hell are you doing here?" A tall well-built man in his late fifties was calling John. "What are you doing here? I've haven't seen you in twenty years. Hell, John, you look the same. Hi, I'm Jack Wagner. I worked with your husband in an undercover operation down in Miami. We were US marshals back then. He saved my life. This man is a hero, a real American hero. I know you must be proud of him," Jack told Morgan while hugging John.

"Yeah…I'm real proud of him. But he forgot to tell me he was a hero, didn't you, dear?" Morgan said while looking John straight in the eyes.

"Well, Mrs. Garfield, we were undercover, and he never told anyone about that. But we were the best of them. Took down some real bad guys. What's your first name? I hate calling people Mr. or Mrs., you know what I mean?"

"Yeah, I know what you mean. My name is Katie. Glad to meet you, Jack. Maybe someday you can come down and tell me all about my hero. He sounds like a real Matt Dillon."

"Come down? You are not living in Virginia now?"

"No, I moved to Dallas a long time ago."

"That's where you met Katie, in Texas?"

"She was born in South Texas. The first time I saw her, I was in Plano, just north of Dallas. Thought she was the prettiest girl I've ever seen."

"Hell yes! She is beautiful. Come here, and let me hug you, Katie. You know, you look very familiar, Katie. Are you one of them news girls that John used to hang out with in Virginia?"

"Jack, all pretty girls look familiar to you. What are you doing here anyway?"

"I'm security here. Heck, they are paging me. I got to go. You make him take good care you, Katie. If he doesn't, you come see me. I will kick his you-know-what."

"You bet," Morgan replied.

Walking to the door, Morgan grabbed John's hand and said, "Well, I didn't know I was being protected by a real live US marshal. Wow, I feel so safe now."

"Well, I didn't know we got married until we came here."

"That's when it happened, dear."

A very pretty lady walked by. She turned around and said, "John, is that you?"

Morgan and John stopped to see what she was talking about, when she walked closer to John.

"My God, it's you, John," she said as she hugged him.

John, looking at her, asked, "Judy, little Judy?"

"Yes, it's me."

"What are you doing here?"

"Lisa got me a job here after you sent me to New York and before she left."

"Lisa King got you this job?"

"Yes. Have you seen her lately?"

"Just on TV. I did talk to her a few days ago."

"Do you ever talk with Karen Carter since she left Dallas?"

"Wait a minute. You know Lisa King and Karen Carter? They are the most popular newswomen on TV. You know them?" Morgan asked.

"Mrs. Garfield, John was engaged to Karen way before he met you, I'm sure."

"I'm sure. You and Karen Carter were engaged? You never told me that," Morgan asked in an excited tone.

"No, we weren't. Everybody thought we were, but I never asked her, and she never asked me. She left Dallas, and the rest is history."

"I'm Katie. I would like to talk with you sometime about John."

"Katie, I can tell you things about your husband that he probably has never told you. I'm sorry, but I've got a segment to do in ten minutes. It was nice seeing you again, John, and meeting you, Katie. Call me."

John noticed a funny, silly type of look on Morgan's face while walking back to their car.

"What are you thinking, Morgan?"

"I'm on TV almost every day for over fifteen years. I work here. I live nearby, and only one person recognized me."

"You're not jealous, are you?"

Morgan, with that funny little look on her face, said nothing and just kept walking.

"Katie Morgan, you are jealous! I can't believe you're jealous of me."

Morgan, putting her arm in John's arm and looking him in the eyes, told him, "I'm so proud to be your wife I just want to cry. It makes me so proud."

"I can understand that," John said while moving his head up and down. "I sure can understand that, but you are still jealous."

"Don't be silly," she said in a low voice, still holding John's arm. She looked up at him with a big smile and said, "Then understand this. You need to feed your new bride, and I know a great place to eat here in Atlanta."

"Now about the honeymoon, dear."

"I'm not that proud. Now feed me."

"Then the honeymoon?" John inquired again.

"We'll see," was Morgan's answer with a sissy look.

"You're kidding, aren't you?"

"You will have to wait and see, but I am stilled proud to be your wife."

She was right. The food and the service were great. She was well recognized there too. John saw no one from his past. They felt so good together. They really didn't want to go home yet, but Morgan insisted on doing so. John took her back to

Landover and her car. She went home to change; John did the same. They were to meet Aunt Annie and Katie back at Anne's Place later. Katie's show would be over at seven. They had a lot to talk about. John went back to the hotel, where he met Mike.

20

Mike Meets the Hostesses

"Where have you been all day? Why didn't you turn your phone on? I tried to call you all day. I took another order for two hundred and fifty thousand this morning. I'm going to get a bonus—a great big Texas-size bonus, right? It was the deal you told me to do. You know, John, I could get used to making a few thousand of them dollars in a day. Sure beats the heck out of running cows up and working at the store at night," Mike said with a voice full of pride.

"You did well, Mike. I'll take care of you. Oh, by the way, your wife picked up a check for eight thousand dollars this morning."

"Did you have any trouble getting Patty to approve it?" Mike asked.

"No, I run this company, and what I say goes."

"You already had it approved before you told me?"

"Yeah."

Changing the subject, Mike told John, "You know, John, those Katies are great. They are so nice and so professional, not to mention they are damned good-looking. Did you see either of them today?"

"I spent the whole day with Katie Morgan. We went to Atlanta to talk with Lynn Tucker of the cable news. Saw some old friends. Katie and I got married. Went to lunch and came home."

"Back up, old buddy. You and who got what, and when did this happen?"

"Today, in Atlanta at the cable news."

"Well, I don't blame you for wanting to marry Katie Morgan, but there's one little thing you two didn't think of. Both of you are married to someone else," Mike shouted at John.

John, laughing at Mike, explained to him, "Everybody thought we were married, and we went along with that thought."

"The people at the cable news are newspeople. They tell the world. Did you think of that? And when are we going home?"

"It's okay. We were just funning around. We told them nothing about Katie, and I don't know when we are going home. I think it might be soon. I just don't know when, Mike."

"I've got a meeting with George, the buyer, at five thirty tonight. You want to come?"

"No, I'm going to meet with Morgan and Katie for dinner. Why don't you join us?"

"Okay, I will. It's at Anne's?"

"Yeah, Anne's, at seven thirty."

Katie Morgan was the first one to show up. Anne seated her in her regular booth.

"Where have you been all day, girl? I've tried to call you. Did you take your phone with you?"

"I had my phone, but it was never turned on, and John's phone was turned off too."

"You spent the day with John?"

"Yeah, we went to Atlanta, talked to Lynn Tucker, and had lunch at the Chester House. John was a US marshal, met the man whom John saved during a drug bust."

"Well, that's fine, but Nicky was in here looking for you. She got mad at Katie and me. She thought we weren't telling her where you were. Any idea what that's all about?"

"No. Did she say anything about Bobby?"

"No, but she said that you were messing up things. Whatever that means," Katie asked her what she meant and she said, "Well, it sure isn't my birthday."

"Oh, one more thing, Morgan. Becky, the redhead who used to work here, you remember her? She was always so nice to you."

"Yeah, I remember her. What about her?"

"Well, she works down at The Doll House now, and she overheard Bobby talking about you. You won't believe what he is saying now. It's really good. But I'm going to let Becky tell you. You might not want Katie or Aunt Annie not to hear this."

"No, that's okay, Anne. They need to hear everything. I'm not going to hide anything from any of them. It might help in finding the killers."

Morgan knew what Bobby must have told them, and she knew it would be worse than what actually did happen. She was smiling real wide, thinking, *This should be a fun night.*

Mike was the second one to arrive. His meeting was long but very good. AHS had accepted his offer of the lower price and agreed to keep John's food line all year. They also agreed to have Mike come back in three months to do another show. Mike agreed to that. There was no doubt in his mind that John would approve of that, and he was counting his money all the way to Anne's Place. He was also worried about the girls. Mike had become very fond of them. They had both gained his respect, not because they were both beautiful and sexy. They gained it by being ladies, by being good people. He had no idea how John was going to save them, but he was hoping and praying every day John could.

Morgan saw Mike and shouted for him to come over. "How are you doing, Mike? I thought you had left town. Join me. I am waiting for Katie and her aunt and another friend of mine."

"John Garfield?" Mike asked.

"Yes. How did you know that?"

"I'm sorry. I guess John hasn't told you yet. He invited me to join you and Katie tonight."

"How do you know, John?"

"I had better let him tell you, Katie."

"Is there anyone in Georgia that doesn't know him?" she asked.

John walked in next and saw Morgan and Mike talking. He knew that Mike had probably told Katie that he worked for him. John didn't know if this was good or bad.

"Hi, Morgan, Mike. You're looking good tonight," John said as he sat next to her.

"How do you know Mike?"

"Mike, you didn't tell her?"

"No, I thought it might be more fun if I let you tell her," Mike said with a silly look on his face.

"Somebody tell me."

"Morgan, I…he works for me," John said in a low voice.

"What do you mean he works for you?"

"I own that Mexican food company that you and he have been selling."

"You own the company. Detective Barker said you work in retail. Now you tell me you own a company of that size."

"It's not that large, Morgan," Mike told her.

"The whole company is right here with you, including the office."

"John, tell me you didn't pull a fast one on AHS. Please tell me you didn't."

"Morgan, everything is okay. A company in South Texas is making the food. Your buyer checked everything out before he was okay with it and placed the orders. Everything is on the up-and-up, Morgan. I wouldn't ever do anything like that."

"He's right, Morgan. Everything is okay," Mike added.

Morgan reached over and hugged John. "I'm so glad you are okay. I don't care that Mike works for you. All I want is for you to tell me the truth. That's all want...I want to believe in you, and I do, John."

She rested her head on his shoulder. Across the room, Anne was watching and wondering what was happening. She had never seen Morgan react to a man as she had to John. Morgan sat up in her seat and stretched the left side of her neck. She saw Katie and Aunt Annie walking in. They saw her and wondered what Mike was doing here.

"Hi, Mike. Nice seeing you again. Are you joining us for dinner?" Katie asked.

"Yes, if you don't mind."

"Don't be silly, Mike. We'll love to have you join us."

"Boy, did I find out a few things today," Morgan announced.

"First, did you know John was a US marshal? I met one of the guys John saved in a shoot-out with drug lords, and Mike works for John. John owns that food company products we have been selling."

Turning to look at Mike, she asked, "Were you a marshal too?"

"No, not me. You said John saved a man's life? He never told me anything about that."

"Well, John is so modest he doesn't like to talk about that, but he's a real hero," Morgan said excitedly.

"And they got married this morning," Mike added.

"They what?" Katie asked.

"It was nothing. We have already divorced," Morgan said as she laughed.

"Enough about you two. Morgan, tell us about Lynn Tucker."

"Yeah, Morgan, enough about our new hero and your wedding day. Tell us about Lynn Tucker. Who's Lynn Tucker?" Mike asked.

Taking a deep breath, she said, "Well…okay, Lynn Tucker applied for a job at AHS, and Nicky got the job. Lynn said she got a call from Jean, telling her she didn't get the job. Jean said that Lynn called her, telling her that she didn't want the job and, of course, we know who got the job, don't we?"

Anne came back to the booth and took their orders. When she returned with their lunches, Becky was walking in the door. Seeing Morgan in the booth, she walked fast to get there sooner.

"Hi, Morgan, and hi, Katie. Hi, everybody," Becky said.

Anne stopped Becky to say, "Oh, Becky, let me introduce you. This is Becky, an old friend of mine. She used to work here. Becky, this is Aunt Anne, Katie's aunt. John Garfield, a former US marshal, now business owner. And his sales manager, Mike Gross. They're from Texas."

"Hi, everybody. Morgan, did Anne tell you what I wanted?"

"Yeah, you can tell me in front them. They're all my friends. They would like to get a big laugh also. It's Bobby and me again," Morgan told everyone.

"It's also about you too, Katie," Becky told Katie.

"This should be good," Katie replied.

"I was taking a break last night about 1:00 a.m. in the booth behind Bobby and some of his friends. The good news is they were too drunk to remember what he was saying. Anyway, Bobby said you, Morgan"—she looked at Morgan— "that last night before you went on the air, you called him. Told him you wanted to be alone with him last night. You were looking 'really hot, superhot,' he said. He kept saying 'superhot and damned good-looking.'"

"He was right about that. You were looking damned hot. Yeah, *superhot* is right," Mike repeated himself.

"Okay, we all agree that Morgan looked good last night. Now get on with the story," Katie told Becky.

Becky looked at Katie, and Mike then smiled and started with the rest of her story. "Anyway, Morgan, you wanted to meet him at his locker, and there was no one there but you and him. Then you suggested you go to the back side where there are no cameras and you could hear if anyone was coming. After you get there, you ran your hand under his shirt, kissed him—a really great kiss that told you were okay with anything—and told him how much you really liked him. You asked for his help in finding a killer. I didn't understand that. Anyway, you then gave him a long, wet, tongue-sucking kiss. And then…you, Morgan, put your hand all the way in his pants. You went far enough to meet Mr. Johnson, if you know what I mean, causing him to come."

"Morgan, she is talking about Bobby Greenwood, right?" Katie asked with a rather loud voice.

"He then opened your blouse all the way down and sucked your breast. Said you would have gone all the way, but you had to get to your show and said your husband was home. That you would do it at later time and place."

"Morgan, did you go to Bobby's locker last night?" Katie asked.

Morgan, who hadn't said a word, shook her head to say no.

"Okay, Becky, go on," Katie said.

Looking back at Katie, she said, "Well, Katie, you will get a laugh out of this. Bobby said that Morgan promised him sex with her and you too if he would help. Said 'three girls are better than one.' That's another thing. He claimed he's having sex with Nicky. Is there any way she would even give him the time of day?"

"You promised sex with me for Bobby?" Katie asked with a not-so-friendly look on her face.

"Look, I've got to go. I wanted to let you know what was being said about you two. I like both of you. Be careful around

Bobby or any of his friends. By the way, I do not believe any of this. Bye now," Becky said as she got up and left.

Morgan still had not said a word.

"Morgan, that Bobby is crazy. Where do you suppose he got that thought from?" Anne asked.

Morgan, still eating her hamburger, said, "I don't know."

"You don't know? Is that what you said? 'I don't know'?" Katie asked.

"He might have got some of that from me last night," Morgan said in a low voice.

"What part might he have gotten from you?" Katie asked with interest.

Morgan, still eating and mumbling her words, said, "I did talk to him last night."

"Last night I saw your show. You were wearing that real short skirt that you said was too short for you to wear. You were also wearing that gray silk blouse, the one that you can't keep buttoned unless you use a pin on it. That's the blouse that you think you look so hot and sexy in. Were you even using a pin last night?" Katie wanted to know.

"She really did look hot and sexy in that outfit," Mike told Katie again.

"Thank you, Mike, and it had a pin there. I never go on air half-dressed."

"What were you doing in Bobby's locker?" Anne wanted to know.

"No, that's a lie. I have never been in his locker and never will be."

"Would you go behind the locker where no one could see you and there are no cameras?" Katie wanted to know.

"How did you know about that spot?" Morgan answered with her question.

"Don't you dare change the subject? This is not about me."

"What about that kiss, the long one?" John wanted to know.

"We never had a long kiss."

"Then you had a short kiss?" John asked.

"No…it was a peck."

"You were pecking on Bobby?" Mike asked.

Everyone turn to look at Mike after that question.

"I'm just putting my two cents' worth in."

"Might as well, Mike. Everyone else is," Morgan said to him.

"Morgan?" Aunt Annie asked. "I know you are having fun, dear, but tell us what really happened. Tell it the only way you can, the truth, dear."

Morgan, still eating and with a mouthful, said, "We talked last night."

"What did you talk about?" Katie asked. "I want to hear about my future love affair with Bobby Greenwood."

"John thought it would be a good idea to get Bobby on our side."

"You thought it would be a good idea, John?" Katie asked as she turned to face him. "A good idea?"

"Yeah, John, explain this," Mike added.

"Yeah…I met Bobby. I don't think he's very bright. Getting Bobby confused will maybe help him to make mistakes. That's what we want," John explained.

"John, Bobby is not calling the moves here. The only thing she did was to get him hot for me. I don't care if he has the hots for her." She looked straight at Morgan. "Thank you very much. You've been a big help, and don't help me again," Katie said with a nasty tone.

Aunt Annie placed her hand on Katie's hand and told her, "Don't be upset with her, dear. She's trying just like the rest of us to keep you alive."

"Well, excuse the heck out of me if I seem to be upset that this pimp sitting over there has just booked me for the rest of my sex life with Bobby Greenwood, of all people. And she might have pimped me with who may be my killer. I'd rather be dead than to let Bobby Greenwood touch me in any way. Look at her eating like a pig and laughing like a darn possum," Katie said, raising her voice and adding a sharp tone to it.

Aunt Annie slipped Katie's neck and kissed her on the cheek. "You don't mean that, dear. Morgan is joking with you. Nothing is going to happen with you and Bobby. Besides, I kind of agree with John and Morgan to get Bobby on our side. I love you, dear," Aunt Annie said to Katie and kissed her again. In a more harsh tone, Aunt Annie told Katie, "One more thing, girl. Don't you ever talk to me like that again, you hear, girl?"

Katie turned and hugged Aunt Annie and apologized to both Morgan and Aunt Annie. Anne was staring at Morgan. Morgan saw Anne looking and asked, "What?"

"Oh, I was just trying to imagine you in your fur coat and a hat with a big feather in it."

Everyone started laughing, and suddenly the stress was broken. They laughed and joked for about another hour. Morgan never did tell the whole story. And that was okay. No one believed Bobby Greenwood's story. For them, it was just a lot of wishful thinking.

Aunt Annie invited all of them over to Katie's house for some coffee and cake.

"Thanks, but I can't. I've been out almost all night and day. I'm going home and take a long bubbly bath and then go to bed. Thanks, though," Morgan said as she turned to face John and Mike.

"What about you, John, Mike?" Katie asked.

"Thanks, I need to do some work before I turn in tonight. Maybe some other time," John said.

"I'll be glad to go. Aunt Annie made that cake sound real good to me," Mike told them.

"Okay, Mike. Come with us. Will you be all right, Morgan?" Aunt Annie asked.

"She will be okay. I will follow her home and make sure she's safe," John told them.

"Yeah, I will be okay. The US marshal is protecting me."

"That's good, Katie, but who's protecting you from the US marshal?" Mike asked.

They all had a big laugh about Mike's remark and said their good nights, hugging each other. John and Mike thought that was the best part of saying good night. They could have said good night for a week. John walked Morgan to her car. Standing beside the driver door, Morgan moved close to John.

"I can't remember the last time I had so much fun in one day. Thank you so much."

"Thank you, Morgan. This has been a day I will never forget. I never thought, never in my wildest dreams did I ever think I would spend a day with Katie Morgan—and have her like it. Thank you for that day, Morgan."

John put his hands on her waist, and Morgan walked closer to him. They hugged so tight and so long. Neither of them really wanted this night to end. Morgan raised her head and looked John in the eyes. They both started moving their faces closer to the point you couldn't put a toothpick between their lips. Morgan saw Anne watching and broke away.

Something about that felt so good to both of them. It felt so right. But they knew that as good as it felt, it was equally that wrong. Neither one of them were rule breakers, especially Morgan, so they backed off. John opened the door for her, telling her he would stay with her until she gets home.

Anne was the last one to drive off, watching John and Morgan until they drove off, wondering just what was happening. This was not like Katie Morgan. She loved her husband too much.

When Morgan drove off, she found herself looking in the rearview mirror. John never took his eyes off the back of her head. When Morgan drove into the garage, he waited to make sure she was okay. Morgan went into the house and turned on the lights. She came back to tell John she was okay. Then and only then would John leave.

About the time John got back to his hotel, Morgan, walking through the living room, stopped and looked at her phone on the oak end table—the same phone that she had used to call her husband every night when she came home. She picked it up and held it close to her heart. But tonight she was still thinking about John. About the fun, about just being with him. She held the phone in her hands for several minutes. Then she put the phone back on its cradle and then went to take that bubble bath she had talked about earlier.

John pulled his cell phone from his pocket. Both Morgan's home and cell numbers were programmed into his phone. He read her name and saw her number. John too held his phone in his hands as he drove back to the hotel. It was several minutes before he would put the phone away. John couldn't get her off his mind.

Morgan sat in the tub and relaxed. She was thinking about this day, the new people she met, the good food she had eaten, the joking with Katie and being called Mrs. Garfield. She thought about that hug at the car in Anne's parking lot. After about thirty minutes or so, she got out of the tub, dried herself off, and slipped into her silk pajamas. She walked to that brown leather chair next to the oak table, picked up a book, and started to read. Her eyes turned to the phone, as if she had heard it ring.

John, walking back and forth in his room, was thinking the same thing: staring at the phone, as if doing so would make it ring. He turned on the TV. Patty, one of the hostesses that he had met the day before, was doing her show. John looked at the phone again. Only this time, he picked it up and called Morgan. It was ringing. It always would ring at least once or twice before the other party could hear it ring. This was ring number three. If there would be no answer by the fourth ring, he would hang up.

"Hello," a pleasant voice that he immediately recognized answered. It was Katie Morgan's voice.

"Morgan, this is John. I didn't wake you, did I?" he asked.

"No, I'm just resting in this big chair and reading a story. John, I really had good time today."

"Me too, Morgan."

"How long can you stay here?"

"Not much longer. A few more days maybe."

"John...thanks again," Morgan said as she pulled the phone away from her ear and put it back on the table.

"Yeah, thank you, Morgan. Good night."

John put his phone down also; they both went to bed at that time. They knew that tomorrow they would see each other again. They believed this to be another good day.

21

They Meet

It was another beautiful morning in Georgia. The sun was just coming up over Katie Morgan's lakefront home, bringing the bright sunlight inside, awakening Morgan. She could smell the coffee brewing in the pot, the pot with the timer she had set the night before. She rolled over in her bed, stretching as far as she could. Managing to finally get out of the bed, she found herself headed for the kitchen.

The aroma of the coffee was too much for her to resist any longer. Pulling a cup from the cupboard and reaching for the pot, she poured herself a cup, walked to the patio, unlocked the door, and walked outside. The lake was so pretty, and the birds were singing. *This has just got be a great day*, she thought. The old worn-looking clock hanging on the north side of the house was still working after almost five years now. Katie had found that clock in a garage sale and just fell in love with it. The same clock was now telling her it was 6:30 a.m., and she knew what that meant. She had less than two hours to get dressed and meet John and Mike for breakfast at Anne's.

Katie and Aunt Annie would also be joining them. Katie had an 11:00 a. m. show. She didn't want to eat at home and be in such a hurry to get to the studio. Morgan was going in for a short time this morning, only to catch up on her e-mail. She had the day off. Morgan had planned to spend some of the time with John, Mike, and Aunt Annie today.

As Morgan got up, she saw that same little girl in that white dress with pink flowers on it. Morgan walked toward her and called her. "Hi, I am Morgan. I live here. Where do you live?" she asked.

Morgan heard a dog barking and turned her head for just a second; then when she looked back, there was no little girl. This wasn't the first time that little girl with that white dress and all those pink flowers on it would just disappear. Morgan wondered how she could disappear so fast.

It was now eight thirty at Anne's Place; and as usual, it was packed, except for that one booth Anne was saving for Morgan and Katie. One by one, almost at the same time, they all walked in and greeted Anne and each other. She had coffee sent over for all of them. Everyone was in a very good mood.

Katie asked Morgan, "You look especially happy today, Morgan. Why?"

"No reason. I slept well last night, and I awoke to a beautiful morning. I'm here with my favorite people. There's no reason to not be happy. Nothing has happened in the last few days. I think this is going to be a fabulous day," Morgan replied with that cute smile.

"You're right, dear. It's a beautiful day, and we are all alive and well," Aunt Anne said with approval.

Turning to John, Morgan asked, "You're meeting me and Aunt Annie back here at about one, okay?"

"Yeah, that's fine. Mike and I need to do paperwork and make a few phone calls. Then you two lovely ladies could show us out-of-towners your town, okay?"

"Great! That sounds like a plan to me, Katie. See you after your show?"

"Yeah...that's fine."

Anne was wondering if John had something to with Morgan be so happy this morning. She seemed a little bit happier than unusual. She wondered whether John spent the night at Morgan's house. Morgan was only happiest in that way because of good sex. Walking back to the kitchen, Anne turned and looked at Morgan and John, and another thought came in her mind. *What am I thinking? Morgan is known to not break rules, especially her wedding vows, or would she?*

A little while past nine, they went their way, walking out at the same time. Morgan and Aunt Annie were together, Katie and Anne walked together, and John and Mike were together. Morgan looked over her shoulder at John while they walked. John got to his car first and turned to watch Morgan get in her car. Anne, looking out her window at John and Morgan, thought, *No, she, well, maybe, no, not Morgan.*

Later that day, Morgan, Aunt Annie, John, and Mike met back at Anne's Place, where Aunt Annie got a call.

"Annie," the voice said, "this is Charles. How about you meeting me for lunch? I have the day off and would like to spend it with you."

"That sounds good, Chucky. Where do you want to meet?"

"How about Lowell's at the mall? I need to pick up something there anyway."

"Lowell's it is. Let's say ten thirty. Okay? Okay, Chucky?"

"Chucky?"

"You know you will always be Chucky to me."

"Oh, okay. Ten thirty."

"That's funny," Aunt Annie said to Morgan.

"What's funny?" Morgan asked.

"He sounded as if I never called him Chucky before."

"He's probably just joking with you," Morgan told her.

John didn't say anything, but you could tell he was thinking. Morgan decided that they would all take her to Lowell's. They drove up and saw the DA standing there, looking for her. Only Aunt Annie got out of the car. John still had that look on his face.

"Why are you looking like that, John?" Morgan asked.

"Oh, I thought maybe it wasn't the DA who really called."

"I thought the same thing, but that's him. I met him the other day. I know that's him."

"Oh, I'm sure that's him. I just hope he made the call himself."

"Whether he made the call or not, Annie is in good hands with him. She's safe. That's what we want for all of us to be—safe," Morgan reminded John.

Morgan, John, and Mike drove off; and the next few hours were pure fun. Mike had Morgan laughing so hard that her side was beginning to hurt. Morgan showed them all of Landover. She too made them laugh hard. It was just a fun day. Everything was going so well. They decided to go back to Anne's place for dinner when Morgan's cell phone rang. It was Katie calling.

"Hi, I'm on my way to Anne's. Y'all coming?"

"Yeah, we are on our way too. See you."

They joked and laughed all the way to the car and all the way to Anne's Place. John thought it might be a good idea to call Aunt Annie and make sure she's okay. The call confirmed that she was safe and having a very good time with her old friend. She told Morgan, "Chucky said he received a call from me." When they arrived back at Anne's Place, Katie was not in sight.

"Have you seen Katie today?" Morgan asked Anne.

"Yeah, she came in and got a drink and some fries. She had to leave to meet Joe Barber at the park. She told me to tell you she will call you later. She left her eating. That's why she didn't call you," Anne explained.

"That's okay, Anne. Can you get us some burgers and fries?" Morgan asked.

The three of them went to the booth, and Anne came with the food shortly thereafter. Morgan was explaining to them why this park was such a big deal. Katie and Morgan had joined together to purchase the now closed park for three hundred and fifty thousand dollars; the property was worth more than four hundred and fifty thousand dollars.

22

The Meeting at Sun Creek Park

Nicky had the day off and was looking for Bobby. She called him on his cell phone, the phone she was paying for, and left several messages for him to call her. More than an hour had gone by, and Bobby had not returned her calls. She was beginning to get mad about this when the phone rang. It was Bobby.

"Hey, honey, what do you want?" Bobby asked.

"Where have you been? I called you over an hour ago. The only reason I gave you that phone was to keep in touch with you at all times."

"Okay, okay, I'm sorry. I didn't turn the phone on this morning. That's all, Nicky. Everything is okay," Bobby said, laughing.

"This is not funny, Bobby. I want you to meet me at the house right now."

"Well…I was going by the auto store. It will only take a few minutes."

"No, Bobby. You go straight to the house. I'm not going to wait all day. We've got things to do today."

"Fooling around one of them things?"

"Quit thinking about sex so damned much and get to the house, or you will never touch me again. Do you understand, Bobby? I'm not happy with you right now, so don't make me mad."

"Okay, okay, Nicky. I'll meet you in about ten minutes. Okay?"

"Okay, ten minutes," Nicky repeated to Bobby with a nasty tone.

Nicky was at the old frame house she had bought last year. No one knew she owned it except Bobby. It was at this old country house that she and Bobby would meet from time to time. Bobby was painting and repairing it for her. The old run-down house in the country was beginning to look new again. They have spent most of their time inside, and nothing has been done on the outside except a new coat of paint to protect her investment. An old broken door was replaced when she first bought the house. Inside were a new air conditioner and a DISH for watching AHS and other shows. A phone line was installed for the computer, which Nicky used a lot. The grounds were a mess covered with dead leaves from years gone by. The grass was dead; the trees needed watering. Nicky didn't seem to be concerned about the yard, only the inside. She didn't stay there very much; she spent most of time in her high-class apartment uptown. This was more of a getaway for her, somewhere she could go and be alone, a place she could meet Bobby and no one would see them together. This was her hideaway.

Sitting on the front porch, Nicky was looking to see if maybe Bobby was coming, but there was no sign of him. She checked her watch. It had been five and half minutes since she talked to Bobby. Nicky got up and walked around, looking down the dirt road that she knew Bobby would be driving down. She checked her watch again. The ten minutes had not passed yet. She walked back to porch, then sat down on an old spring seat, watching for Bobby. She had a lot on her mind today. Unlike Bobby sex was not one of those thoughts.

Things had not gone the way she had expected. Nicky had heard about Bobby's bragging of Katie Morgan. She didn't believe much of it. She really believed no woman could take any man from her, certainly not Katie Morgan, of all women. Nevertheless, it did bother her that Bobby was talking with Katie. Bobby knew too much to be talking with anyone, especially Katie Morgan. She heard a sound from the distance. It was a truck. She knew it was Bobby's truck. Nicky watched for it to turn into the driveway. She was right. It was Bobby's truck. He pulled next to her car and got out. Nicky walked to the truck to meet him. Bobby immediately hugged her and gave her a big kiss. He tried to touch her, but Nicky was in no mood for sex. She pushed herself away from him.

"Listen, Bobby. There has been a change of plans," Nicky said.

"Okay, honey," Bobby said as he grabbed her and kissed Nicky again.

"Damn it, Bobby," Nicky said with a nasty tone. "We are not going to have sex, so get your little mind off it."

"All right, what do you want now?"

"We are going to kill both of them," Nicky said with a stern look on her face. Bobby had never seen this look before. He had never heard that tone either. It was like she was someone else.

"What did you say?" Bobby asked with a loud voice.

"You heard me, Bobby. There's been a change of plans."

"I heard that. What the hell are you talking about killing them? You told me all you wanted to do was to scare them. You never said anything about killing them, Nicky."

"They are not scared. They act like this was nothing. They are too stupid to know that they are alive because I'm letting them live."

"Nicky, you are crazy? You don't mean that."

"Don't ever call me crazy again, Bobby. I'm not crazy. You know I'm not crazy," Nicky said with that same strange voice. "I'm not crazy, and never call me crazy again."

"Okay, Nicky, I know you are not crazy. I'm sorry I said that. But, Nicky, you can't go around killing people."

"Why are you taking up for them, Bobby?"

"I'm not. I don't want any part of this."

"You think Katie Morgan is going to be so thankful that she's going to jump in bed with you and bring Katie with her?"

"I don't care, Nicky," Bobby said as he turned away from her and started walking to his truck.

Nicky started unbuttoning her blouse and calling to Bobby. "Bobby, come back. Let's talk this over," she said in a familiar sexy voice. This was the voice that Bobby knew well. Every time she spoke in this tone, sex was to come. Sex was what Bobby lived for. He had fantasized about almost every girl in town, and he had his fair share of them.

"You will not talk about killing them?" Bobby asked as he slowed down and turned to see Nicky with her blouse open. He walked to her. She reached out for him; they kissed, hugged, and touched until Bobby tried to take her pants off.

"No, no, Bobby. We can't do all this now. But tonight we can do everything you want. But first we to have to kill them," Nicky said in that sexy voice while she was stilling kissing him. Bobby backed off. He wanted nothing to do with killing them. He wasn't the smartest man in town, but he was smart enough to know no one should be killing people.

"No, Nicky, I won't help you kill them. They are good girls. They do like me, and I know what Morgan said, and I know I will never be with her. I was just playing with her. She doesn't mean anything to me, Nicky. I love you. I don't want you to get hurt."

"Bobby, we are both going to jail for what we have already done. Who do you think they will believe? Damn sure not you, Bobby."

"I'll go to jail for what I did, but I won't let you kill Morgan and Katie," Bobby told Nicky as he started again walking to his truck. Nicky pulled a small gun from her purse and aimed it at Bobby's head.

"I wouldn't do that if I were you, Bobby," she said in that strange voice.

"What are you going to do about it?" he asked as he turned and saw the gun pointing at his head. "No, Nicky, don't do that," he pleaded with her.

Nicky was walking closer to him. "Do you want to give up all this?" she asked as she pointed to herself. "Bobby, you have never had it this good before, and you will never have any better than me. You never had so much money to spend. Do you want to lose all this just to save two girls that don't care for you the way I do?"

Bobby reached for the gun. Nicky fought back. She was kicking him. They rolled over and over in the yard. Bobby got the gun away from her and managed to get back to his feet. She then kicked him in the stomach, and Bobby fell to the ground. He had landed on closed water well. The wood had been there for years and could not support his weight.

Bobby fell into the well. Nicky ran to see. Bobby was about ten feet down. He was not moving. She yelled to him. No sign of life was coming from Bobby. Nicky looked for her gun. She couldn't find it. The gun had landed with Bobby in the well. Nicky had nothing to lose now. This made two people she had killed. She knew that she must kill Morgan and Katie now. She didn't need Bobby anymore; he was to have been the fourth killing anyway. Nicky didn't like messes. She covered the well back up, drove the truck inside the old wooden garage, and locked the doors. She would deal with this later. She had a plan, and for it to work, it had to be carried out today. She had already started working on this plan earlier today.

Nicky went back into the house and cleaned up. She picked up her cell phone and called Jack Gram, a man whom she had dated a few times. Jack owned a Cadillac, with the same color and make of Joe Barber's Cadillac. He had always wanted to drive Nicky's new Corvette. She never let anyone drive it. This time she needed the Cadillac, and she knew how to get it. Jack answered and was pleased to hear Nicky's voice.

"Jack," Nicky started to say, "I'm been thinking of you a lot lately. What are you doing today?"

Jack was so happy that Nicky had called. He said with excitement, "Nicky, I haven't heard from you in over a month. I thought you were mad at me."

"Don't be silly, Jack. I've been working a lot lately."

"I saw all your shows. You know, Nicky, people don't believe me when I tell them we have dated."

"I don't know why they wouldn't believe you. When I tell people that we dated, they believe me."

"You tell them we dated?"

"Of course, Jack. You know how much I love to brag."

"Nicky, you always make me feel so good."

"Well, Jack, maybe this will make you feel even better. How would you like to do me a favor?"

"Sure, anything for you, Nicky."

"I've got a lot of running around that I have to do today, and my car has to go in for service. Can I trade cars with you and you take mine to the dealer?"

"You want me to drive that new Corvette? You won't let anyone drive it. Darned right, Nicky, I'll trade cars with you," Jack said in a very excited tone.

"You sound more excited about driving that car than seeing me," Nicky said in an innocent tone.

"I'll take you any day over that car, Nicky, but that car is a good second-best."

"I will be by in about an hour, okay?"

"I'll be waiting. You really are going to trade cars with me? You know my car is five years old, and that 'Vette is new."

"That's all right, Jack. I can drive any car. It's only a car."

"Yeah, a brand-new Corvette is not only a car."

Nicky traded cars and some good sex with Jack for another hour. Jack was so happy with the way this day was turning out. Not only was he driving a new Corvette with less than five thousand miles on it, he was also with the prettiest woman in the world. Jack Gram was happy.

If it was one thing that Nicky could do and do well, it was make a man happy. Nicky, on the other hand, was happy too, but not for the same reasons. She hated driving anything older than one year. And having sex with Jack didn't mean as much to her as it did to Jack.

Nicky now had a Cadillac that looks just like Joe Barber's car. She called Katie and pretended to be Joe Barber. She told her about the deal and to meet her at the old Sun Creek Park. Katie thought she was talking with Joe Barber and agreed to meet with him.

Nicky got to the park first and parked the Cadillac in view so as to make Katie feel more at ease. She knew that Katie would recognize her Corvette and maybe not come inside. Nicky couldn't afford to let that happen.

Katie drove up and parked next to the caddy. Nicky was right. Katie was at ease. She really believed that Joe Barber was inside, and with him was the contract to sell this old park.

Katie looked around at what she thought would be hers and Katie Morgan's soon. They had been working on this deal for more than six months now. The financing was all set. The bank was more than willing to go along with this deal. The park was worth more than the selling price, and both girls were more than good for the money. The bank had nothing to worry about on this deal.

Katie walked to the office door on the back side of the building. Still looking all over, she opened the door. There was no one in sight. She could see some paper lying on that old metal desk and a jacket hanging on the wall. Katie was spooked out.

"Hello? Mr. Barber…hello? This is Katie Richard…Mr. Barber, are you here?" she asked louder. Katie thought he might be in the restroom. She walked to the desk to look at the papers. Thinking she had heard something, Katie left the desk and walked by a wall—the wall by which Nicky was waiting for her to walk. Nicky placed her hand over Katie's nose with a cloth full of chloroform. Katie was out fast. Nicky then pulled her limp body into the other room and tied her to that old wooden chair with most of the finish coming off. She then placed duct tape over her mouth. Part one was over with now. Part two was getting Morgan to the park. The same technique would be used to achieve this as well.

She had pretended to be Dianne, and Morgan went for it. Nicky knew how much this deal meant to them. This was going to be easier than she had thought.

Morgan, John, and Mike were looking over some of Morgan's notes from her reporter days when she got a call from Dianne, another very beautiful hostess on AHS. Dianne was also a licensed attorney. Morgan answered her cell phone. "Hello."

"Katie, it's Dianne. Katie called me a little while ago about the deal on the park. Well, it seems that Mr. Barber is ready to close. Katie asked me to read over the contract and have you meet us out there as soon possible. Okay, Morgan?"

"Yeah, that sounds good. We'll be right there," Morgan said with excitement.

"We? Katie, there's not much room out there, and the air conditioning is not working. Besides, Joe Barber doesn't like strangers. Maybe you should come alone. Or I could come by and pick you up and we could go together."

"No, that's all right, Dianne. I will go by myself. I'll be there in about twenty minutes."

"It will take me about that long too. See you later."

"That was Dianne. You know her, Mike. Anyway, we are closing the deal on that park. Katie has made a deal with Mr. Barber, and Dianne is going to read the contract for us. I'm so happy. I just knew this would be a fabulous day." Morgan reached over and kissed John on the cheek.

"Wait! Are you sure everything is okay?" John asked.

"Yeah, Dianne is okay. She's also a licensed attorney. But she's right. Mr. Barber doesn't like strangers. When he first met me and Katie, he didn't recognize us. It was his wife who called and asked if we were the ones on AHS. After that, we were okay. His wife knew us well from TV. I've got to go."

"Morgan, listen. Call me when you get there, and let me know everything is okay. If you don't call in twenty minutes, we're coming after you," John told her.

"Okay, Dad, I'll call you when I get there. Okay?"

John, placing his hands on hers, told Morgan, "Be careful. I don't want anything to happen to you or Morgan."

Morgan, looking John in the eyes, said, "I know you don't, John. I will be careful, and I will call you. If you don't hear from me, please come and find me." Morgan kissed John again.

"When we get back, I will treat all of us to a great restaurant."

Anne, overhearing what Morgan had said, replied, "What! This not a great place to eat?"

"Of course, this is the greatest, Anne. You know what I meant."

"I was included in the dinner, wasn't I?" Anne asked.

Running out the door, Morgan hollered back to Anne, "Of course you need a great meal too."

"Thanks a lot," Anne said.

John watched Morgan walk out the door. He watched her all the way to her car, and he watched her drive away.

"She's married," Anne said as she looked down at John.

"I beg your pardon, Anne."

"Morgan, she's married," Anne repeated herself.

"I know."

"Okay, as long as you know. Would you two like anything else?" Anne asked before she walked away.

John knew what Anne was referring to, and he made no other comment about it. Mike, however, did say, "I guess you get told."

They both said no to Anne's offer. John picked up Morgan's papers and notes. He started reading them again. Mike helped to read some too. John was reading about Nicole Parson. He kept thinking NP, Nicky Pearson. He remembered what Morgan had said—that she thought Nicky looked so familiar. John was reading that Katie Morgan, Katie Richard, and Nicole Pearson were all there together.

Together at the Miss National Journalist Pageant. The pageant that Kathryn Turner, now Katie Richard, won. Katie won the crown under the name of Kathryn Turner, and she didn't want to talk about it. This was a great honor. This was something to be proud of. But Katie didn't tell anyone about it, not even her best friend, Katie Morgan. John was totally immersed in his reading. Mike reminded him, "It has been twenty minutes since she left. She said it would only take twenty minutes, John."

"Let's give her a few more minutes, Mike," John told him as he started reading of Morgan's notes again.

Katie Morgan drove through the old worn gates and around the back side of the park. She had been there before and knew where to go. Parking next to Katie's new T-Bird and Mr. Barber's old Cadillac, she noticed that Dianne's car wasn't there yet. Katie turned off the engine and pulled her cell phone from her purse and called John. She knew he was waiting for that call.

"John, I'm okay. Katie and Mr. Barber are here. I don't see Dianne's car, yet everything looks good."

"Morgan, call me in twenty minutes, and don't turn your phone off. If I don't hear from you or you don't answer, we will come out. Okay, Morgan?"

"Okay, twenty minutes. Bye."

Morgan got out and walked to the door. She took the same look and deep breath that Katie had taken a short while before. She opened the door and looked inside.

"Katie, Mr. Barber, this is Katie Morgan. Katie, are you here?" she called out loud.

"Katie, you come out now," she demanded of her.

Morgan was not feeling at ease. Something was not right. She turned to go back to her car, lock the doors, and call for help. She immediately turned and headed for the door. Morgan had not come in far enough for Nicky to grab her the way she did Katie. Nicky knew she had to make a move and make it now. She ran out from the hall with that cloth full of chloroform. Morgan heard something behind her and started running. Nicky caught her, trying to put her to sleep too. She missed Morgan's nose. Morgan hit Nicky in the side with her elbow and started running again. Nicky grabbed her by her belt and pulled her back. Morgan turned and hit Nicky in the face. Nicky fell back somewhat, and Morgan was once again headed for the door. Nicky grabbed her by her long hair. She threw Morgan into the wall, and she fell to the floor. Blood was coming from her head. Nicky jumped on Morgan's back and locked her arms down. She then pulled Morgan up and forced her into the room with Katie. Morgan was fighting all the way into that room. Nicky finally hit Morgan hard, and Morgan fell into one of the old wooden chairs. Morgan's face was covered with blood. She could taste it. Morgan was not scared any longer. She was now mad, damned mad. Morgan

John Gardner

looked up and recognized Nicky. She looked to her left and saw Katie tied up with that tape over her mouth.

"What the hell is going on, Nicky?" Morgan shouted at her.

Nicky was walking to Katie when she saw Morgan getting up.

"Sit down now, or I will kill her," Nicky told Morgan in a nasty tone while pulling a knife from her pocket. Morgan saw the knife and sat back down. Nicky took the tape off Katie's month and walked back to Morgan. She picked up some foam rubber, cloth, and some rope. Nicky tied Morgan's hands together behind her back. With the cloth and foam rubber.

"Why are you doing this, Nicky?" Morgan asked.

"Her name is not Nicky, Morgan. Her name is Nicole, Nicole Pearson," Katie told Morgan. "And she wants to kill us."

"What's with the foam rubber?" Morgan asked.

"She is going make people think you and I killed each other. The foam rubber with the cloth will not leave any marks," Katie's explained to Morgan.

"That's good, Kathryn Turner," Nicky said to Katie. "You were always good at figuring things out.

"You are Nicole Pearson from the Miss National Journalist Pageant."

"I was Miss National until Kathryn Turner took it away from me."

"She never took anything away from you. You were in a car accident and could not perform your duties as Miss National.

Katie had nothing to do with that. You won't get away with this. People will be looking for us," Morgan told her.

"I will get away with this, and, no, Morgan, they won't. I'm going to call Anne and tell her that you and Katie had a big fight. You think she might kill you. Katie believes that you are the one trying to kill her and for her to call the cops. By the time the cops get here, I'm gone. And you two are dead," Nicky said as she walked around the room, waving the knife in her hand.

"Do you really think people will believe we killed each other?" Morgan asked Nicky.

"Yes! People believe what they are told to believe."

"Anne won't believe you," Katie told Nicky.

"No, but she will believe you, Morgan."

"Hi! This is Morgan," Nicky said in a voice just like Katie Morgan's.

Both of them were worried now. Morgan was hoping John would try to call and not be able to get through. This was the only hope they had. John and Mike would have to come out there.

Morgan was thinking. She could not let Nicky call Anne's. She had to keep talking until John called. They both knew if Nicky talked to Anne, then she would have to kill them immediately. They also knew once the phone rings, help would be on its way.

"Nicole, we will make a deal with you. Kill me and let Morgan go. She has nothing to do with this. She will give you her word that she won't tell anyone about you," Katie pleaded with her.

"I will not!" Morgan shouted back to Katie.

"Morgan, give her your word," Katie pleaded with Morgan.

"No, I'm not going to give her anything," Morgan told Katie.

"It wouldn't make any difference anyway. She wouldn't keep her word," Nicole added.

"I've never gone back on my word in my life. Just tell me one time I didn't keep my word. Just one time," Morgan said with a nasty tone.

"Morgan, this is no time to be discussing your honor. She means business," Katie shouted to Morgan.

"No, she's going to kill us anyway."

Morgan and Katie continued to argue among themselves, stalling for time. They knew the longer Nicky waited, the better the chance they had of staying alive.

John and Mike were still reading over Morgan's papers. They discussed a few things in her notes they talked about Nicole Parson. The cell phone lying on the table began ringing. John knew it was Morgan. This would be a relief to them, knowing that both Katie and Morgan were okay. The deal was fine, and they would be coming back soon. John grabbed the phone fast and said, "Morgan?"

"No, it's Lisa," the voice on the other end was saying. "John, is that you?"

"Yeah, it's me. Lisa, how are you? Did you find out anything?"

"Well, hello to you too," Lisa said with a silly voice.

"I'm sorry, Lisa. I was expecting a call from a friend."

"That's okay, John. Look, I did find something. The initial NP stands for…"

Before she could tell John, he told her, "Nicole Parson."

"Yes, then you also know that Nicky Pearson and Nicole Parson are the same. But did you know that Kathryn Turner and Katie Richard were the same? Nicole thinks she has killed a judge named Joe Rolland. Only no one could find the body. Six months ago, the judge showed up in Friendswood, Texas, using the name Jack Brunson. He has been running from the law. Parson did threaten him. That's why he disappeared. He wanted Nicole to get the blame for killing him. A young reporter named Katie Mason wrote a story about this. It made the police look at Nicole. She also wrote that Nicole was trying to kill Kathryn Turner. She said that Nicole was sleeping with more than one judge. Nicole blamed Katie for taking the crown from her. She told everyone that Katie was sleeping with Rolland and the other judges. No one believed this. All the reporters started looking into Nicole's life. This made Nicole mad. Katie and Nicole traded limos the night of the accident. It was not Katie's idea to do so. The limo that Katie was supposed to have been in was in a crash, killing Shelley Parson, Nicole's baby sister, and cutting Nicole's face to the extent that she had to have plastic surgery. Shelley ran and jumped into the limo at the last moment. A woman named Alma Thief, the mother of Laura Thief, ran her car into the limo. Alma Thief was upset because she had paid Rolland and another judge named Phil Mead to vote for Laura. Nicole did not know this. She thought Katie had something to do with this too. She threw a reporter named Kathryn Morgan out of her hospital room. She accused her of writing lies about her. Morgan was a cub reporter. This was her first assignment. She checked and double-checked everything she wrote. She said nothing about anyone that was not true and could be proven. I think she got her and Kathryn Mason mixed up. It hurt Morgan's feelings. She tried several more times to interview Nicole. Nicole would not listen to anything she had to say. Morgan and Mason both left town about the same time and put this story behind them. Only John, a reporter, never really puts a story behind them, especially if there are loose ends. Mason kept writing about Nicole, and she could not back up what she was saying. Mason later got fired. Got another job and got fired from that one too. Today she's working with the National News Group under the name of Kitty Smith. Oh, by the way, John, Kathryn Morgan has changed her name to Katie. That was probably who you thought was calling, right?"

"You're right."

"Well, that's not the end. Nicole never got over losing her sister. Both her mother and father were also killed in a car wreck less than two years after Shelley's death. They left all the money to Nicole. But Nicole could not handle the loss of over ten million dollars in cash and a company worth millions. She cracked up. She was institutionalized for four years. She got out about three years ago. She was still blaming mason. Only, she confused the name with Morgan, so she has spent the last part of her life thinking that Morgan and Katie were the cause of all her troubles."

"What's going on down there? My sources tell me someone is trying to kill one of the American home-shopping girls. There seems to be a major cover-up. My sources tell me this has been going on for a few months now. Level with me, John. You got two girls in the same place as the one who blames them for everything. Is Nicole trying to kill them?"

"You're right. They are keeping this quiet. Nicky, as she calls herself down here, is trying to kill Katie and put the blame on Morgan."

"John, you be careful. Nicole is not all there. She could freak out at any time and kill both of them and you too if she thinks you are against her. Remember, Nicole is very intelligent. Her IQ is higher than yours and mine put together. She is also an impersonator. She's good at it. She can impersonate either man or woman."

"Wait a minute, Lisa," John said as he put the phone down. Anne was standing next to him.

"John, John," she said nervously.

"What is it, Anne?"

"I called Morgan. It's been thirty minutes, and she was supposed to have called back in only twenty minutes."

"Yeah, what happened?"

"She didn't answer her phone. I called Katie, but she didn't answer either. I think we need to go there," Anne told John and turned to see Dianne walking in.

"Aren't you with Morgan and Katie?" Anne asked.

"No, why?" she asked.

"Lisa, I've got to go. Something is happening."

"John, tell me if I need to have a news crew there. Where is it? You owe me that, John."

"Okay, but keep your crew out until it's over, okay?"

"Okay, now where?"

"Sun Creek Park, an old closed-down park outside of Landover on Highway 678 south. I've got to go. Thanks, Lisa."

"Keep in touch with me. I'll keep this line open for you. I don't want any other news source to get this first, you hear, John?" she said, as John agreed. Hanging up the phone, they headed for the car.

"Anne, you know how to get there?"

"Yes, I'll drive."

John, Mike, and Anne ran out the door as fast as they could. They realized that time may not be on their side.

"I will call the police," Anne said with an excited voice.

"This is Anne. I need to speak with Detective Barker."

"He's not in now. Could I take a message for him?" she asked Anne.

"Yes. Tell him it's about Katie Richard and Katie Morgan. They are in danger. Nicky is with them too. They won't answer their phones. They are at the old Sun Creek Park. On the back side. Please tell him. I'm headed there now. I will need help. Thank you."

"Sun Creek Park, back side. Okay, Anne, I'll tell them."

"Be sure you do! I know I will need help."

"They're coming, Anne?"

"Yeah, Barker was out. She said she would tell him?"

"Hey, Marshal Dillon, you do have a plan, don't you?" Mike asked. John, looking out the window and thinking, said nothing. "You don't have a plan?" Mike asked again.

"I'm thinking. I'm thinking."

"Do you have a gun?" Anne asked.

"No."

"Do you have a gun, Mike?" Anne asked.

"No."

"No plan, no guns. What the heck are we doing? How can we rescue them without a plan or guns?" Anne asked with a very concerned look on her face.

"Yeah, John, just what are we going to do?" Mike asked.

"Don't worry. I will think of something."

Seeing that Anne was worrying, Mike spoke up, "Anne, don't worry. John always comes through. He's not going to let them get hurt. He's just not the fastest thinker in the world. He'll take care of this."

John was forming a plan, but it would depend on what he saw when he got here. He has to find out what the conditions were there. *Does she have a gun? Or just what is her method of killing? What room are they in? How easy is it to get into the building?* Once he learned all of this or some of these things, then he could put together a plan.

It was dark and cold, and bugs were crawling over his body. Bobby appeared to be dead. Nicky certainly thought so. But he was not. Bobby was knocked out cold. He had a broken leg and cracked ribs. Bobby started moving. The pain was bad. He couldn't sit up. Bobby knew if he didn't get out of this well he would die, for sure. As he rolled over, he could feel something beneath him. It was the gun that Nicky had, the same gun that she would have shot him with and the same gun she was going to shoot Katie and Morgan with too. He was glad he had the gun and not Nicky. Bobby could feel something else in his pocket. It was his cell phone. The cell phones that Nicky had given him. Bobby pulled the phone from his pocket and called 911 for help.

"Help me. I'm in an old well. I can't get up help," he pleaded with the operator.

"Take it easy. What's your name?"

"Bobby Greenwood."

"Where is this well?"

"The old Carter farmhouse on Farm Road 134 south of Route 655."

"Okay, Bobby, help is on its way. Do not hang up until they get there, okay, Bobby?"

"Okay, listen to me. Call Detective Barker, and tell him I'm here. Tell him that Nicky is planning to kill both Katie and Morgan. I don't know where, but please call him. I don't want anyone to get hurt. Please!"

"How do you know this, Bobby?'

"She told me."

"Why would she want to kill them?"

"Damn it, lady, quit asking so many questions and call Barker. You're wasting time. Nicky left about an hour ago. There may still be time to save them. Call now, damn you."

"Calm down, Bobby. I have already called him."

"I hear the siren. They are here," Bobby told the operator with excitement in his voice.

"Okay, Bobby, you are going to be all right."

"Hey, I'm over here. Be careful. I'm covered up. I'm here," Bobby kept shouting. He could hear them all around him. A little bit of light came into the well. It was a beautiful sight for Bobby to see. More light came, and he could now see the rescuers. They went into to the well and put Bobby on a stretcher. Bobby was safe now.

"Where is Barker?" Bobby asked.

"He's on his way now," he was told. Barker and Park arrived about three minutes later.

"What do you know about Nicky killing them?" he demanded of him.

"Where is Nicky now?"

"I don't know. She said she was trading cars with Jack Gram. I don't know why."

"Jack who?"

"Jack Gram. He has an old Cadillac. I don't know why."

"Where can I find him?"

"He works at the old mill store on old Highway 678."

"I know that place." Turning to an officer, he said, "Put an APB on that Corvette of Nicky's. And that other old car. Send a car to the store. We got to find those girls. Neither one of them will answer their phone."

A call came in from headquarter for Detective Barker.

"Anne called. Said Katie and Katie Morgan were in trouble. She needs help."

"Where are the girls now, and what happened?"

"I don't know what happened, but Garfield told Anne they were at the old Sun Creek Park."

"Okay, thanks. Park let's go. You two come with us."

The old park was about twenty-five minutes from the old farmhouse, even with the siren blaring. He didn't know what to expect. He only he knew he had better get there fast.

John, Mike, and Anne got to the park first. John told Anne to slow down and turn off the lights. They could see the three cars parked out back. The office door was open slightly.

"Anne," John said, "is there any windows in this building?"

"Yes, one in every room, almost."

"How many ways can you get in?"

"There's only one other door. It's on the other side."

"Can you get in without making any noise?"

"When I was a kid and worked out here, I found out that when the door appears to be locked, but if you turn the hander just right, it would open."

"What're you thinking, John?" Mike asked.

"Well, this is the plan. We'll look in the windows to see if we can find them."

They got out of the car, closing the doors very lightly so as not to make any noise. Anne took them to the office window. They did not see anything, so she took them to the old office of the assistant manager. Looking through the dirty window, they could see Morgan and Katie, both tied up. Nicky was walking around the room, holding that knife. Nicky was talking to Morgan.

Both Morgan and Katie knew they had to keep her talking. They had heard the phones ringing earlier, and they knew help was on the way. There were two ways to get into that room, both from Nicky's back side if she was facing the door she had forced the two girls through. The door, which John would be coming through.

Now John has a plan. Things were falling into place. John told Mike and Anne to wait until he gets Nicky far enough away from the girls before walking in and cutting the ropes. Anne took Mike to the back side and showed him how to get into that room. John waited for them to get in place before he made his move. After about a two-minute wait, which seemed more like a two-hour wait, John went into action. He walked into the room where Nicky was walking. John pulled up a seat and sat down by the door.

Morgan and Katie were glad to see him. They didn't say anything. They just looked at John, wondering what he was up to and how he was going to rescue them.

"Hi, Nicky," John said with a friendly Southern voice.

"Hi, Morgan, hi, Katie. I see y'alls are all tied up right now. Maybe I better come back another time."

John got up from his chair and started walking to the door when Nicky hollered at him.

"You come here, you hear?" Nicky demanded of John.

John waved his hand in the air, waving good-bye to her.

"I will see you later, Nicky. I just had something I wanted to talk with you about, but it can wait," John told her while still walking.

Nicky walked to Morgan and put the knife at her throat and said to John, "I will kill her if you walk out that door. Damn it, I mean it. I will kill her right now."

John stopped. He could not take that chance. He turned around and faced Nicky. He pulled that chair back to him, this time a little bit closer to the door as to give Mike and Anne time to cut Katie and Morgan free.

"I'm sorry. I thought y'all are just having some kind of game, and I didn't want to interrupt you."

"Who are you, and what do you want with me?"

"Oh, I just found out a few things. Thought you might like to know. You know things about them."

"You know them?"

"Well, I don't know them. I don't know them any more than I know you. I know that all of you are on TV. I know y'all are very pretty, and you, Nicky, are certainly sexy."

"If that's all you know, I might as well kill you too."

"No, no, Nicky. You don't want to kill me. Maybe them, but not me. I'm your best friend. I'm going to help you get out of this mess, so you can get away with this."

"You're my best friend. And you want to help me. How are you going to help me kill them?"

"Look, I don't care about them. Dead or alive, doesn't make any difference to me. I'm concerned about you."

Nicky was close to John now. Mike motioned for Anne to go to Morgan, and he would go to Katie. They both got behind the chairs when Nicky turned around. She didn't see them. Morgan and Katie knew someone was behind them. They didn't know if it was help or if it was Bobby.

The both of them just sat there very quietly, hoping whoever it was back of them were the good guys.

"What is it that you think you know about me?"

"Well, I know your name is Nicole Pearson."

"So you know my name. They knew my name too, so what?" Nicky said as she walked around the room, looking at Katie and Morgan.

"I know you are wrong about the judge, about Katie, and about Morgan."

"You want to explain this? Katie stole the crown from me. This little one with the big mouth wrote lies about me. And you're telling me I'm wrong?" Nicky asked with a mean look on her face.

"He's right. You're wrong, Nicole, or whoever you are. I never wrote anything that wasn't true about you," Morgan shouted out at Nicky.

Nicky walked to Morgan, told her to shut up, and slapped her across her face.

"Take the rope off, Nicky, and let's see how tough you really are," Morgan shouted back at her.

Nicky walked back to Morgan, grabbed her by the throat, and told her, "I will. Then you die." Morgan spat on her and told her to get out of her face. Nicky hit Morgan again, and new blood came from that hit. John motioned for Morgan to keep quiet.

"Leave her alone, Nicole, and let's talk about you," John pleaded with her.

"It doesn't make any difference if she lies or not. I don't like her anyway, and I have never liked her. You know how stupid she is? She thought she could take Bobby away from me. You know what she had to promise him? Sex with both her and Katie. She wasn't a woman enough to take him on her own. She had to promise him sex with Katie too."

Morgan started to say something when Anne putt her hand over her mouth and told her to shut up. Morgan was relieved to see Anne. Katie saw Anne also. She now knows that Mike must be behind her chair.

"Nicole, you are right. Katie Morgan is not the woman you are. She never will be."

Morgan, having a real hard time keeping her mouth shut, looked at John as if to say, *What are you talking about?*

Trying to keep Nicky's eyes off Morgan, John continued, "Heck, Nicole, she's not as pretty or anywhere near as sexy as you. You know, Nicole, I hear that she has a low IQ. But look, Nicole, let's talk about the pageant and that night. It wasn't Katie's idea to change cars. She had nothing to do with that or Shelly getting killed. She hated it as much as you did."

"She slept with the judges. And Morgan told everyone I killed that judge named Joe something, and everyone believed her."

"Nicole, Joe Rolland is alive. He was running to save his own neck. Alma Thief had paid him money to vote for Laura. She thought she was running into Katie's limo. It was you that made that switch on the limo, not Katie. They couldn't find the judge. Katie never slept with anyone. She didn't want the crown. Not the way she got it. She believed it was always yours. She felt bad about it, and a reporter named Kathryn Mason wrote all those bad things about you. It was not Morgan," John explained to her.

Anne cut Morgan free, and Mike cut Katie free. Mike and Anne told them to leave now. Katie said no. Morgan said no.

"I'm not leaving John with her. Besides, there's some unfinished business to take care of," Morgan told Anne.

"Don't do anything stupid, Morgan," Anne whispered to her.

"I'm okay. I won't do anything stupid, Anne."

Nicky was thinking about what John had said. She was now confused. She was beginning to believe him. Then she heard the police siren. She flaked out. Holding the knife up above her head, she ran straight at John.

"You lied! You lied to me! You were only waiting for the police to come."

Nicky was moving toward John faster than John could get away. The old chair John was in collapsed. Mike, helping Katie get loose, saw what was happening and started for Nicky. Morgan, now free from her rope, ran faster than she had ever ran before, jumped up, and grabbed Nicky's hand. The knife fell to the floor. Nicky turned, and Morgan hit her in the face. Blood came from that hit. Morgan grabbed Nicky by her hair the way Nicky had done Morgan just a short while ago. Morgan had her fist closed and ready to hit her again when Katie came up. She grabbed Morgan's arm. "No, don't hit her again," Katie told Morgan. "It's my turn."

Katie hit her so hard that she hurt her hand. Nicky fell back down. Morgan put her foot on her throat. Katie joined her, with her foot also on her throat.

"Do not ever put a knife to me again," Katie told Nicky.

The door burst open before Morgan could say anymore. Detectives Barker and Park, along with two other cops, came in with guns in their hands. News reporters from Lisa's network were there too, with cameras.

Morgan, looking up and seeing the cameras, said, "That's just great. I'm going to be on the six o'clock news with blood all over my face and torn clothes. Who told them about this?" She was asking John.

John came over and held Morgan in his arms. "You look beautiful, Morgan. Don't worry about the news reporters."

The paramedic came over to check her cuts. They cleaned her face and bandaged her head. A jacket was handed to her to cover her torn blouse. Katie felt better now.

The police placed the handcuffs on Nicky and read her rights to her. They let the paramedic check her head. Then Nicky asked if she could talk with Morgan and Katie. She was told it would be okay, and they agreed to talk.

"What you said and what he said, was it the truth?" Nicky asked with a sad look.

"Yes, Nicky," Katie told her, "everything. I would never do anything to hurt you. I felt so bad being Miss National. I never wanted it that way. I tried to keep in touch with you, but I couldn't get to you. I never wanted to leave you alone. I wanted to help you. But your people wouldn't let me get near you, Nicole. I still want to be your friend. Please get some help, Nicole. I will help you. I will be with you if you want me to."

"I feel the same way, Nicky, I mean Nicole. I don't hold any hard feelings toward you. I saw what it did to you. I don't want that to happen to me. We will both be here for you, Nicole, but please got some help," Morgan said with a sincere voice.

"I'm sorry for everything. Detective Barker, Bobby is in a well at my house. He's dead. I didn't mean to kill him. Will you get him out? I will pay all the expenses?" Nicole asked Barker.

"Well, Nicole, I've got some good news for you. Bobby is not dead. He was knocked out. Bobby called, asking us to stop you. Bobby is okay. He's in the hospital now with a few broken bones."

"Bobby helped save us, Morgan," Katie said. "You know what that means, don't you, Morgan?"

"I'll take care of that, Katie. Don't worry."

"No, we will take care of that, but not the way you promised, though."

"Okay, we will talk to him."

"What are you two talking about?" the reporter asked.

"It's nothing. Just a little joke between us. That's all," Katie told her.

"Okay, Lisa the computer is on," the reporter said.

"Yes, I can see you. Can you see me?" she was talking to Lisa King, who was in New York.

"Yes, I see you. Find John Garfield for me, will you?"

The reporter was looking and asking for John. He was found next to Katie and Morgan. The reporter told Morgan and Katie that Lisa King wanted to talk with them before going on air.

"Lisa King is doing the interview?" Morgan asked.

"Yes, is that okay with you?"

"Yes."

The reporter told them to look into the monitor and talk with Lisa.

"I've one question for you, Lisa," Morgan said to her.

"What is it, Morgan?"

"Do you really know John Garfield?"

"We are old friends from Texas. He helped me get here. If it weren't for John, I would have a nine-to-five job today. Why?"

"No reason. I just wondered."

"Are you and John…?"

"Oh no, no. We're not anything," Morgan answered before Lisa could ask.

"Okay, Morgan. John, I know you don't want to be on camera, but I need you to be here for me. Morgan and Katie, I need you two here too. John, you are not going to let me down, are you?" Lisa asked in a low sexy voice that Morgan picked up on.

"Yeah, you're not going to let your old girlfriend down, are you, John?" Morgan said in her low sexy voice of her own and with a strange look on her face.

John overheard what Morgan had said and just smiled. Anne also heard her. John agreed to going on camera, something he hated to do. Katie and Morgan gave their version of what happened. Mike called home to tell everyone to record this newscast. The girls and Mike did most of the talking. John did as little as possible. Lisa was kind to him.

The police, the news crews, and the paramedics were all leaving when DA Charles Albright and Aunt Annie came in. Charles Albright was called and told what was happening. He and Aunt Annie came as soon as possible. Aunt Annie ran inside as fast as she could, saw Morgan first, and hugged her so hard. Then she continued to hug Katie, Anne, Mike, and then John. She was so relieved that everyone was okay.

"Morgan, you're coming home with us. I don't want you left alone tonight," Aunt Annie told Morgan.

Morgan said, "Okay, Aunt Annie, I will."

As she walked over to John, Morgan put her arms around him, hugged him so tight he could hardly breathe, but John wasn't complaining. It felt so good, and he was so happy that she was okay. He was also happy that everyone was okay, even Bobby. Still holding John in her arms, she asked him to come with her to Katie's house. Aunt Annie, hearing that, said. "Of course, John. You and Mike and you too, Anne. Come over, and let's all of us be together tonight and give thanks that we are all okay."

Morgan put her head on John's shoulder and stood there holding him. She felt safe in his arms. Anne, watching her, asked Katie, "You don't think any…"

"No, Anne, Morgan is all right. She will always do the right thing. Right now John is her hero. That's all this is."

"John is enjoying that moment. Right now he's thinking he's in heaven. It can't get any better than this, and that's for sure. He feels so good about today," Mike remarked.

"Mike, I'm so sorry. Come here," Katie said to Mike with open arms. She held Mike so tight. He thought too he was in heaven with John. It felt so good, not only to Mike but to Katie also. The hug was great, but as great as it was to them, the fact that everyone was alive and okay was a greater feeling. Katie kissed Mike. A long kiss. He held her even tighter and returned the kiss. Morgan was still holding John with her head on his shoulder. She looked up at him, and with tears in her eyes, she thanked him. She then gave him a kiss. This was not just a thank-you kiss. It was a *thank-you kiss*. The kiss lasted awhile. Aunt Annie and Anne, watching them, said, "It may be awhile before we can leave."

The night went well. Aunt Annie sent out for a fine meal. Everyone stayed late. Morgan asked John not to leave town in the morning, to please stay another day. John and Mike agreed to do so, but they told her they would have to leave then.

23

The Next Day

The night before was full of good food, good wine, good friends, and good family. The night was full of laughter. No one wanted to be serious. It was a night to give thanks.

They laughed. They joked. Someone one said that Bobby's face would crack from grinning so hard. Someone else said there would be no living with him or working around him now.

Morgan was laughing as hard as anyone, making jokes about the deal she had made with Bobby. Anne was still wondering how Morgan would look with that fur coat and that big feather in her hat. Katie even laughed about it. She said Bobby would never want her again, guaranteed. Mike was so happy that he had come and that he did help in the rescue. Morgan even referred to him as "Macho Mike." John seemed to think it was funnier than the others. Aunt Annie looked at Morgan and Katie with pride. She was so glad they were okay. She was so proud that they were her girls, even Anne, tonight. She loved them so much. Aunt Annie also had a strong love for Anne, Mike, and, of course, John.

Morgan was finding it hard to sleep. She was thinking about Bobby and that deal. She had never gone back on her word before. She knew this was not a real deal, but what would Bobby think? She certainly could not have any form of sex with Bobby, and Katie didn't even know about the deal. She knew she would come up with a way out of this without sounding like she went back on her word.

That wasn't the only thing bothering her, though. John was on her mind as well. She was having thoughts about someone whom she had never had before, and she didn't know what to do with them. Morgan wanted to be with John. She wanted to hold him and kiss him. She also knew she couldn't do this. She had never cheated before, not even mentally cheating. And as far as she knew, her husband had never either. John was different. He made her feel good about herself. He made her feel sexy. He made her feel like a woman, and that was a good feeling that could not go on; it has to end, but how could it and when could it end? She wondered why something that felt so good and so right was so wrong. Tomorrow would be the day. She would have to do something. Right or wrong, tomorrow she will have to do something. The problem was, she knew the answer but hated it.

Katie awakened to the aroma of fresh coffee brewing and maple bacon frying on the stove. It alone walked her to the breakfast room, where Aunt Annie was setting the table. Katie walked to Aunt Annie and kissed her on the cheek.

"Good morning, Aunt Annie."

"Good morning, dear," Aunt Annie replied.

"Morgan sleeping in?" Katie asked.

"I went in and called her about ten minutes ago. She said okay or something."

"I don't think she slept well last night."

Walking into the room with her eyes half-open, still in her PJ, and yawning, Morgan said, "I didn't, but I'm all right. Good morning, everyone."

She walked over and kissed Aunt Annie while getting her first cup of coffee.

"I thought we would go to the hospital this morning, about ten or ten thirty. What do you think, Morgan?" Katie asked while taking another sip of her coffee.

"That's fine. Let's go as soon as we eat."

"Well, you girls can go now, but you won't get there this morning," Aunt Annie told them.

"Why? What hospital is he in anyway?" Katie asked.

"Oh, he's in Landover General."

"Well, we've got plenty time."

"I hate to tell you, dear, but it is eleven thirty now," Aunt Annie informed them.

"Okay, let's go this afternoon. Do you have any more eggs?" Morgan asked.

It was after one o'clock before they got dressed. Aunt Annie decided to stay home. She thought the girls would like to talk to Bobby alone.

Morgan still did not know for sure what to say. Bobby did try to save them. He tried to do the right thing at the end. But there was no way they were going to honor that deal.

Pulling into a parking space at the Landover General Hospital, Katie asked Morgan, "You know what you are going to say?"

"Let's see what he has to say first, and I'll take it from there. Okay?"

"Okay, but I'm not going along with that deal or whatever you called it."

"Okay, okay, me neither," Morgan told Katie with a funny little look on her face.

"I mean it, Morgan."

"I know. I will take care of this."

"Or I will," Katie added.

They walked to Bobby's room and found a police officer outside the door. The officer recognized them and let them in the room. Bobby had a cut on his face and a bandage on his waist. His leg was hanging from a bar above him. He really didn't want to see them. Bobby felt bad about the role he played in hurting them. They were his would-be friends.

"Hi, Bobby," Morgan said.

"How are you, Bobby?" Katie asked.

"Look…I'm…so sorry about what Nicky did to y'all," Bobby said with a sincere look on his face. "I never wanted to kill you or hurt either of you. I thought we were only going to scare you a few times. That's all I thought we were going to do. I'm so sorry."

Morgan, coming closer to his bedside, reached out and touched his hand. "Bobby, thank you for doing the right thing. You did help, and we appreciate what you did."

Katie, moving to his bedside, held his other hand.

"Thanks, Bobby. We really do appreciate what you did. Thanks so much…Morgan wants to talk to you about that conversation you and her had a few nights ago, don't you, Morgan?"

Morgan, giving Katie a you-know-what kind of look, said, "Yes! Bobby, we need to—" But before she could finish what she was going to say, Bobby interrupted her.

"Morgan, I know you meant what you said that night. I know you 'ways keep your word."

"Bobby…I—" Morgan was trying to say something again, but Bobby was not letting her talk.

"No, Morgan, wait. I can't take you up on that offer, and you know how I would love to be with you and Katie. I can't do it, Morgan. What I did was so wrong. Please forget that we ever talked. I will never tell anyone again about our talk, okay, Morgan?" he asked of her with tears in his eyes.

"Are you sure, Bobby?" Morgan asked.

"Morgan, he's sure! Bobby is a man of honor," Katie spoke out loud to Morgan in a strong voice.

"I don't know about honor, Katie, but I'm going to change. I want to be more like y'all. I want to do right from here on. We almost died last night."

Morgan reached over, rubbed his face, and gave him a long kiss. Katie looked on and thought, *That's great! Now I'll have to kiss him.* Morgan raised her head back and looked Katie in the eye and motioned for her to do the same. Katie reluctantly reached over and kissed Bobby, a kiss slightly shorter than Morgan's kiss.

They said their good-byes to Bobby. Walking back to the car, Katie asked, "Are you sure about that Bobby? Are you crazy, Morgan?"

"Well, how about, Morgan wants to talk to you about sex with us," Morgan came back at Katie.

They both started laughing and put their arms around each other. Morgan told Katie she wanted to go home and change clothes. She would see her later. Katie went to Anne's Place with Aunt Annie. John and Mike were there. Everyone had heard about this on the news and was asking questions. They got away from their fans and started talking with Detectives Barker and Parks.

"Hi, Detectives. Hi, John, Mike. Everything all right?" Katie asked.

"Yes, ma, everything's okay. Just had a few questions I needed to ask you and John. Everyone is okay?"

"Yeah, we are fine, Detective. Thank you for asking," Katie said.

They asked a few minor question of them, then said, "Well, we have got to get back." Then Park's cell phone rang.

"Park here. Oh…hi…Kim. How are you? I'm okay, thank you. Tonight, your place…are you sure, Kim? I love to. Seven, at your place. Yes, I know where you live. See you tonight," Parks was saying to Kim, who was always his favorite hostess.

"What was that all about, Parks?" Barker asked with a smile.

"Oh, nothing…doggone it. She called me…Kim called me. The prettiest girl on TV called me."

Parks hadn't been this happy since he won a thousand dollars in a lotto winning three years ago.

Walking around in circles, Parks realized what he had said. Not wanting to offend anyone, he looked at Katie and said, "You're pretty too, Miss Katie…You are real pretty."

"That's all right, Detective. I know what you meant, and Kim is beautiful. I don't know about the prettiest one on TV, but pretty," Katie said while laughing.

24

The Boy Goes Home

"I'm so glad you two came up to help. If it hadn't been for you two, I might not be here today. Thank God you came," Katie said with a lump of sincerity in her voice.

Aunt Annie and Anne agreed with Katie. Aunt Annie added, "We are thankful for our new friends, and if we never see you again, you will always be remembered in our hearts."

"Thank you so much for that. The people we met here will always be in our hearts too."

"You're right, John. I can't remember when I have met such wonderful people as all of you," Mike said with a lump in his throat.

"Let's go back to Katie's house. I know Morgan had asked you not to leave until she got a chance to talk to you again. Where is she anyway?" Aunt Annie asked.

"Oh, she got in her car and went home to change," Katie told them.

"Okay then, let's go. She will come on over when she's ready."

"You are coming too, aren't you, Anne?" Katie asked.

"No, I can't go until three. Jamie called in sick this morning. I've got to wait here before I can leave. Jan will be here at three. I will see you later at your house. Tell you what. I will bring one of my cheesecakes when I come."

"That's great. I love those," Katie replied.

They all left for Katie's house. Mike drove his pickup, and Aunt Anne drove Katie's new T-Bird with Katie by her side, while John rode with Mike.

Morgan was trying on different clothes, changing her hair, looking in the mirror. She finally decided to just wear jeans and a nice blouse—let her hair down and be herself. She was happy with what she saw in the mirror.

She walked to the kitchen and poured herself a glass of iced tea. Morgan had often carried a glass of iced tea out to the patio. It had a calming effect on her. She could look out over the lake. It seemed so peaceful. She walked to her favorite chair, the old baby blue one that she had picked up from a garage sale. Katie Morgan had only one thought on her mind. It was John. The feeling she had for him, the feeling she believed he had for her as well. She knew these feelings—as good as they might feel today—must go away. She could not and must not keep them. She didn't want to say good-bye. That was the last thing she wanted. Maybe this is okay, and maybe that is not okay. Other people do this all the time, but Katie Morgan was not other people. Her parents taught her what was right and what was wrong. Those were the only choices you had. You make your decision. You live with it. It's like when you take your kids to a store and let them play on the merchandise there, and all you can say is they're not hurting anything. But you know what they are playing on is not yours and maybe they could get hurt.

Morgan was having a hard time with this feeling. She had never had to make excuses for anything she had done before in her life. She looked at her watch and saw it was getting late. John and Mike were leaving sometime today. She couldn't let them go without seeing John one more time. Morgan picked up her cell phone and called John's cell phone.

"John, how are today?"

"I'm fine. How are you?"

"I'm well...John, I've forgotten to water a friend's plant the last couple of days. Would you like to ride over there with me? I want to talk to you before you leave."

"I would love to, Katie."

"Great! Where are you now?"

"I'm at Katie's house."

"I'll call you from the car when I get there...I don't want to go in right now, okay?"

"That's fine. See you in a few minutes."

John closed the cover on his cell and placed it back in his jacket when Aunt Annie asked, "Was that Morgan?"

"Yeah…that was Morgan. She's coming over, and we are going to water somebody's plants. She's not coming in. I'm meeting her outside."

"Oh, yeah, Jody is out of town this week," Katie explained.

"I hope those plants are not dead. Morgan will be buying her all new plants."

"Yeah, at the depot. You know how much she loves that place. We are always going there for something."

"And that cute little John working in the inside garden always makes me feel so good," Katie added with a smile.

"He's a flirt, but he is cute," Kim added.

A few minutes went by, and John's cell phone rang again. It was Katie Morgan in the driveway. John said good-bye and left to be with her.

Jumping into her car, John remarked, "Wow! You look great, Katie. What's that word you like to use? Oh yeah, *fabulous*. That's the word. You look fabulous today."

"Well, thank you so much for that. I'll buy you a drink for those kind words."

It was a short trip to Jody's house, and the conversation was good. They both laughed about the week. John reached over and grabbed Morgan's hand. She squeezed it back, as if she was giving permission to hold it.

"Here we are, John, and here is the key. Shall we go in and feed some hungry plants?"

"Yeah, let's."

Morgan grabbed his hand this time as they were walking to the house. Both of their hearts were racing. Neither one of them were thinking of the plants. They were thinking of each other. It only took about fifteen minutes to water all the plants. The last plant was in the bedroom. They both looked at the bed, not saying anything. Then Morgan said, "Let's put this watering can away, okay?"

"Yeah...okay."

Morgan took John by the hand as they walked back to the pantry and put the water can back on the shelf. She turned to John and walked him back to the den where she sat down, and John seated himself very close to her. They both started laughing at the same time. Morgan was thinking, *God, I want to kiss you*, and John was thinking the same. She got up and walked around the room, stopped, and looked out the window.

"John...I...I'm going to miss you when you leave."

"I'm going to miss you too, Morgan. I'm going miss you real bad."

Morgan, walking back to the sofa, sat back down.

"No...you don't understand, John...I'm going to miss to you way more than I should. You know...what I mean?"

"Believe me, Morgan, I know what you mean."

John placed his hand on her face and rubbed it so softly. Morgan, placing her hand on his, turned her face and kissed his hand. John was not taking his eyes off her. He continued to rub her face. His hand slid down her neck. John, looking Morgan in the eyes, knew this was the time to kiss her.

Morgan, looking John back in his eyes, knew the same. Their lips touched—pressed together so hard it would take a heavy bar to separate them. Morgan held him so tight. This felt so good to each of them. The kiss came to an end, and he placed his hand back on her neck. Morgan was more excited than she had ever been. She pulled his head back and kissed him again. This time the kiss was longer, wetter, and better than the time before. They kissed and held each other so tight and so long. John moved his hand down to her waist. Morgan moved her arm out of his way. She was telling him anything would be okay with her, and he was giving the same signal. Morgan, holding his face in her hand, asked, "You want to go in there?"

"Yeah...I do."

John for her hands, pulling her into his arms—their lips touching, their hands rubbing each other's back as they stood there holding each other so tightly yet so gently. Morgan started to pull away. John pulled her back, and Morgan kissed him again. But this time, she insisted and walked to the window. Looking out, she saw nothing outside; her thoughts were not on the outside of the house. They were in her heart. It was as if she had two angels sitting on her shoulder. One was telling her, *It's okay. Do it. Everybody does it. It's okay.* And the other one was telling her, *No, it's not right. You must not do this.*

Morgan stood there, while John walked behind her, placing his arms around her waist. She rubbed his hands, turned, and kissed him again. John began to unbutton her blouse. She did nothing to stop him. He opened her bra and rubbed her bare breast. But John knew something wasn't right. She was feeling the same. His thoughts on right and wrong were the same as Morgan's. It was right, and it was wrong. It was nothing else.

"John, I…I…can't do this…I want to, but I can't," Morgan told John in a sensitive voice.

John dropped his hand back to her waist and, in a low voice, told her, "I know, Morgan. You…you are right. Neither of us has the right to do this."

"You have to be a president to do this," Morgan told John and started laughing.

"He didn't even have that right. He just took it. Morgan… I…I understand how you feel, because I feel the same way."

"Do you really, John?"

"Yes, I really do, Morgan."

"You know, at this very minute in my life, I love you so much. I just love you so much, John, and I feel so bad about loving you that much. Does that make any sense to you, John?"

"Yeah, it…it really does. I love you too, Morgan. I love you so much it hurts."

"Then why are we here? Why do we feel this way? I never thought once about cheating. I have had guys, damned sexy ones…I would have enjoyed, but I said no every time, never thought about them again. But you, John, well, you are different. I can't get you off my mind. I don't know what to do about you. When I thought about you leaving today, I'm so frightened that I will never see you again. Will we ever see each other again, John? Can we not take that chance? I don't know these answers. All I know is, I love you, and I can't love you. I want to make love to you, but I can't make love to you," she said with tears running down her pretty face.

Morgan walked to John and placed her arms around him. John held her and kissed her on the neck, pushing her long brown hair back.

Looking into her eyes, he said, "Morgan, I don't know the answers either. The only thing I know is, you're right. We love each other, we want to make love together, and, yes, we will miss each other so very much. Morgan…there will never be a day in the rest of my life that I won't think of you. You will never be out of my heart. Maybe we should agree to not calling, writing, or e-mailing each other…oh, what the hell. We could e-mail once in a while. Maybe call every now and then. I can see you and hear your voice every day on TV, but you can't see or hear mine. I don't know, Morgan… I just… not talking with you again."

John kissed her on her neck again, and Morgan raised her head and looked into his eyes, and they kissed. This was not a sexual kiss. This kiss was an "I love you" kiss filled with passion. This one told them both what they had just said: *I love you, and I will miss you so much.*

After that kiss, John pulled a hanky from his rear pocket and began wiping the tears from Morgan's face. Smiling at

John, Morgan told him he had some makeup on his face. She cleaned it off for him.

"Well, I guess we had better get back before they start thinking that we are doing something we shouldn't be doing," Morgan said with a grin on her face.

"Yeah, we wouldn't want them to think that, would we? But it will be more convincing if I help you with your clothes."

Morgan slapped John on the shoulder and told him, "Okay, I do need some help. It's time to put these babies away."

After John dressed her, she was still in his arms. They looked at each other; it was only natural that a kiss would be coming.

Backing out of his arms, Morgan said, "Let's go."

Anne arrived shortly after Morgan and John left. She was asking, "Where are Morgan and John?"

"They went to water Judy's plants. They will be back soon," Katie told Anne.

"You let them go over there by themselves? Are you nuts?" Anne shouted.

"It's okay, Anne. They will be right back."

"How long have they been gone?"

"About an hour or so."

"Let's go," Anne said as she started walking to the door.

"No, Anne. We are not going over there," Katie said.

"We can't let them," Katie interrupted her before she could finish what she was about to say.

"Morgan will do the right thing, Anne. If we try to stop her, she will never forgive us. I've known Morgan for a long time. She always makes the right decisions. Morgan would never do anything like that. Believe me, Anne, she will be okay."

"Yeah...Anne, she's with John, not me. If she was with me, she wouldn't have a chance, but John? They all turn him down. So don't worry, Anne. Morgan is okay. I've seen John in action. He's not very good. She really is okay," Mike informed all of them on John's ability to handle women.

A few minutes later, the door opened. Morgan and John walked in, saw Anne, and greeted her.

"They are okay. Everything is okay over there. It was cold when we got there, but we turned up the heat. It got really hot over there. Had to turn the air back on to cool it down," Morgan told everyone.

You could hear Anne saying underneath her breath, "I'll bet it got really hot over there."

Not hearing what Anne had said, Morgan asked, "What did you say, Anne?"

"Oh, it was hot over here too."

"I hate to say this, but we have to get on the road. It's over a six hundred miles to home," Mike said as he stood up.

"Yeah, he is right. We do have got going," John agreed with Mike.

"Here I have fix all some food for the road." Aunt Annie handed it to John.

They walked to the pickup together. Anne and Aunt Annie kissed both John and Mike good-bye. Katie kissed Mike. This was not just a kiss. This was has been said to make hair grow on his bald spot. Morgan kissed John, another long and passionate one. Anne elbowed Katie in the side and pointed to Morgan. Then Morgan went to Mike and kissed him. It was a good kiss, but nothing like the one she had given John. Mike wasn't complaining, though. He had just received two great kisses from two of the prettiest girls in the world. There would be no complaining from Mike on the quality of either one of those kisses.

Mike started the engine, and the pickup rolled out of the driveway. Morgan stood there, watching them drive off. John had turned and looked out the rear window. It was as if they were sixteen all over again, and one was leaving for the summer. The pickup rolled out of sight. Morgan was still looking. There was nothing to see, but Morgan could still see John's face.

Katie said she would have a talk with Morgan. Aunt Annie said no and told them to go inside, she would talk with her. Aunt Annie walked to Morgan's side, placing her arm across her shoulder.

"We are going to miss those two cowboys. They are one of a kind."

"You don't know how much I'm going to miss them, Aunt Annie."

"John kind of got to you, didn't he?"

"Aunt Annie, it hurts so badly. But I know I did the right thing. Why should doing the right thing hurt so badly?" she asked with tears flowing down her face.

"I don't know, dear. But doing the right thing is always the best thing to do."

"You're right…but it still hurts so badly."

Aunt Annie offered her some tissue. Morgan wiped her face and started smiling, then hugged Aunt Annie.

"What am I going to do, Aunt Annie?"

"You will do what you have always done. You will take it one day at a time, and you will do the right thing. The pain will go away."

"How would I know just what the right thing is for me?"

"You'll know. You have always known what was right and wrong for you. That's a decision that only you can make for yourself."

"Can I? Maybe I will make the wrong decision. Maybe I won't even make one. I just don't know, Aunt Annie."

"This is a decision of the heart, and they are always the most difficult ones to make. And people don't always make the right decisions. Think things out, and you will be all right."

"You're right. It may be just a now thing. I don't know where I can go from here. I have always believed that there are no gray areas. Only right or wrong. Now I don't know."

Holding Morgan in her arms, Aunt Annie told Morgan, "You told me once—and you, not Katie—that there are no gray areas. A gray area is only a way of justifying a wrong."

"Yeah, I did say that, and I still believe that."

"Neither you nor I know what tomorrow will bring. But you know, I see you as the CEO of a big corporation soon."

"Yeah, a corrupt corporation with my luck."

"Whatever. But you know some of my thoughts come true."

"That's what worries me, but a CEO? We'll see about that one," Morgan said with a smile. Looking up at Aunt Annie, she asked of her, "Aunt Annie, if you don't mind, I would like to be alone for a few minutes. I don't want them to see me crying, although I see them peeking out the window."

"That's okay, dear. They just care about you too. When you come in, get yourself a piece of Anne's cheesecake. It's the one you like best, chocolate swirl."

Thank you for buying and reading *The Hostesses: The Case of Who's Trying to Kill Them*. And be sure to read book 2, *The Case of from Hostess to CEO*. This is the beginning of the main mystery.

Note: If you are planning on buying a new house, be sure to read my book *Thoughts*. It will tell you all about the HOA or as I call the local dictatorship zone.

Please e-mail me at gardner196@gmail.com.
Let me how you like the story.
Which character did you like best?
Give me your thoughts on a new story.

CPSIA information can be obtained
at www.ICGtesting.com
Printed in the USA
LVOW01s0136210916
505491LV00003B/4/P